AUTOMATONS

AUTOMATONS

AUTOMATONS BOOK ONE

BY **BP GREGORY**

THIRD EDITION

Acknowledgments

Thank you to my patient and diligent proofreaders Jason, Diane, Martin, Ahren.

Automatons cover image by NinaM, Something for Everything cover image by Extradeda, , Flora & Jim cover image by Marcel Jancovic all courtesy of Shutterstock.

Old Skipping Rhyme is by Ahren Daniel Morris and used with permission. Ahren Daniel Morris retains all copyright on the rhyme.

For more information, more stories, or to stay in touch visit www.bpgregory.com.

Content Advisory

This story features adult themes including addiction: alcoholim, addiction: drug use, animal violence, child neglect, sexual harassment, and sexually explicit scenes. It may not be suitable for all readers.

TABLE OF CONTENTS

CHAPTER ONE

AUTOMATONS

Hard Plastic Candy

THE TIN KEY rasped around its slot in the toy mouse's humped, die-cast back and rusted cogs squealed so shrilly you would think that Joyce was killing it. She bounced the little metal trinket in long fingers and squeezed as she had once done selecting avocado or peaches from rough market stalls, testing the soft swelling of ripe fruit, choosing from among plenty.

Bailed up by memory she could almost smell meat, fish and vegetables, citrus and sweet doughnut sugar all trampled into the Sunday Market's hard earthen floor. Saliva welled pointlessly through grimy molars—but reminiscence, no matter how vivid, would not stuff her writhing gut.

The tin key rotated. Today was yet another drawn-out day, and despite the brave assumption that they must be achieving something the parts had long since forgotten their purpose. There was nothing left now but to grind down aimlessly.

Bummer, hey?

'I was just sitting back a little, you know?' Joyce's whine carried a long way into stillness; complaint broadcast to the big fat nobody listening. Even monsieur mousie's pinkie-sized ears were merely welded on, not much for anything more than decoration.

'I was taking what I might mention was a well-earned snooze. Not robbing any banks. Not coveting my neighbour's ass. It must have really broken hearts to see me resting for a change!'

Sorrow a voice had murmured, rousing the near cataleptic Joyce spitting and swearing into the chill light of morning. No rest for the wicked, eh; although a sympathetic soul might have hardened to hear it was nine-thirty am, so not exactly the crack of dawn.

Still, "chill" morning? Long delayed reports came in from the frontline: it was cold; bloody bloody ass shrinkingly cold! Joyce yelped pitifully like a stuck hyena; sitting up in the road she could feel traumatised nipples trying desperately to burrow back into her chest.

'What ..?' A croak, a cough; that was not much shake. Vocal apparatus burned. She cleared it and tried again. 'What do you want?'

Sorrow the voice had murmured again right in her ear which was damned creepy, even if you were used to it. The voice trembled with unshed pathos, it thrilled Joyce's ragged nerve endings until tears squirted to her marbled yellow eyes. Such a voice could whisper *grow* to the moss squirming in the pavement and up would shoot an obedient oak. Hell, a forest of them!

Some organic matter, however, was feeling less co-operative. 'Get stuffed,' Joyce replied succinctly, yawning wide and wider until her jaw creaked.

It was not as though this promised to be a cracker of a morning at any rate. Great fistfuls of sleep-flakes ground beneath Joyce's swollen eyelids and when she went to scrub them away, the headache that had been lurking in the wings was inspired to full molten glory. Arteries throbbed palpably beneath her chill palms.

'Sorrow, hey?' She grimaced: even her voice tasted vile. 'I notice that nobody seems particularly sorry for me.'

Sorrow.

'Yeah, I heard you. Shifting, aren't I? Want to see me dance?'

As Joyce hauled herself upright joints popped like Chinese New Year. Even such a brief flirtation with exercise brought about hands on knees and a spot of heavy breathing.

'I'll find your sorrow,' she puffed. 'Don't I always?'

Easier said than done, said the rabbit to the priest. Despite Joyce's confidence the city was one big mess to go sifting through on foot, and it was not going to help that your piddling sorrows typically swung more weight than a Shakespearean tragedy writ large across the sky.

Skyscrapers curved wearily over the crumbling street. A few of the cinderblock idols had given way and tumbled, so long ago that their remains were streaked in exhausted white spoor. As Joyce wandered listlessly from rue to boulevard the buildings denied her pallid face even a whisper of sun; buried in their shadow she hugged her bones and wished herself baking on a stretch of beach somewhere.

High up was a glimpse of blocky wings threshing the light. Nary a living feather to be seen down here. It was likely for the best: if tempted she might have taken a stab at eating air rat, and those germ factories had good likelihood of making the living tongue drop from your head. Joyce squinted: besides, those pigeons looked all wrong. Too square about the outlines, and all that uniform ash colour. Not a speckle or a band among them.

Here and there a few ground floor windows remained intact and, bored, Joyce heaved chunks of bitumen through them. Although the sound failed to travel her reflection crashed and scattered gratifyingly. Staring, glaring eyes: SMASH! Flesh hung off a frame of outsize pointy bones: CRACK!

Exposed in a blown out lobby a vending machine hummed briefly. Joyce paused, trembling, the only other sound her breath. The machine's radiance filled the grey lobby with the promise of sweetness, hurting her eyes. The prospect hurt her modern, sugar-addicted body. Chocolate. Lovely dark rich melting chocolate. Her taste buds moaned with desire. She wanted to lick the images.

Against all better judgment she ducked inside, hurrying eagerly to give fate yet another opportunity to smack her down. Yep. The machine was empty. She wondered if this was how homeless people had felt, to be surrounded by such dispensaries: a thousand flavours for the masses and none for me.

Joyce unplugged the vending machine for good measure and its golden siren glow winked out. The cold grey world took over.

'You see that?' Her shout rang off the concrete sky; a little pathetic á la Hamlet but building in power and volume as she went. 'I even take out defenceless chockie machines for you! Are you proud? Poor little fellow will never play the piano again …'

Before Joyce could go on an invisible spring coiled her gut into spasms. She just about made it back into the open, praying desperately *don't puke, don't puke*, and buckled from her considerable height to the verge. Her right hand landed square on a spatter of broken glass, the very same glass that she herself had broken. The left, not to be outdone, shot into an unnecessarily spiny weed. The jury remained out over which hurt more.

'Steady on there Joycie,' she chided herself and whiffed hard through her nose until the cramp eased, incidentally jetting wet nose-goblins over the pavement between her stinging palms. The ground, as seen through a long tunnel, seemed to buck and roll wildly.

The stupid belligerent weed had some sort of allergen in its arsenal. Little inflamed bumps were already beginning to march up the tender skin of her wrist.

'Have to get some vegies in the old diet.' Since nobody listened, Joyce would damn well cheer herself along. 'Or even some *food*, wacky as that may sound. Yeah. On the to-do list. Get some food in my diet.'

Wasn't it traditional for champions of life in extremis to get some kind of miraculous water cracker? It were not as though she were demanding that the knowledge of good and evil be popped back on the buffet, but a slice of bread and a fish stick would not go astray.

All poor Joyce had for comfort was the smell of her own feet. She snivelled a bit, sitting alone in the deserted street but it was clearly not getting her anywhere. Also, the atmosphere this close to the end of her with toes hung sour with a heavy yeasty odour.

Wow that was nasty! Her shrunken stomach flopped over. More than anything else in the universe: more than her personal quest, or not wanting to die in the gutter, it was the need to escape her own feet that got Joyce moving again.

'Death by foot cheese,' she panted, reeling a bit until she caught her balance. 'I'm sure that would look all kinds of dignified on my headstone. Here lies Joyce, who has gone on to a better place. May they never be short on soap.'

At the thought of better places a sour scowl crossed her face and was gone, like a resentful shadow. But never mind better places, she had her own troubles to worry about.

It could have been hours later—long, numbing hours, when Joyce finally rounded the right corner. She had been tiptoeing to avoid a clump of desiccated dog poo that might have been a hundred years old, looked up, and there was the sorrow in the middle of the road. The sorrow! Idling before a traffic light.

The sorrow was a smallish car and it was weeping.

The car's ultra modern engine (or was that antique now?) produced little more than a polite cough and the sobs came through clearly. Joyce gnawed her cheek worriedly before advancing and a pale lump crumbled beneath her incautious foot, some asshole dog owner reaching down through the mists of time just to piss her off.

She knocked tentatively on the hood, 'Hello?' and the car's window scrolled down with a smooth electronic sigh.

'Help me!' the car squeaked. Its voice might have been

funny in the days of Saturday morning cartoons but in the here-and-now it set Joyce's teeth on edge. 'Please, I have to get her to the hospital!'

'Her?' Puzzled, Joyce ran both hands across her scalp: prickly black fuzz; and hunkered down for a look through the windscreen. She shot up again a damn sight more quickly: 'Ugh!'

The car's pitiful little passenger lolled against beige upholstery, cradled in her steed's seatbelt arms. Bathed in the steady glow of a stop light which with modernity's typical duplicity should have looked warm, but wasn't. Her teeth were still so white.

Joyce found herself very, very glad that none of those rear windows stood open.

'Look.' She paused: oh, how to put this. 'I'm really sorry, I am; but I suspect things might be a little too advanced for a doctor now.'

'No, no, oh no! She'll be ok if I get her there, she has to be ok!'

'I'm telling you no hospital would take her! A taxidermist wouldn't take that!'

Damn. There had been no call for unkindness. Joyce was *trying*, but the reserves of tact had dried up long ago.

Chrome tears leaked through the front grille. 'It's all my fault!' the car moaned. 'I was taking her to the hospital, but the light just wouldn't change and, and I couldn't; she needed me to save her and now …'

It was never fair, that was the problem.

Groaning at the slow protest of cartilage Joyce sat herself down in the road. The traffic signal was still lit up red. Had not so much as flickered since her arrival.

Here died the last child of the old world in her absurd pink tissue paper dress. Killed by a faulty traffic light.

Joyce fought the urge to smash her sour reflection from the car's wing mirror. She found herself fighting down a lot of such urges these days, and it was like shovelling sand to hold back the tide.

'Why didn't you just go through?' As if she did not already know.

'Through the light?' In the tortured whine of gears she heard that the failure was not through lack of trying. You might as well ask a human to stick their hand in a welding torch: *better*, because a person conceivably *could* to save a child.

'You poor bastard.'

That shocked the little vehicle right good and the sobs petered out into disapproving silence. A respectable upper-middle class sedan, it had probably never been so spoken to in what passed for its "life".

'Can only do what you were designed for, right? No less and certainly no more. Just think: the dumbest human jerk on the planet could have saved that girl, whether or not you could count on him yanking his shorts up after a crap. But not *you*.'

'Who are you?' The car managed and outrage was evident, g-rated vocabulary or no. But to its surprise the tall woman sitting by its wheel merely laughed acidly.

'Me?' Joyce snorted as though genuinely tickled; 'Who am I? I'm the mote in our Creator's bulging great eye, the fleck of crap on his boot heel. No, no; I've got it—I'm our era's damn night janitor, that's what I am. I come along after the party on my hands and knees to clear away all of the vomit, burnt sparklers and dribbly knotted up rubbers so that everything is squeaky and clean for the next lot to come along.' She sighed, enthusiasm leaking away. 'Hope they manage a better job of things than we did.'

The car shrank away as Joyce leaned comfortably back against its panelling. This big intersection seemed to be the only place in the entire city where the sun touched down, and she loved it: the alloy behind her protruding shoulder blades was warming nicely. For the first time today Joyce was finally beginning to feel human. Gregarious, even.

'I mean, I don't see why I'm stuck explaining this; it's not like I don't have better things to do. Places to see and so forth. For instance you'll never guess what I happened on last night.'

Your sanity? The new gospel scribbled on a toilet door? It could be anything, her tone promised revelation. 'What?'

'A bar.' Joyce whistled pleasurably through her teeth; then frowned and tried to scrub the back of her incisors with her tongue. 'An honest to mergatroid real life bar. A gem, tucked down some side alley. They're usually picked clean these days but I'll bet that even when there were folk around to drink up nobody could find this beauty. I had me a pretty special time, let me tell you.'

She sure had … at least, from what she could dredge out of the depths of memory. Bits of recollection came untucked from her story like a handkerchief from a sleeve. There had been the dark and a candle jammed in a straw bottle, very rustic, very romantic.

Moderation not being a strong point Joyce had knocked back six-odd shots of something like molten honey. Then some fancy microbrewery beers from the bottom cupboard, cement dust on them. Toasting the little pool of light with a bottle of inky red, no glasses but never mind, this was the end of the world, she could get by. At some point late in the proceedings Joyce had then stumbled and slithered her way back up the narrow staircase, erupting out into the night with her breath in great frozen clouds around her.

Out in the street she had yelled at whatever constellations peeped down through the skyline … and it had been warm. Unseasonable heat that beat against her hands and face, the exposed skin. Hot enough to raise a sour alcoholic sweat.

Did she set fire to the bar?

Aw nuts. She must have, using that handy little romantic candle. Romance this! Joyce remembered blurry orange flame in the night, a defiant signal to those cold, distant perfect stars. Toasting with the only bottle that had made it out by lucky circumstance of being in her hand: champagne, drink of champions, from the actual Champagne region. With her back roasting and her upturned face frozen.

The gutter was where the voice had woken her with all of its "sorrow" nonsense. With past history as a guide she had most likely tripped and then decided to go to sleep, since she was already down there on the floor and all. Joycie, you are one real classy dame.

'I've seen your type before.'

Joyce was not even aware of having drifted off until the car recalled her. As an audience it sounded a long way from being impressed.

Nonetheless, a brief thrill of mingled joy and fear raced through the tall woman. They had been here! They must have!

Whoa up there Joycie. Past victim of hope she dragged herself up short. There was no way that the bringers could have been through this city. Not with this car, this "sorrow" clogging up the works; she was quite literally getting ahead of herself. The bringers only ever trailed along behind, followed when Joyce's work was done. She was alone among the buildings.

Something gooey and white and just that little bit gross was coming off her teeth. Joyce grimaced and wiped it on her sleeve. Bloody hell. She was falling apart.

She feigned disinterest like a cat: 'You have?' and while she was talking lay flat and began to work her way beneath the car, shirt ruching up to expose ribs as broad as girders.

'Sure thing. Your lot are everywhere. Wandering the suburbs, chatting up street lights and clutching rancid trash jealously like it's your own treasure. I've seen plenty of you.'

'Hardy ha ha. Please stop before my sides split.' Joyce was holding her nose while speaking: things smelled pretty oily and foetid beneath the chassis, enough to leave the whiffy issue of her feet in the dust. She tried not to think about how some of that aroma must be drifting down from the sad little passenger above. 'You know, once upon a time the screws would have said talking to a car was crazy.'

'That's "shrinks" you mean, right?' The car doubted her tall tale, anyway. It had never met any vehicle who failed to respond when spoken to, and could not imagine one so rude.

'Nah, it's screws. They screw around with your nut, see; which works out for them 'cause you'd have to be pretty screwed up to screw one.'

Not even a titter. In the awkward silence Joyce scalded three knuckles on the exhaust, the white domes of blister rising like icecaps. She banged a chunk of freed metal irritably against the undercarriage. 'Sneer all you want, but I am doing important work here! Stuff that you won't catch your average Nutty McNut-Nut doing.'

'Like what?' the car wondered. 'What difference can you make? I couldn't even go through a red light.'

Then Joyce finally pulled something vital. As she yanked the cable free a neon spark arced between her hands—it paid to be well grounded. The engine's discreet cough died and for the car all worlds, failing or new, were finally over.

She answered anyway. 'I end things. I clear out what can't go forward, make way for the new world. Endings are all that's left for me. My job. Like you, I'll never get to be part of the new world that they're bringing. I'll never even dream it.'

Unvoiced in the darkening bruise that was her mind she whispered "I'm sorry".

This is how it was all over the world. Depots of buses waited desolately for somebody to take them touring again on the beautiful open roads. Airplanes dreamed, tipped over to one side so that one wing pointed to the clouds they longed for even as they sank into the overgrown earth.

An automatic teller machine could not question its place in life and take up art. A food processor could not find fulfilment in literature once nobody was around to want frappé any more.

Of course it was not fair! So what was the point in apologizing to one? The abandoned world had no rhyme or reason left; only a blind, grinding inevitability.

To crawl from beneath the steel corpse took almost more than Joyce had. There were worse tombs she supposed, the streets were lined with them but ennui did not alter the fact that she had a job to do.

Joyce squinted up at the sky, all hint of sunshine gone. Only the pavement-coloured clouds, their heavy guts swagged low enough to be stuck through and through by the most enterprising of the skyscrapers. As an afterthought she smashed the traffic light's panel open with a rock and disconnected that, too.

And that was when Joyce had spotted the glow of the toy shop.

Both front windows had been busted in and bright detritus flooded the footpath like hard plastic candy. The fading of the city's other establishments had not diminished these Christmas reds, burning Van Gough yellows and deep Whiteley blue. Once upon a time these things must have been marvellous.

Their clockwork life was so enviously easy. Nobody was born in candy land. Nobody lived in dread of dying at the end of all of their hard work—that's it, game's done. No, a giant hand merely wound you up: it wound and wound and off you went until it all ground down again.

In good conscience nobody could blame humanity for being dazzled, and for trying to run with the dumb fidelity of their own dumb machines. After all, for a while it worked and those people wrought miracles.

But then in a very un-clockwork fashion they began to break down. Humanity threw a cog, to draw an analogy, from international politics right down to the cellular level.

For example Joyce must have been what, fifteen? sixteen? when her friends donated their first major organ. Happy Birthday Joycie, they sang. Blow out your candles. Have a kidney.

Finally the struggle within the tin mouse she was holding stopped. Black glass eyes glittered up at her. With a final groan of defiance an old spring snapped out to bite her hand.

'Oh you dirty bastard!'

Vindictively Joyce pitched the toy back into the general junk, a faint crunch as it landed somewhere inside, and inspected her palm tremulously. A torn ridge of skin peeled up, neatly bisecting what might well be her life-line. Or heart. She had never been very good at palm reading hippy crap.

The skin curled on itself like a white pencil shaving. She bit it off; teeny squirts of blood on her tongue like old rust. Was it HIV that you caught from injuries on machinery? Or was that lockjaw?

'Steady on old girl,' Joyce told her tingling fingers. 'It's all psychosomatic, anyway.'

Sssand.

Joyce's old buddy. The sibilance stretched out, intensified until the spoken word became less a signifier and more the sheer embodiment of sand, of hot grains rubbing together. For a moment she felt the skin of her face tighten, its moisture sucked out as though she had plunged into an oven.

Then grey day returned. Joyce spat the piece of skin out. Poor abandoned scrap of my body, nobody needs you any more.

'You know,' she said conversationally and with what she felt was immense restraint. 'I notice it's never "Caribbean Resort" hissed at me in the ooky-kooky voice. Not for Joycie. For me it's just crap and awful things and more crap.'

Sss …

'Oh shut up. I got it the first time.'

The toy shop's bell jingled cheerfully with her exit.

Some time, a goodly time after the big noisy woman was gone the toy shop's tumbled brickwork came alive.

An army of real brown mice squeezed their soft little bodies from hundreds of cunning hidey-holes and came darting down the rubble. Frail, ordinary mice with tiny pink hands and quivering ears. Apt to drop dead from too much hot or cold, or from just sheer fright. Even capable of eating themselves to death given the chance,

Although Joyce was now long gone it took them a long time to be brave. A bit at a time they timidly crept close and then settled in to shiver and peer superstitiously into the blank bead eyes of the discarded mechanical mouse.

CHAPTER TWO

AUTOMATONS

INSANELY HUGE CURSIVE

THIS WAS the desert. Welcome to the crimson heart of fuck-all. Red sand in all directions.

Young (enough), full of spunk (or at least feeling it), Samuel tipped back his head and sucked in the kiln-thick air, his sweaty chest expanding against backpack straps. Loaded backpack and all, having achieved an amble in his overworked boots, Samuel was following the highway—although to call it a "highway" was a little like trying to pass off Niagara's chief attraction as a gentle summer mist.

Glistening black and straight as a bolt the highway shot out over the sand, seventeen lanes across, dunes on either side. Superheated air boiled from its midnight surface like cappuccino froth. In this heat the asphalt stink was threatening to corrode Samuel's nose right off his face.

Although it had looked inhumanly flawless from a distance, now that he was up close and personal Samuel found that the highway was actually a ruin. Only the great road trains could hope to travel its fractured surface now, where chunks of blind asphalt reared their heads like tarry bergs. Easily thirty or forty trailers long, some of the road trains: towering on futuristic suspension no honest vehicle outside of the military could hope to match.

But it had been a hell of a long time since Samuel had seen one of those roar past, and he listened for them closely—you had to get your ass over the hill right quick when they came. Perhaps trucking was dying out, too, finally defeated by the degrading face of the highway.

For Samuel his journey had begun in the town that the highway had set out from, and ended … who knew? There could be no better reason in his learned opinion to hoist a pack and find out. So far as the eye could see and quite a bit further there were only two things to the entire world. Hot, dead sand and road.

He did have company, though. Of sorts. Against all odds, little blobby things lived in the desert. They had once been something like bugs or worms; perhaps an illicit lovechild of the two; and they lived out their swollen little lives on the underside of stones where there was just enough cool to sustain them.

As the man passed they squidged further down into their hidden niches. Foremost on what was only a few steps removed from a true hive mind, they wondered together; "What the hell is he doing out here?"

Samuel's legs hurt. His shirt was sticking to his back. He had never felt so God damned alive and life was glorious.

In celebration he sucked back another scorching, enthusiastic lungful. 'Hello the desert!'

'*YAAAH!*' Came the unexpected response. Samuel glanced up in time to see a woman hurl herself off the top of a sand dune.

Still screaming, silhouetted between burning sky and sand she skidded perhaps ten meters triumphantly upright and in that instant was a Valkyrie, invincible, arms braced wide in classic surfer stance.

Then one foot lagged and she went over all at once, tumbling and rolling like a bowled octopus.

Samuel bolted forward, the pack thudding his spine, mouth dry (and wasn't *that* funny in the desert)—certain that the insane idiot had just killed herself. Wouldn't that be typical: the first face to talk to in weeks and she promptly goes and carks it.

But the woman lurched panting to her feet before he could reach her and punched a fist at the sky. 'Yeah! A road! How do you like that; a bloody *road*!'

Samuel took a reality check. Then another, to be on the safe side. Way back in the recesses he could still remember the grinding machine of the fashion industry with its endless parade of catwalk kitties; however, he had somehow never translated the grotesquery of such female proportion into real life. This goddess in the middle of nowhere soared awe-inspiringly into the stark ether, even sans heels. Graceful only in certain poses which she seemed to strike without thinking: a hand on her hip, one long thigh dropped.

Lacking the great leveller of cosmetics, despite being stretched mid-grin the woman's over-lipped mouth still pouted, an idiot bow that teetered beyond the bounds of good taste. Her skull bulged almost cephalatically to accommodate the huge eyes. Those eyes! They were what bothered him the most: they seemed to gape blindly through him, sun blasted and utterly strange. Hair that should have been a silky waterfall was instead dark, crudely hacked off fuzz. She looked like a mutilated doll.

Samuel glanced about bemusedly, half expecting a pack of paparazzi to come mincing down the dune in pursuit to hunting cries of "darling!" and "fabulous!" but the woman was all alone.

A good conversation starter eluded him. 'Um ...'

'Hi!' The stranger paused her victory dance long enough to turn that bright dizzy smile on him, so dizzy that it made him queasy. One front tooth was rotated slightly, a flaw that steadied him. 'Fancy seeing you here.' She might have been handing around canapés at a cocktail function, one ankle tucked coquettishly behind the other. 'Got anything to drink?'

'Um, sure.'

As he un-slung his canteen the tall woman's hands opened and closed compulsively by her sides: not that he found eagerness unattractive in a lady, mind. She was sunburned and peeling, with grim highlights such as her nose glowing as oxide red as the sand.

That was what was so wrong here! Samuel almost dropped the canteen handing it to her. There was nothing on this woman but her clothes! She might have been magically plucked from street or studio and plonked down here on the sand. He could not believe it. 'You didn't come all the way out here like that?'

'Uh huh.' The lady was chugging like a uni student already, shuddering and gasping as her body rejected this shocking new input. Still she forced the water down greedily, as one used to such insurrection from the ranks.

'But ... but this is the desert! You can't just stroll into the freakin' desert with no food, no water—look at you! Not even a bloody chap-stick ...'

Samuel was saved further outrage as a rush of sunspots caught up with her. Oooh yeah. She had definitely drunk that way too fast. Every cell whispered its prayer: *water, water*. Dazed and temporarily blinded she swallowed hard and concentrated on not fainting as the nausea-tsunami ripped through.

'Wasn't my idea,' she croaked. The words had to be eased past a pre-vommie lump. She shook on her feet like a boneless rag. 'Sent me. Said "sand". Jerk never says "holiday".' Icy sweat she could ill afford to lose broke out all over.

Samuel was quick to rescue his canteen before she could drop it. Relieved of responsibility the woman thumped to the sand in a sort of half-sit, half-fall, her gangly legs stuck out in front. He supposed she would be safe enough there for the moment and climbed, slipping and wallowing up the dune that she had surfed down.

Sand, hey? Well if that was the woman's mission she had certainly got her fill of it. All that he could see was glaring desert, with an occasional rock thrown in for good measure. The arid landscape pressed and sucked hungrily at his eyeballs.

Not that Samuel expected a tour bus, mind; but the desolation nailed home just how bizarre the woman's sudden appearance was. She did not fall from the heavens, either: there went her footprints, meandering in great aimless loops like a sleepwalker's. Estimating distance was not easy when the world looked so generic but that trail led over the hill and far, until his eye lost it in the rippling heat.

Had Samuel been able to get higher, perhaps to the soaring altitude of one of the rare desert eagles he would have seen something to really split his gasket.

In insanely huge cursive the footprints that appeared so drunken from the ground spelled "Joyce". At least eight hundred meters high to a letter, her name stamped on the desert's face like a fancy cattle brand.

C'est impossible, as the French would say. Those wacky French.

Shaking his head Samuel climbed/slid back down, only to discover that his fair damsel had effected a recovery and set off down the highway.

He jogged to catch up and while she did not wait, she did not speed up any either. 'Hey. I'm Samuel.'

'NicetameetyaSam.'

He winced. 'Just Samuel, please. Nobody calls me Sam.' A helplessly expectant pause which it became clear she was not about to break. 'And you are …?'

The woman shot him a comically suspicious glare: who wants to know? But oh, right, he had already given his credentials. 'Joyce. My name's Joyce. Although I'd imagine that folk call me whatever the hell they want.'

'Right. Joyce it is.' At their backs her giant name was being slowly blurred away by a desert that would not suffer any traveller to leave their mark. If only he knew. 'So, Joyce. Who wants you dead so badly?'

The veiled glare was open now; 'Why would you say that?'

'Nothing much. Only that when someone sends you into the big red on foot sans gear, you're generally not expected to see the other side. It was a time-honoured punishment for rustlers back in the day. And not to stick my nose in, but that then makes me wonder what a lass like yourself might have done to cheese anybody off so hard.'

Smirks were beginning to show through the gloom. 'A girl like me? I'll have you know that I can rub folk the wrong way as well as the next man.' Better, actually. 'Come to mention it, though, what is on the other side of this sandbox?'

'Spill the beans and I'll share: who sent you out here?'

'What does it matter anyhow? Who remembers the past these days? Half the populace out there can barely remember what they ate for breakfast this morning.'

'Interesting and totally unhelpful philosophy. Well, for my turn so sorry but I haven't the foggiest what might be out past the desert.'

Joyce goggled like a kid caught out by a magic trick. 'You don't?'

'Haven't been there yet, have I?'

Damn it, he had her there on logic. She hated that.

After a few moments of stewing; 'So where's your car then?'

'Car?'

'This is a road isn't it? I'm not mistaken?'

'Highway,' he corrected. 'One of the last great ones. Pretty slim chance of a car coming this way any more, some of the cracks are big enough to drop a car into. This is a trucking route.'

'Sure am glad the road monitor was here to set me straight on that one. So show us your truck then.'

'Don't have one.'

'Come again?'

'I'm about this the old fashioned way,' he elaborated. Then elaborated further: 'Walking.'

'Well crap.' Joyce exhaled wearily. 'My blisters have got blisters. The scenic route isn't nearly so much fun as I'd hoped.' Her careless heel kicked over a rock and unnoticed by either of them, twelve or so poor blobby things writhed agonising deaths in the hard afternoon light. Late afternoon sky, although in the desert every hour felt like noon.

'The scenic route … is it at all possible you were dropped on your head as a baby?'

She shrugged. 'Anything's possible.'

The sun was beginning its task of rolling down the heavens. With the horizon on fire and crimson sand below the world became a nightmarish blaze of red. Joyce's eyes watered under the assault; she found herself focussing narrowly on the cool blue of Samuel's eyes merely for the relief. He was far from discomforted.

'You hungry?'

'Dear lord yes. Yes.'

'Well I'm about ready to settle in and make myself dinner, camp, the lot. You're welcome to join me.'

A sort of smirk stirred her generous mouth. 'Gee Sam, I dunno. I did leave reservations at the Sheraton, and you *know* eight-thirty's cocktail hour. But guess I could stay seeing as it's for the pleasure of your company and all.'

'The name's Samuel. Keep up this Sam crap and it'll be nothing but a lump of coal and a spanking from Santa this Christmas.'

'Ah, but what sized lump?' Squatting comfortably in the

sand with no inclination to assist she watched him work. 'So what brought you out to this sun kissed wonderland?'

'I'm writing.' Samuel measured spirit into a little stove with the care of a bomb technician. 'Sort of a travel-diary-come-guidebook. About the way the world's become, I guess.'

'Why bother?'

'Come again?'

'I mean, nobody reads anymore. Folk wipe their asses with books, burn them, or use them to insulate their shacks. And it serves Mr Lovecraft quite right for frightening the pants off me when I was nine.'

'Serves you right, I'd say. What's a nine year old doing reading Lovecraft?'

'Well who's going to read your travelogue?'

'Somebody. Maybe thousands of years from now somebody will pick it up and go wow, so that's how things really were back then. That Samuel sure was a champ for writing it all down. Let's name a country after him.'

'You're wasting your time.'

'What makes you so sure?'

Joyce looked down evasively, doodling in the sand with a gnawed fingernail. 'Say stuff changes, gets better. Then the way the world is now won't matter anymore. None of us will matter. You ought to wait a bit and write about new things, not old—the old world's going to get left in the dust.'

She wiped away her sketch, the little stick figures, enjoying their obliteration and switched topics. 'What are you cooking?' The bubbling pot assaulted her nostrils without delicacy, but in a good way.

'Curry. I've had to make something to stick most of the veggies in; even dehydrated they're dying in the ass out here. And watch out if it's crunchy: the desert's no place for gourmet cooking.'

'It smells wonderful.' At this stage anything would. As Samuel was spooning out dinner Joyce felt her salivary glands kick into Pavlovian overload and it was a good thing that he handed over fork before plate, otherwise she might have just stuck her head straight in and inhaled it. Which would be a pity: first impressions were so important.

Even so, she seemed to be making an impact.

'Do you always eat so ... enthusiastically?'

'Compliments to the chef,' she snuffled. 'How are girls like me s'posed to eat?'

'Now that you mention it, I don't know. Side-saddle, I guess.'

'This really is fabulous.'

'Really?' he said, pleased. 'You're not just saying that?'

'Sam, do you have any idea when I last saw a vegetable? I haven't taken a crap in months, it's like my ass is glued shut.'

'Charming,' he conceded dryly.

She grinned unabashedly, still shovelling it in. A fair degree of sand was sliding down too. The sides of her cheeks, the insides where she bit and bit nervously, fizzed and stung—but it was a nice kind of hurt. Sort of curry-cauterising.

Unfortunately if Samuel were planning on scintillating discourse ... which was admittedly unlikely on the heels of her last comment but he would not mind understanding how the hell she got out here; he was to be sorely disappointed.

One moment the lady Joyce was ramming the meal's tail-end in: food, glorious food! The next she lay face-down in the sand. A thin, reedy snore began working its way out her nose.

Samuel dropped his spoon back in the pot. Only one fork and one spoon: he had not come prepared for company. Overhead the remainder of dusk's fierceness had pinkened and begun to leave the sky, pushed by an advancing wave of deep eggplant. Tangy runnels of sweat cooled in his shirt.

'What am I going to do with you?'

Snnoore. Like wet gravel shifting.

In lieu of an answer Samuel went right on and finished up both his meal and the camp, laying his sleeping bag there by the highway. Every now and again he glanced over but Joyce had dropped into sleep like a puppet with the strings cut. She did not even twitch.

A horrible thought occurred but checking her pulse he found it reassuringly steady and unimpressed with the trials of the day. He suppressed an evil schoolboy urge to dip her fingers into warm water, turn about for the fright she had just given him.

'Fine, you can just sleep there. You're too big to move.' Although he supposed he ought to make her more comfortable.

With a fair amount of shoving Samuel managed to get the tall woman into the recovery position where there was less danger of smothering. A bag jammed under her neck relieved that grinding snore which was a boon not only to his ears, but to untold numbers of nearby blobby things as well.

Joyce's skin was horribly sunburned: fiery, with blisters clustering about the delicate parts of her face. She looked an awful lot like a British tourist at the beach. All Samuel had in his pack was sunscreen—a first aid kit would have been an awesome idea, but is the sort of thing nobody packs until they have needed one.

He dubiously scanned the tube's ingredient list with their spiky-sounding names. Rumour had it the stuff was loaded with heavy metals which was not great, but perhaps the aloe vera had something to offer?

Under his fingertips Joyce's dreaming face felt hot and hard. Up this close she exuded a sort of salty animal smell: not something you would find in a Parisian salon but you could not precisely call it nasty, either. It mingled uneasily with the sunscreen tang, producing a potent third that was absorbed by his hands as they massaged the vulnerable line of her jaw. Infiltrator, from there it crept through his bloodstream to saturate and drown his body.

The lotion could not cool her. Her flesh was as sparse as could be managed while still leaving a real person inside. Samuel stared, fascinated. His grip on her frail neck could easily lock all the way around. Her collarbones looked sharp enough to slice him wide open. A deep swallow forced a little more moisture to his mouth.

Her shoulders rolled smoothly, leading his hands down. Her steady pulse became his new reference point as it lubbed, lubbed. Half-hypnotised, he would have ventured further but Joyce stirred and mumbled unhappily in a voice blurred by sleep.

'They're coming.'

Samuel's hands stopped their creepy creeping. That was it: he snapped the tube shut; no more. Another man perhaps, but not him. With the chaste care of a physician he tucked her long limbs carefully under a blanket.

'Following,' she groaned again in her sleep. The word ached with all the vulnerability of unconsciousness' longing. 'So beautiful. And I can't be there. I don't want to be left behind.'

'I won't leave,' Samuel answered brusquely and flushed as soon as he said it. To cover the embarrassment he wormed briskly into his sleeping bag: it was getting cold now. 'Just … get some rest.' And turned over to do just that.

Samuel might not have dropped off so tranquilly had he known that although the night looked peaceful, every cranny seethed with life. For a short time the blobby things were liberated from the tyranny of the sun.

Crossing between neighbouring rocks they met and gossiped—in pantomime, having no voices—they warred and fucked. Not surprisingly a good part of the gossip revolved around the two sleeping intruders; but having eavesdropped on only a thin instant in the couple's lives it was all hearsay.

In the midst of it all Samuel rested limply for a few hours but it was not an easy sleep. Rather, he sank all the way to the bottom as though thrust and pinned under by a powerful hand.

He had been subliminally aware of sobbing for some time before fighting his way back to the surface.

'Joyce.'

Unwilling to abandon his sleeping bag he commando-crawled in it over to her.

'Hey. Hey, it's ok.'

'It's not okay,' Joyce hiccupped in exhausted dry heaves, her poor body too parched for tears. 'It'll never be ok again.' In the dark all of the blobby things had become rapt listening statues, frozen in attitudes of rage, love and interpretive dance.

Dim starlight picked out her unhappy rictus of a face. Samuel's heart skittered: as though by compensation for her eyes the lower half of her face ran wet and bloody and her hands were just as bad, sand-encrusted from her attempts to staunch the flow.

Oh thank God ... it was just her nose, only from her nose. No reason to run about in a panic, he told himself sternly.

Joyce fought Samuel's insistent comforting until it because obvious that he was not about to let go: and then she let go, all at once, a bony tower of cards falling into his arms. She slumped so limply that had he not held her up and in she would have sunk into the sand and dissolved away.

Fetching his canteen Samuel urged another round of water into Joyce sip by sip until a touch of fluid squirted to her scratchy red eyes, daring enough to be wasted. All he could wish was that he stood in a more dignified position than hunkered down with his sleeping bag puddled around his ankles.

'Better? Joyce, are you ok now?'

'What?' Joyce's reaction could not have been more abrupt had he stuck a molten poker up her ass. She snapped all the way awake with a jerk, zero to one hundred and shoved him loose, yammering fast enough to blur the words together. 'Of course I'm ok, I'm fine, the only thing not fine 'round here is you, who the hell are you?'

'Look Joyce—just calm down! You were dreaming ...'

'Who?' She insisted shrilly. To be frank, waking terrified in the night was not groundbreaking stuff for Joyce but at no time in living memory had somebody been *right there* holding on to her.

'I'm Samuel. We met on the highway, you remember? I made curry.'

'The road, right.' Embarrassment wiped its feet and came right on in. 'Sam. Sure I remember, I ... oh gross, did I have a nosebleed?'

Fundamentally torn between correcting Joyce on the name or the highway thing, he went with the gripe that had dogged him since childhood. 'It's Samuel, actually. Here, take my hanky.'

'Thankyou.' It was difficult to remain mortified with a man who not only pocketed a flat ironed square of plaid but who actually called it his hanky. Wiping, Joyce reasoned she should probably be grateful that he did not just hock one up in the handkerchief and fall to scrubbing her face himself.

'I'm tidy.' Or close enough—as good as likely to get. 'Can I have some more water?'

'Here, but take it slow. You nearly passed out last time …'

'Yes, thankyou Mum.'

'Fine, fine.' The lady obviously harboured pretensions of being some grade-A hard-nut. In Samuel's sage experience girls like that were all mouth no pants: Xena on the outside, orphaned kittens within. He listened to her gasping and slurping in the dark.

In a sense it was a pity, all that water. As the lightness receded Joyce was left tied down in the depressing bedrock of her body. Walking for so long in the sun she had begun to feel so lovely and swimmy inside her skin. Free from life's little concerns.

Joyce handed the canteen back. 'I came out here because … well, a voice sent me. It's part of my job. Instructions only I can hear. You don't need to know anything more than that.'

Never was a embargo less likely to be honoured. Beyond their charmed circle a couple of blobby things nudged each other and leaned forward eagerly to catch Samuel's reply.

But whatever the reasonable, clean-cut young man might have thought was lost forever as a shattering bellow rolled out across the desert.

The couple's bones and gritted teeth reverberated to the brassy sound and, somewhat redundantly, Samuel jumped. Joyce with her more highly-tuned instinct for self-preservation was already fifteen meters away. Samuel watched bemusedly as she slid to a halt in the sand on the rather shamefaced realisation that, as awesome as the sound was, it had originated some ways off.

Cold start sprinting probably was not the best idea; it had been years since Joyce had indulged in such athletics. As she leaned gasping on her knees Samuel came to stand beside her, wondering if he ought to pat her back or something. 'Air horn.' The distant mechanical beast lowed again.

Straightening her spine Joyce winced at the second insistent blast although the shock value had mostly gone. 'Don't suppose you know Morse Code?'

'Don't ask like everybody knows it! Do you?'

'Not so much, no. I don't think there's enough pattern for it to be a code anyhow, it's just going "blaaah, blaaah".'

'Could be an SOS dumbed down for neophytes like us who don't get Morse Code? Save Our Souls.'

'Air horns don't have souls,' she snapped, as though the very idea was upsetting. 'Anyhow, we're awake now, so ... oh come on. You can't tell me you're not even a little curious.'

'I'm coming. Just give me a second to pack up.' Things were all right for girls who just collapsed and slept where they fell, he grumbled to himself.

Joyce watched curiously. Only a professional boy scout could have crammed the lot back into one pack with Samuel's neat alacrity; whereas any normal person would just go stark raving mad. In record time he had all and sundry swung on to his back. Joyce applauded dryly, and he saluted with his middle finger.

The eerie hoots: distress calls, or whatever they were; continued as the two of them walked down the highway together. Joyce had not been kidding about blisters on her blisters and they could only make slow progress: the woman was a wreck. Her body slipped and juddered when in motion like a broken down old cement mixer.

The tarmac was obligingly treacherous underfoot but was still better than either would go on the sand. Samuel seemed to remember that athletes used to deliberately train on the bloody stuff for the extra workload, and if that did not prove humanity was cracked nothing would. He kept the pace gentle, but could not guarantee the same for his tongue.

'So. Voices, huh? Is this a God thing?'

Joyce set her jaw in a gesture that any wise man would have known to watch for. 'I never said that.'

'Old Testament, or New? What?—it's a valid question.'

'Quit being a dick.'

'So that makes you … seraphim? Cherubim? Not one of those chubby little angels who don't wear underpants; you know, I see you as more of the smiting type.'

Joyce's big mouth opened up for retaliation but then some memory of her dream caught at her thoughts, hers being a mind that loved to fling such things in at the worst moment. She was treated to a glimpse of colour and bright music as though some heavenly host really had brushed by, but the remembrance brought no hope. Only a sickening twist of jealousy. Suddenly the angel gibe was not so funny anymore.

'No,' she answered curtly. 'Not me.'

'Save our souls. Is that it?'

She snorted grittily, recovering her equilibrium; 'Are you kidding? I've got more than enough trouble managing my own. Souls are pretty much the only things out there that aren't my problem!' And whose fault was that, that her sad electronic victims had no souls? Science? Engineers? The ever-popular government?

Samuel was so engrossed in watching judgment roll in across her face that looking where he was going went right out the window along with his footing. He did not go down gracefully.

'Oh dear.' Joyce kept right on, cattish affront in every stride. 'Hurt yourself, have you?'

He grimaced and rolled up his pants leg: a gritty scrape oozed through dishwater blond hair. Rubbing fingertips in slick blood he regained his feet. 'I'll live. Just.'

'I'm not some nutter if that's what you're thinking!'

Samuel grinned, hobbling to catch up; at least now they made more of a matched walking pair. 'God forfend.'

'It doesn't make me special or anything, quite the opposite. Were it up to me none of this crap would even be happening.'

'Thank God.'

'Were you born this funny or did you take lessons?'

'Lessons. Elementary A-Hole One-Oh-One.'

Joyce laughed, surprising herself. The impending apocalypse evaporated from her expression leaving only clear skies. 'You're a good man Sam.'

'Samuel. I aim to please.'

She pondered a little shyly, limping along beside him in the dark. 'Sam?'

'Samuel.'

'Can I hold your hand?'

He was not sure he had heard her right. 'Why?'

'Because it feels nice. Because you're a nice guy and you just fell down, and I haven't held anyone's hand in a really long time. Just because. Don't you ever do anything for no reason?'

Joyce's hand did look kind of empty down there, swinging by her side. Samuel took it. He had to admit that it was kind of nice. The tall woman's fingers were cool, at odds with her sunburned skin. Now should one of them find a ditch worth tripping into odds were that they would both go: all-for-one and all that. The comradeship was comforting.

The air horn groaned again. Up ahead they could finally see its source: a cluster of points looming against the sky. All orange, yellow and red as though a giant lit Christmas tree had been laid on its side. Target in sight Joyce picked up the pace, pulling eagerly as though Samuel were a reluctant extension of her arm.

Towed briskly along, he wondered if he had ever spent such an eccentric night in all his life? Probably once or twice at university.

The lights defied all sense of perspective. Even approaching it took a while to decipher the illusion: they had found a truck, and the damn thing was massive. It tilted crookedly, slewed onto the highway's verge with gargantuan treads on one side gouged deep into the sand. Only sidelights. The engine was a deep low throb that you could hear in your spine.

'Hello?' Samuel ventured and the horn blast cut mid-way, leaving their ears ringing. The cab door stood open. It creaked a little in the night breeze.

Entirely lacking his imagination Joyce pulled free and ran forward, her eyes shining like stars. Years peeled back to leave mainly child. 'Wow! Oh wow. He's beautiful!' She reverently patted the hauler's snout, unmindful of the filth coming off on her fingers, and then tried to hug it.

BANG! The truck's high beams blazed on, evaporating her in a detonation of light.

BANG! BANG! Then off, leaving pristine midnight.

On again: BANG! The world bleached sterile. Then off.

'Joyce!'

'I'm here.' Sitting on her tailbone in cool sand she shook her head blearily. Neon sea creatures swam before her eyes.

'Ben!' The scolding, grizzled old-man voice drifted out of the dark. He sounded gasping and weak for all his amused chastising. 'You really gonna holler help, then get cold feet at th' last second you big ole tease?'

Samuel found him. The trucker lay sprawled a meter or so from the cab, with his finger of reproductive flesh hanging limply from his fly. The sand was clotted all around with the uric reek of piss. One hand crabbed loosely at the old fellow's barrel chest inside a roomy flannelette shirt; what should have been ordinary everyday breathing had become an uphill marathon.

'Son, you mind tucking my snake in 'fore the lady gets herself an eyeful?' Embarrassment thickened the patois.

Always the gentleman, Samuel considerately obliged without expression. The old man's flesh felt cool, boneless and somehow dead in his palm, and the crinkly hair that he nestled it back in amongst was as scratchy as dry straw.

Heaving the now decent trucker upright, he got a breathless laugh in return. 'Hell, you seem like a decent type. Ain't many guys'd give that handshake before a proper introduction. Here,' he offered his hand. 'I'm Geoffrey.'

'They don't look like hope to me,' a sonorous voice countered. 'Hope's easy to recognise; it arrives bright with colour and laughter. Something altogether different sneaks out of the dark.'

'Well excuse me all to hell …' Joyce started.

'Can it Ben,' Geoffrey wheezed. 'And while you're at it, light the candles.'

The headlights flicked on again at a grudgingly low level. Enough for them to finally see the hauler sitting by the side of the highway: fire truck red, fabulous and bold, calling to mind adventures and heroes lost. Against it Geoffrey's sick face was the colour of old cheese.

'My truck, Ben,' he gasped the introduction. 'Don't mind his rot; literary pretensions an' all that you know. My Ben's a poet.'

CHAPTER THREE

AUTOMATONS

THE JUDGMENT DAY DINER

'I THINK HE'S had a heart attack.'

'Had?' Geoffrey wheezed, wincing at the knobbly jut of Samuel's knee beneath his head. '*Having*.'

Ben could accommodate all three passengers with Geoffrey lying down, so long as they were willing to get cosy. The trucker had his head in Samuel's lap, jolting wildly as they began their ascent up hundreds of gears, cresting the broken skin of the highway.

Man and truck must have journeyed together an awfully long time. Beneath their jouncing buttocks the upholstery exhaled decades of breathing, sweating and farting saved up into one noxious miasma. Joyce thought rather uncharitably of ancient, scabrous tomcats on heat, or of those withered zoo apes who scream and pump wildly at piss-soaked bars.

Poor Geoffrey looked no better since they had bundled him into the truck's cab; Samuel heaving, and Joyce shoving grimly with a face-full of chunky trucker ass. Worse, rather. His skin was greying out in the way of the bottle (cancer-sticks induce jaundice, but the really heavy alcoholics go stone grey, their abused bodies finally fading out on them. Clothed in ashes).

With his eyes slitted, focusing on the narrowing confines of his chest the trucker hissed on every out-breath like a deflating balloon, already unready for the trial of taking more on board. The oxygen seemed to just flow impotently in and out without reaching where it was needed. Still, it was better than lying in the sand like an upturned turtle, splattered with his own whizz.

And never mind that a life or death situation may not be the best moment to discuss comfort zones, but while Samuel was normally a fan of having his crotch investigated that was by invite only. Another man's skull butted into his groin was not how he had pictured this evening panning out.

With Geoffrey unable to take the wheel it fell to Joyce to tackle the behemoth truck's controls. In lieu of skill she managed with an Amazon's violent love-struck glee, and sober circumstance aside a manic grin threatened to pop out and disgrace her any moment.

She crunched a gear, missed, and then rammed that sucker in. If metal could flinch the entire cab would have recoiled around her. 'Sweet mother! Be gentle, that's my butt you're mangling!'

'Does. This. Look. Easy?'

'Yes, actually.' The truck switched his attention to where it really belonged. 'Now you just hang in there Geoff, we're getting you to the hospital ...'

Get her to the hospital, a pathetic squeak of a voice moaned in Joyce's skull and her gut twisted, the cramp drawing her knobbly spine up and painfully sideways. All the memories were starting in for a piece of her now, all of those pleas accumulated over the years into a great stinking heap, pouring its misery into her chest.

Yeah, well my cup runneth over, she snarled to herself. What she heard was the universal misery of mankind, a hapless phobia distilled tenfold in their creations: Don't leave me alone!—What will I do?

She wondered if either of the men had heard the terrible restraint that Ben lashed around his quietly spoken words. And all the while the engine was thundering, winding up to a run, an all-out sprint across the desert. Perhaps going through crisis without adrenaline, reflex or fleshly instinct left a machine with nothing but sanity.

But somehow, from the sound of him, she doubted that. Machines certainly had something akin to hysteria. Ben's cab might fly apart around them any second, casting them into the chaos of the truck's passage ... only that would mean no hospital for Geoffrey. So Ben gathered it all up and held it together by sheer will, as though fidelity still meant a damn thing.

They were rolling at a good clip now and a fond glow lit the trucker's streaming eyes, momentarily eclipsing even his body's tightening vice. He laid a gentle hand on the console. Joyce recognised the tenderness there, as foreign as it was to her nature—she reasoned her way to it as the blind might to colour.

'Come off it Ben.' Geoffrey coughed, and the stunning pain it brought dropped another ten years on his bowed neck. 'Even if we traipse all th' way out there do you really think anyone's left? Some doctor twiddling their thumbs, just waiting to patch my pump?'

'The hospital …'

'Shh. Come on now. We've had a damn time, haven't we? Better 'n I deserve.'

'Don't give up! Not yet!' Joyce's interjection was chopped staccato by feet pummelling pedals. Even with Sammy-boy glaring at her the clamour in her skull demanded that she speak. 'Hold on a little longer. There's a whole new world coming!'

'What've I got for any new world?' Geoffrey might have been waggling his finger fondly at some errant child; 'Too much already of this one.'

'But people don't get to just give up!' It was not fair.

'Can't expect you t' understand. Ain't no reward for doing the right thing, no matter who you do it for. Only the next day, an' the day after that …'

'But a new world! Don't you deserve all the new things, the same as everyone else?' Everybody but me, her traitor heart whispered. When you have all gone on I will be here alone.

'Nobody gets their heart's desire in th' end, missy. What I deserve is to stop and rest. I'm glad for all your marvellous hope that's coming, but rest is all I'm for. Not to have to think or to be anymore. And now's my chance.'

Joyce's arguments were not going to do any good. Waiting so long and fruitlessly for hope had left Geoffrey broken in some fundamental way. Terrified of having to endure what days were still stacked against him.

'Geoff.' Ben found his voice. 'Stay with me. We made promises—you promised.'

These conversations always came in duets: the abandoner and the bereft. The voyager and their victim.

'Ah, see now,' Geoffrey murmured wryly. He had never imagined doing this in front of a couple of gawping kids, but so be it. 'Never trust a poet: always blurting their heart out.'

'Fuck you!'

'Ben … if there's anything in this world worth stayin' for, it's you. But I'm so tired. I feel like if I don't take this chance it'll all grind down, everything that's left, *including* us. Then you'd have reason t' hate me.'

'I hate you now!'

Ben marvelled bitterly at what an idiot he must have seemed for all those years in his joy. How much of their time together had Geoffrey been rehearsing this? Flirting with this excuse or that, the words on his tongue like wine. Geoffrey had taken to not wearing the driver's harness lately, his pulse cut off from sensors that might have seen this coming. He had been cut off from Ben. Why hadn't he worn it? If Ben had teeth he would be grinding them.

But then, panicking: 'No, I don't hate you Geoff, I don't!' Feeling the edifice that was *them* totter. Let Geoffrey live with tearing it down if he could; the truck was unwilling to kick so much as a brick out himself.

It appeared that Geoffrey would not have to live with anything for very long. The trucker smiled tenderly, loving Ben, still intending to play the low-blow all the way. 'You'll let me go 'cause it's what I need. Won't hate me after, neither.'

He gasped, the worst sound they had heard from him yet. In the same moment the yellow hot blaze of dawn broke the horizon ahead, slamming blindingly through the windscreen. Joyce yelped and flung up her hands; not the best driving tactic but Ben rescued the steering with all the smoothness of a pro.

Out of all the chaos only Samuel knew what was happening. His legs were under the trucker and he felt something snap in the old man's body like stretched elastic. New lines of shock etched themselves around Geoffrey's mouth: the very near future graven in white marble. They ran on, the engine pounding.

Too impatient for farewells the sun's hot ball seemed to claw into the sky, touching the tips of sand ridges aflame to either side of the highway.

Tough as cured tendon Geoffrey reached for his sunglasses clipped to the shade but they were too damned high and it was beyond him now to sit up. Thankfully the young fella with the earnest eyes stretched and sat them on his face, freeing his hand to drop back to the dash. He was determined to be calm and spoke to his truck with simple dignity as though there were nobody else in the world. Behind the sunglasses a bright pyre glowed.

'Knowing there's some new world for you to go into is good, makes it easier.' Oh sure this was hard for Geoffrey but spare a thought for Ben—to be on that train outta dodge was miles off having to stand alone on the platform and watch it leave. Geoffrey chuckled to himself, a humour of tearing agony. 'You're the best my life's ever had.'

Then the blazing sun leaped free of the horizon. It was a glory that burned, never intended for frail human flesh. Staring into it Geoffrey sighed and died behind his glasses, swimming in the dawn's fierce light.

Those that he abandoned travelled on at juddering speed at least twelve hundred meters in moments before Ben realised his loss. By then Geoffrey's threadbare soul had been left far behind standing by the side of the highway. Did he feel anything anymore? Warm? Cold? Watching after them, mouth open as if to call out; did he wish at the last moment to have done life differently?

The only one to see Geoffrey's revenant was a lone desert eagle floating high above.

Should any observer have sailed with the bird they would have noted that its cruel beak hooked a shade heavier than Charlie Darwin would have liked, the wings were a touch too primitive, the eyes nearly blind from the sun. Trail the eagle back to its nest and you would find open-mouthed chicks with traits more rudimentary again, even less likely to survive than their predecessor. Thus the great rolling back of the world continued.

The eagle itself did not give a flip for tragedy. It could not assuage the constant, exhausting harassment of its chicks with ghosts and it could barely see the food that it had to catch. Ignoring the lonely sight of Geoffrey's dissolving phantom the eagle slid away across the sky.

'*Geoff?*' Ben's anguished cry was like a stab to Joyce's over-abused heart.

Seizing the wheel she slammed both feet down so hard that her calves groaned like strummed girders: the brakes hissed and boomed. Tyres locked up. As they slewed across the highway the cab's occupants were tossed painfully about and the logistics of actually bringing their headlong charge to a halt fell to Ben. The only person Ben cared about no longer felt anything at all.

Grinding, and a jiggling that chattered teeth. Then finally

they were still.

For a moment everything was quiet and awestruck. The juggernaut had been halted, blocks of highway torn up and tossed free behind.

Then hot metal boinged. No tragedy in the world could avert inappropriately humorous noises should physics dictate them.

Joyce wrenched Geoffrey from Samuel's lap by his shirt collar, angrily dashing water from her eyes before boy scout could see and start his smart mouth flapping. The limp body came unwillingly and her back pinged and twanged warning of unhappiness later on: the trucker's solid gut and the corded strength of his arms that had attested to life lived were now just one ungainly, lifeless lump. No need to unclip herself, she had never bothered with the creepy over-complicated seatbelt.

All that Joyce could hear was her internal monologue endlessly recycling her sins. Save them. Save us. Do not leave me.

Exerting all the leverage of her long frame she toppled backward with the trucker out of the cab, avoiding Samuel's hands as they tried to reclaim their burden. Forgiving hands, that was how they looked. Even twisting in the air she wanted to forsake breaking her fall to slap them aside: how dare Samuel forgive anything!

The air felt so much cleaner outside the cab. Well, likely it stank of asphalt but all Joyce asked was the world be blessedly clear of the fusty reek of old man. Impact. On the sandy verge, luckily: the road would have smashed her spine. Samuel was descending after her mouthing something, but with Ben's anguished groan all around like a scaffold warping to fall she could not catch a word. It was unlikely to be anything so congenial as "Merry Christmas".

'Lay him on his back,' Joyce recited from rote, chewing and spitting the words as though they offended. During CPR she had been more concerned with fake soul-kissing the mannequin to the appalled delight of her classmates—who could have predicted this situation ever arising?

'Head tilted; obstruction in the airway?' An investigative forefinger found only a loose tooth. The trucker's tongue was warm dough, wet buds that sprang up and down beneath her nail. A quick series of shudders ran down her spine.

Compressions: *breathe.* Sucking in the already toasty morning air Joyce flavoured it with her own life and drove it into the trucker's flattened lungs. That he would not want it, would have recoiled from the offering was beside the point. People did not get to just give up. From behind she heard Samuel climbing down and the furtive deep breath as he took in the clearer air: they could still enjoy such pleasures but none for Geoffrey, not anymore.

Breathe. Geoffrey's mouth was surprisingly fresh and minty; to feel pleased at the discovery felt very, very wrong. Come back you bastard, Joyce snarled between the count. Harder, press harder. Her hands quivered, cupped crossways as though trying to comfort each other during this violent task. She kept wanting to gag at the feel of his slack unresponsive flesh.

Bastard, get back here. It will all be new. *Breathe.* Again. Still again, damnit.

But bugger all was happening. For all she knew this pummelling away at Geoffrey's shop-worn frame might be driving him off rather than bringing him back, but she kept on as her world narrowed. Soon it was only as large as her rather knuckley fingers cupped on a barrel chest where the flesh hung so slack she could feel the curved ribs beneath.

Joyce blew into lax lips, the pressure smearing Geoffrey's weathered features all over what no longer formed a face: they had broken into separate elements and were slowly sliding apart.

'Joyce!' Samuel sprang up at her shoulder like a shock-in-the-box. Remaining quite rational within her body's beating shell Joyce understood that Sammy was not really swimming in flashing purple dots: she was failing to keep enough air for herself, and failing to save Geoffrey, simply failing.

'It's not fair,' her protest slurred out. 'New!'

'Just cut it out.' Capturing her cramping hands he hung onto them while she knelt in the sand panting in shallow gasps. No breath to wrest them back from him. Who would have thought oxygen was so handy?

Inwardly Samuel was rolling his eyes in exasperation: was the woman constantly on the verge of falling apart? But his outward face stayed all concern. 'Stop. There's no point keeping him going. There's no more help coming. We were it, we were the help.'

'You were the help,' Ben agreed softly.

'I'm sorry.' She was only gabbling now, as though something had rattled loose in that cropped skull of hers. 'I'm so sorry, I'm sorry.'

'Joyce stop it. Really.' Samuel considered slapping her; therapeutically, of course; but ruled a reluctant no on the very certain ground that she would smack him back twice as hard. 'You can't help him.'

'Why not?' She bellowed, finding some extra oomph down around her toes to rally with. 'Why should I only ever get to end stuff?'

'Get over yourself!' Samuel bellowed back. Growing up among sisters had prepared him rather admirably for bellowing. 'You are just a person, same as any of us and I hate to break it to you but nobody gets specially hand-picked to do anything. Not to save, not to kill, or any of it. On any given day people have to get up and decide what sort of person they're going to be, all on their own.'

Joyce wrenched sullenly out of his grip; there would be no more holding hands after that one.

'Fine.' Samuel stood, having had about enough of female histrionics. A set of boobs did not give one carte blanche to chuck a wobbly whenever circumstance invited.

Joyce had settled for staring sullenly at the ground which was very useful. Samuel un-kinked his spine and took a moment to stare around at the big fat nothing. Grains of sand rattled against Ben's wheels. They were the only help, that was for damned sure.

Geoffrey's body looked less real by the unforgiving light, lying in its impact crater. More of an impression in broad strokes by an artist who had failed to capture the man.

'Ought we to bury him?' Once the words were out not even Samuel fancied the sound of that. The highway was no place to be left behind. It was no place at all.

'No.' Ben was shocked to find that he had an opinion, even on this. That first wild agony was swiftly becoming an ache in his vitals, one that felt terrifyingly permanent. *No!* Ben's heart leaped up rebelliously: *I want to live!* But then in its darkest chambers it sighed *Geoff*, and were still. 'I can't leave him here.'

'I'm sorry Ben.' Now Samuel was on the sorry bandwagon, the inadequate words dribbling out feebly but what else could you offer?

'Who cares about some glitzy new world? I wanted him in this one.'

Wilfully ignorant that sometimes it is better to be kind than truthful Joyce rather tiredly dropped the second half of her bombshell. 'There's no place for you in the new world, Ben. It's for people, not machines. Geoffrey would have had to go without you.'

'Damnit Joyce!' Samuel snapped, wheeling around; 'What the hell is your problem?'

'People like you are my problem! You're everyone's problem!' She had sat smoothing the sand about Geoffrey but now stood, infused with new purpose, shaking red grains from her fingers. 'Let's put Geoffrey back in the truck.'

They began to heave doggedly, round two of this particular task but never having really understood the term "dead weight" before now. Joyce must have been leaving the bulk of the work to her homme, as she found the wind for an ongoing tirade. 'You think because Ben's speaking words you understand him? He thinks he cared about Geoffrey ...'

'I do.' Ben. Quietly. Standing firm against the moment he would have to adjust to reality, relax back into its flow and be carried along without Geoffrey.

'... do you even get what that means? Because if you think you do, you don't! He's a truck Samuel! It's worse than opposing cultures trying to get an idea across, only about a billion times worse and we were oh-so good with that in our day. A truck doesn't have hungers or a subconscious or needs like we do because it's a *machine*. The *opposite* of us; we're just little feathers of intellect floating on a vast churning reserve of organic craving.

'What Ben is we can't even imagine because it's the antithesis of our entire basis of *everything*; so don't you go assuming that because he uses our words they must mean the same thing! What the hell does it mean when he says he cares for someone?'

'Expert on love, too, are you?' Samuel clipped the last restraint into place to hold the trucker's body upright in the passenger seat. An ordinary seatbelt, unlike that of the driver's side which sported the sorts of straps and buckles you would expect to see on an amusement park ride.

Geoffrey's sunglasses had slipped and Samuel paused to replace them. Those dead, dead eyes boggling at the ongoing argument were disturbing but he could not bring himself to close the lids or, worse, ask Joyce to do it and unleash another torrent of derision. One black glasses lens was marred by a hairline crack. As they jostled Geoffrey about it caught the light like a wry wink as though reminding Samuel not to take Joyce to heart: just be cool.

'Joyce, surely you realise how utterly full of shit you are.' Ignoring his shoulder angel Samuel was going for broke. 'Whining and tossing in your sleep 'cause life looks so bad—think there's only endings in store for you? Well this is a real ending right here. You, you get to walk about and talk and *live*, if you'd only pull your thumb outta your ass long enough to try it; while Geoffrey sure as hell doesn't, and Ben …'

'What they had was fake!' Inside the cab, having successfully dodged the ass-shoving position this time, Joyce's anger had been mounting with the heat until both were strangling. 'It's all fake, do you understand? We made *things* that look and sound real, and then got attached because that's what sentimental lonely humans do. We made the fake safer to love than each other: we dug our own trap! Sign up for a machine instead of a pet, a friend, a baby—what? The cities are empty? Best bring in more machines then, make them cuddly. God forbid that the last human jerk left on the planet should ever feel lonely!' She laughed wildly.

Like a small island nation although excluded from their war Ben was still vulnerable to the fallout. 'If I even thought I was bad for Geoff, don't you think I'd have left?'

'Could you have?'

'He left me.' Which was no answer at all.

'You're not everything you think you are Ben. It's not your fault: nobody had any right to pretend that we could just hand out souls. Nobody bothered to think about it—just sat around applauding each other, with no idea of what we had done …'

'My Geoff wasn't thick! We were together for forty-six years for heaven's sake; in all that time wouldn't he have twigged if I weren't real?'

'Not if he didn't want to, he wouldn't.'

Listening to the rubbish pouring from Joyce's mouth Samuel's good ol' boy patience finally passed its use-by date. 'So Ben isn't real, huh? So says the great Joyce; and so of course some soulless hunk of programming can't really be suffering right now, he only thinks he is, so it's ok to say whatever the hell we want. How could I ever have doubted such flawless compassionate reasoning?'

'What is the weather like on your planet?' she hissed. 'No, really, please tell me: you, you wander about the rubble like some middle-class pomp touring the third-world from an air conditioned bus, drivelling into your little book … look around Sam! Everything just tickety-boo with the world? And you think that people need some holiday diary to make their lives better—are you utterly nuts?!'

'At least I'm making something!' Samuel could not believe who he had just copped the crazy card from, and tickety-boo to boot! 'Better than shitting all over what others have spent their lives building! You're … you're inhuman, that's what! Just heartlessly keeping on and on without stopping to care for one minute how anybody else feels. You reckon Ben here doesn't know if he's real or not? Well I know who I'm casting my vote for because out of the two of you, you're far more the candidate for being a damned machine!'

Hideous fireworks exploded. There were no words, Joyce was that enraged. Stiff-armed she shoved Samuel square in his scrawny chicken chest, longing for the might to fling his skinny ass right away across the desert. Surprise wiped pomposity from his face as he flew backward from the cab, arms pin-wheeling with just enough time to think "ouch" before the impact hit home.

Carpe diem! Joyce slammed the door shut while on his hands and knees Samuel tried to compute what had just happened. Her heart thumped with exultation and dread all layered up together like a birthday cake. 'Ben, we are leaving! Right now! Go!'

'Whoa, whoa!' Ben protested on both the ex- and internal speakers for the benefit of all involved—good old Switzerland, the other trucks had called him, mocking his failure to engage in the spats that they loved so well. 'I don't pretend to understand what sort of hormonal crazy you two have going on here but I am telling you right now missy, there's no way you can abandon Samuel out here.'

'Actually, I can. Absolutely I can.' Trembling—excited of course, not scared, Joyce wound down the window. 'Well ol' Sammy. After all our precious time together what can I say, except: sod off.'

Samuel looked measuredly at his hands planted in the sand, taking the time to collect himself although a muscle in his jaw twitched angrily. He now had sand up his nose and all through his hair, and a nice gritty scoop of it had somehow ended up in his mouth. The sand was hot. It sure seemed that when you touched a nerve with Joyce you yanked that sucker good and brought on a wave of reactions, all of them set to holocaust. How on earth had such an emotional disaster area ever made it to adulthood?

He glared up into Joyce's eyes, probing. The dawn light was

too harsh to see their colour but as for the expression, well: he would not have thought that "you stupid jerk" could be spelt out visually but hey, there it was. Women tended to draw back from such a frank examination but Samuel could read no hesitation in that stony face, not a flicker of uncertainty. If she loathed him now, then according to that look it went right down to her toes.

She was good, he had to give her that. She would be a dab hand at poker. Anyone would think that she actually meant to leave him here!

'Fine.' He crossed his arms.

Ben slipped up a hysterical notch. 'Don't be crazy man!'

Samuel patted the truck's big wheel reassuringly, although still glaring challengingly up at Joyce. 'She's not going to leave me. Not out here in the desert.'

Unmoved by all the shouting and hoo-ha Geoffrey's sunglasses stared ahead through the windscreen. One lens gravely considered what distance remained to be travelled while the cracked one winked.

Ben's engine cycled up reluctantly and Samuel had to step back from the juddering wheels as they fought to drag inertia from the verge, dangerously close to the highway's edge— once again Joyce's failure to notice even in passing how her antics endangered others.

'Look, Samuel …' Ben began to call over the rumble but Samuel flapped a nonchalant hand.

'She's so not going to leave me here. Go on. You'll be turning around before you've even hit the skyline.'

The engine really started to roar, blotting out what the truck was yelling and off they went. Samuel refrained from giving an ironic little wave.

The great red truck had been vanished over the horizon for several long humbling hours before Samuel started walking.

At first he had stood waiting keenly, not wanting Joyce to catch him appearing bored or God forbid, worried. He planned to look all casual when she swung that behemoth around and rolled contritely back.

That plan stuck for a while and then a while longer of shifting from foot to foot. Eventually physical discomfort won out over pride and he sat.

Samuel's core temperature, comfortably flattened by Ben's air conditioning, began to soar. Gradually the stupid waiting prised open a sinking pit of quicksand in his stomach. If asked, he would put patience on a list of his top ten virtues (the only difficulty in getting him to stop at ten); but just as pride gives way to physicality, so even his thick donkey stubbornness had to eventually bow to fact.   That bitch, that … Samuel's pack was still in the truck, stuffed into the foot well and likely forgotten by Ben's new captain as she steered on into her mad destiny.

Now Samuel was the one without food, water or even a chap stick; precisely the state that he had found Joyce in. Their fates had done some bizarre sort of do-si-do. He was going to die here.

Even worse, she had driven off with his damned book!

So Samuel walked. What else could he do? He only had the highway to follow now: even the cloud that had boiled in Ben's wake had settled. Silent, shifting sand presided.

His head hung low under the glare of the sun; it was exquisitely difficult to think. He wanted water, already. Badly. And to think only yesterday he had trod this selfsame highway heading in the same direction and all, but what a difference the right equipment made! In order to exist the modern human lugged about a veritable arsenal, or arranged the environment to provide them. But turns out when your number came up, to die all you needed was yourself.

Sweat, humid and unhelpful, seeped copiously about Samuel's bowed neck and shoulders. Realising that he was doomed his body's traitor water was fleeing for a more productive future elsewhere. Sweat was chafing his armpits and favoured pant-related spots something vicious; it stung his eyes and lips, filled his breathing air with salt.

Doomed. Such a flashy, ridiculous word. Surely folk shuffled modestly off the coil all of the time without being *doomed*. The tarmac was a brisk chemical burn to the tender pink inside of his nostrils.

'Kiddo, you're gonna start hallucinating soon. Not enough juice. Brain'll shrivel up like a walnut.'

'Thanks. A bit on the obvious side, isn't it?'

'Isn't it?'

Samuel did not bother to look. The last he had heard of his father was some years back when an otherwise charming blond the size of a wren had slipped him a roofie and stolen his shoes at a New Year's rave. Already in a foul mood, instead of enjoying himself he had then wasted the night demanding to know why he had had to be telephoned by one of the old man's nervous snivelling tarts to say Daddy had passed away in a hotel room.

Bastard probably went out with a smile on his face. He had that sort of life.

'Everybody knows that people hallucinate about their parents before they die, *Dad*. Unresolved issues and all that. Personally I always wanted to sneak back in the night and take a big steaming piss on your grave, you know that?'

'Real firecracker, isn't she?' Startled this time Samuel did glance up in time to catch one of his hallucination-Dad's bright blue eyes drop a conspiratorial wink.

'Dad! This is not one of your "hobbies" we're talking about—this woman has deep bizarre issues that I for one believe should be medicated! Possibly using a tranquiliser gun!'

At that Dad cracked up, uproarious guffaws echoing off the sandy flatness. Samuel did not wonder at all that he remembered that laugh so well; for a long time before he learned better it had been the crux on which all the joy and disappointment of his childhood had swung. His gut tightened angrily.

'Always one for the safe option, hey Sammy?'

'I have a proper name. You ought to know, you named me!'

Only imagination could have transplanted that wistful smile from more congenial soil onto his father's hard bright features. 'Still battling the nicknames then. You oughta have learned by now that in the unlikely chance that a man gets remembered at all, he's got a bee's dick's chance of dictating what for.'

Samuel shook his head in disbelief. 'Seriously, my dead father pops up after so long with, mind you, his pants buttoned for a change and this is the best wisdom I get?'

'Still.' Without its bantering edge Dad's voice scarcely carried further than a whisper. The slight man pacing the verge left no footprints. 'You have to use your noggin now. It looks like there might be important stuff going on here, of the earth shattering kind even, but you have to ask yourself: What's important to you? Really important. Because if you get this one wrong you can sure forget that travel book of yours.'

'Thank you very much. Ignoring the fact of your final ambition being to get your miserable old rocks off that one last time, that made about all the sense I'd expect from a million expiring brain cells.'

'Take it as those fatherly pearls of wisdom you were always hankerin' for. It wouldn't hurt you so much to pick what you want and go after it.'

'Like you did, huh?'

'Merely wanting anything for yourself is already a betrayal of those around you: their needs and their wants and their plans as to your role in getting it for them. The least you could manage would be to see something of your own into the bargain.'

'You selfish old fuck.'

'Well excuse me all to hell. And hey, would you look at that!' Dear old Dad, ever the topic-switcher, was pointing to a black blob on the horizon. When Samuel looked back he had gone.

'Ooo-kayee.' Samuel let out a long whistling breath. So far as his confused stinging eyes could tell the unexciting blob was no more than it looked, except that the highway appeared to lead to it.

Motion, even pointless motion was still better than waiting for salvation that would never come so Samuel set his head back down and resumed trudging. He was getting pretty good at the ol' trudge, all things considered, what with the lost backpack and all.

Or at least he thought he was. At some point it filtered through to Samuel that he was actually laying full length, limbs trembling as they tried to accept his commands to walk. The sand was as hot as a sauna bench and he breathed dry fire.

He should have pulled his shirt over his head for shade right from the get-go, rather than assuming he had already given up. He should have waited for night. Should have done a lot of things.

Well this was rubbish, he was not going to get far on his belly! Samuel raised his head but everything more than a meter away ran in a weeping blur. Even such small elevation squeezed his arid skull and he laid it back on his arms. The breeze stirred his sandy hair.

A sound was throbbing, pulsing the in the gut more than the ears. Initially distant, as distant as Samuel was from himself, it swelled with eager speed and in turn forced Samuel back to himself to deal with it. The sound became close and wrackingly harsh, bludgeoning his poor burned senses back to consciousness whether he chose it or not.

Samuel peeled his cheek blindly from the sand and a voice in the ludicrously friendly cant of the north coast said: 'There now mate. You just take it easy.'

And water was put into his mouth.

Flying down the highway pillion on a motorcycle, the wind brought Samuel the rest of the way back. And hallelujah, his enquiring mind came too. 'I thought that only trucks could travel the highway,' he shouted over the engine's roar.

'Trucks—and this baby,' the impossibly lanky biker bellowed back, tall frame sagging into the road monster as though they belonged together. Samuel had always imagined a motorcycle to be something elegant, like a flying droplet turned sideways; whereas this throbbing, grinding mount resembled an industrial production-line on wheels. Machinery of brute force barely constrained, that if you put a foot wrong would gladly chew you up and spit you contemptuously onto the road.

As the biker was talking with his helmet turned a crater loomed ahead. Samuel bit his tongue trying to scream, but the motorcycle bucked of its own accord and almost seemed to leap the gap. They landed with a hip-dislocating crunch, never mind the state of his terrified bladder.

Did not seem to bother the biker any though, he crowed with delight. 'Anyways, Ben said you was out here so I put my hand up an' said "why don't I shoot out and collect ya". We all appreciate you bein' there for Geoffrey, for tryin' to help. Everybody liked him. He was … a good sort.'

'Thank you.' Chit chat at the top of scorched lungs was not easy but Samuel was no quitter. 'Ah, who's "everybody"?'

In a gesture eerily reminiscent of his hallucinogenic father the biker pointed ahead to where at speed the nondescript blob was resolving rapidly into a nondescript oblong. Then a much less nondescript building.

Finally they were close enough to read the incongruously pink neon sign perched on top like a lewd guiding star: near-invisible by day, it must blaze at night like a call to Vegas. JUDGMENT DAY DINER.

'You like that? Did the wiring myself. Stopped melting shoes around the third try—Missus was ready to scream the roof down by then but I told her, sweetpea, that sign's got good chi.'

The judgment day diner was a trucking stop crouched by the highway, with perhaps a dozen of the road giants in a block of compacted dust out front. There were all sorts of trucks to Samuel's uneducated eye: some looking down long noses, or snub with the engine behind the head, gleaming as-new chassis or well-pitted with rust. The least of them would have topped six hundred forty tonne.

The biker rolled to an easy stop on the flat pan, and there alongside pin-neat rows Ben had been left slewed in a careless space-eating diagonal. Because some things never change somebody had written "wash me" in the thick dust of his flank.

In one elegant move the biker kicked down the stand and swung off, leaving Samuel feeling a bit ridiculous sitting up there on his own. The biker shucked his helmet and dusted down his knees, so thin as to resemble a modern mummy wrapped in faded brown leather as cerements. 'I'm gonna grab a beer after all that. Come inside, the guys'll wanna meet you.'

Regaining his own two feet Samuel jiggled a bit, trying to encourage reluctant testicles to drop back out of his lower colon. 'Absolutely. Be with you in a minute.' Alcohol was awesome for sunstroke.

He wandered in amongst the trucks' sleepy gossip. 'Hey, thanks a bunch Ben.'

'Samuel!' Recent history aside the truck sounded genuinely, innocently pleased to find him there—which was fair enough: Samuel felt quite pleased himself. 'Hey, everybody, this is the young fellow that I was telling you all about. I *said* he was a stayer and would make it, had that look. The world likes him too much to let him die.' And then slyly: 'Not so bright, though. I knew that she meant it.'

'Well I think it's revolting!' A lime green hauler chimed in nasally and uninvited. She sounded disturbingly like Samuel's grade nine sex ed teacher, a citrus-faced woman wound so tight she could not sit down for fear of sucking up the furniture. 'Leaving another human out there! It takes so very little and poof! they're gone … uh, sorry Ben.'

'Don't mention it,' came the polite answer but Samuel got the suspicion that should repercussions and the like not factor in, Ben would not mind "poof"-ing the mouthy green truck. If only Ben could have met Samuel's old teacher: he would have rolled right on over her.

Still, the green truck's thoughtless blundering had nudged

the great red hauler into a melancholy mood. 'Geoff liked to talk like he was invincible, you know how humans are. He was so alive that I guess I went and believed it too, for a while. The only one who really knew better in the end was him.'

'Uh, Ben?' This really did not seem the best moment to interrupt but Samuel was dying to know. 'Do you still have my pack with you?'

'Sure. Your lady friend had a brief gander through it.' That put a squeeze on Samuel's heart.

The cab door creaked obligingly open and suddenly his guts shrank in tight with poor mistreated balls shrieking falsetto because for a moment he thought Geoffrey was still sitting there, cracked glasses winking down at him—hey you made it buddy, care to join me?

Which was crap of course, the only thing there was Samuel's overstretched imagination. The odd seatbelts swung free, restraining no one, and all that remained was Samuel's rather battered pack. He clutched it down eagerly.

Travelogue: check. Thank God. After deeming it inedible Joyce had not touched it. Samuel allowed himself a tight sigh of relief, a little smile. Every day his travelogue grew like a Japanese movie monster, pages upon pages. He did not like to think about the day that he would have to choose between carrying supplies or paper, since both sustained him in their own way.

He whiffled through notes with his thumb, already longing for a quiet spot and a pen. The Diner in the Desert. What a great title for a chapter.

While Samuel took stock of his few possessions and of life in general, Joyce was dying in a restroom cubicle.

She was taking a crap. The sort of shattering bowel movement that weakens the knees and makes your head all light and swimmy. Joyce was firmly convinced that she was dying; to faint would be a blessing, but she wanted her head no nearer to the sheer horror of what was going on down there. Space-time itself warped around the cubicle from the awfulness.

Her clammy, blanched features were pointed at the ceiling, lips moving in a silent litany of blasphemy versus prayer, when the outside door banged open. That in itself was no surprise—likely death's angel was coming for her, or the horsemen of the apocalypse, or the centre for disease control if any of those guys were still kicking around anymore.

What she did not expect was to hear Samuel's exclamation echo around the tiled bathroom. 'Oh sweet Jesus, that's just not human!'

Joyce mentally smacked her forehead against the cubicle wall in despair. Why? Why of all people must it be him?

Of course there were any number of reasons why Samuel should not be in the ladies bathroom, but his personal ethic twisted in a curious series of crossways and loopholes. He knew for virtuous fact that he would never *actually* peek under a toilet stall, fondle a sleeping damsel or fail any of the other moral dilemmas life might throw at him. He loved the secret interior image of himself too much to do otherwise. Securely girt by principal, he then saw nothing untoward about banging the door open and strolling right on in. Creepy bathroom stalker? Other guys, sure: but not good ol' Samuel.

'It was the food,' Joyce said mournfully. 'The people at the diner gave me the trucker's special. I ought to have known better but all those elephantine bastards were gromphing it down by the bucket-load.'

'Now you know what's so special about it.' He could not help himself. Still, smart-assery aside Samuel shuddered picturing Joyce pitting her matchstick frame against a meal intended for a hundred and fifty kilogram truckers. 'Do you know what was in it?'

'Beans, I think. Mostly beans. And onion. And a lot of red stuff.'

'Well you know what, serves you damned well right!' Like a rock rolling downhill Samuel began to gather an avalanche of indignation as the exhausted jumble of the day pushed its way to the surface. With sleeve over his nose he was also striving to become the world's first anaerobic man. If this did not put the final nail in the Breatharians' coffin he did not know what would.

'What sort of lunatic goes and leaves people in the middle of nowhere to die, just because you had a tantie!'

'Quit your bellyaching Sammy.' She shifted gingerly; it was a poor choice in terminology. 'You're alive ain't cha? And here.'

'No thanks to you!' he raged. 'My pack, everything I needed to live was in that truck! You took everything!'

'Look, it's over now and you survived. Are you going to stand there winding yourself up over what's been and done, or will you make yourself useful and pass me in some more toilet paper?'

Samuel squeezed his eyes shut and counted to ten just like the self-help books suggested. Then backwards. And forwards again. When he opened them he could finally unclench his teeth enough to talk.

'What I intend to *make myself useful* doing is to go hit the bar and drink about twenty litres of water. Then I intend to eat something that doesn't napalm your intestinal tract, *then* book a room, have a nice cool shower and get some sleep.

And since you're so practiced at it and all, I fully intend to leave you to look after your own damned self!'

'You're leaving me?'

Ah, now that was what Samuel wanted to hear. Perhaps now Joyce could appreciate a little of the raw panic he had felt at being abandoned out on the highway. But en route to the door he paused. Joyce really was suffering in there, no doubt about it. Maybe he shouldn't be such a jerk.

'Come on Sam—don't be such a jerk.'

She ... she was impossible! 'Enjoy your night Joyce. At least that's fixed your vegetable problem.'

Even basted in cold sweat and as trembling sick as a dog Joyce could appreciate a parting shot. Peals of her shaky laughter chased Samuel's offended back from the restroom.

CHAPTER FOUR

AUTOMATONS

Poor Man's Dystopia

In the solemn quiet of morning a watery smear peeped between Joyce's pale thighs. Secretive, a fox's plume vanishing into the underbrush. She found herself literally dumbfounded. It had been so long between crimson intermissions that she had come to regard herself as retired, those tender figs of ovaries flicked away by providence: you won't be needing *these*.

The air of the enclosed bathroom was stuffy with damp towels left to lie, cracked tile and blobs of a rough floral shampoo in dear wee complimentary tubes. Billowing steam fingered everything, coating surfaces in fragrant droplets and prising up the paintwork to slip subversive spores beneath.

Joyce's wrinkled white digits squeaked across the mirror. She frowned into her reflection and wiggled those severe eyebrows as solemnly as any child savage confronting her image for the first time, lifted her chin before deciding that yes, it really did seem to be her. The unnerving dislocation of the familiar-unfamiliar.

Just left of vanity, of particular interest was the progress of Joyce's nutritionally facilitated revival. Get some food in the old diet indeed! She had stacked on a few kilograms that had, wonder of wonders, migrated to all of her favourite landmarks first. Call them potential tourist attractions in the topography of her body. An eyelid pinched down saw red tributaries spilling onto the jellied white floodplain: *white*, not yellow!

The occasional nosebleed still cropped up—she had resignedly taken to scrubbing her sheets in the basin and stringing them across the furniture where they dried in the shape of chair backs and had to be pummelled back to softness—but that aside she was practically healthy!

Joyce plucked absently at her towel. Being the same general dimensions as Samuel's staid plaid hanky it left little to the imagination, but you could not fault the diner's linen for being virtuously clean. Redolent of lavender like an old ladies' home with "JDD" picked out neatly in lemon thread. Towels, scented soap, showers. Such luxury!

Like health, the judgment day diner itself made Joyce uneasy. Its comfort threatened to become familiar, disrupting the masochistic links between self and circumstance she needed, for without self-blame then everything inflicted upon her happened entirely outside of her control.

But the diner. What sort of folk barricaded themselves in a place like this with all the wide world out there? The building clothed itself in beige like some badge of respectability: colourless carpets, protective camouflage. A forced plainness that did all but scream "Don't look at me! I'm ordinary!".

Of all the décor it was the carefully inoffensive paintings that got under Joyce's skin the most. On every wall hung these awful, awful artworks in their heavy rustic frames; nostalgic drippings of cane ripening, cows mooing and other barnyard friends enjoying whatever meat experienced between spawning and the table.

Some nincompoop had been longing for a pastoral utopia when they tricked out the diner. A slower, more fulfilling world. Where everybody donned akubras and adopted ludicrous accents, and never mind that in reality you would be facing a good trampling by livestock, or your tractor rolling, or plugging up with stones and no emergency department for days in any direction. The Simple Life: when dreamed of it was an impossible wet dream of modern convenience and rustic charm. None of which changed in the merest iota the reality of being clacker-deep in sand out here.

'Sand,' Joyce's reflection muttered scornfully, biting her lip.

'Can we move this along?'

With a squawk Joyce spun to find Samuel loitering in the doorway—aghast audience of one as she slipped and crashed spectacularly to the tiles.

'Oh my God I'm sorry! I didn't mean to scare you.' With the tiny towel and everything there did not seem to be any chivalrous way to assist so Samuel had to settle for hovering and wincing.

True to form Joyce would have plenty to say if it weren't for the silent screaming: her jaws gaped wide without so much as a whine escaping. Her rather fleshless state had made the impact the equivalent of a giant all-over whacked elbow. Finally air rushed back in like the tide between her white lips. Rummaging, she found the word and the word was: "*OW!*"

Dignity being long by the wayside Joyce solved Captain Wonderful's dilemma by seizing his arm to haul herself up. A quick inventory found no bones punching out through the skin, so presumably no real harm done.

'Holy crap!' Samuel could not credit how rapidly the purple, black and jealous green blossomed in Joyce's skin. Rotten colours, like dye injected into watered milk. 'I am so sorry.'

She blew on a rapidly darkening elbow and snatched at the towel: whoops, almost unleashed a nipple on the world there. Decency was clearly impossible; it was more a case of knowing the strategic zones to conceal. 'Sure you are. Delicate, lamb-like poppet that I am and all.'

'Well you need to delicately hurry it up some. There's no such thing as being fashionably late to a wake.'

'Fine, fine.' Joyce turned back to the mirror-mirror on the wall and flapped a long-boned hand at him. Droplets flung from her fingertips pattered his cheek. 'Clear out then. I'll only be a second.'

In the reflection Joyce caught Sammy's exiting appraisal of her, the dirty perve, but was entirely unprepared for her own reaction to those warm eyes. Resurrection! Hormones she had written off as extinct sprang to life and began pouring excitement into her bloodstream.

I am going to get groinal with this man, Joyce admitted to herself with a quiver of wonder. Not *immediately* this second (although impulse shrieked "Do it!" gleefully), but it would be inevitable.

Eager queries tumbled in to her long starved imagination. How would his weight feel, this flosser of teeth and trimmer of pubes. Would the rich musk of his crotch captured in his underpants be nice or nasty? *Nasty, nasty!* imagination hooted.

And if Joyce were to be completely honest with herself there was no hurry—for after doing the wild thing Samuel would likely no longer be on her side. Assuming that he was now.

To be daunted by all this went against everything Joyce stood for; not an option if she was to ever look boy scout in the face again. With a matador's flourish she flung off the towel, bold challenge in the turn of her wrist as though baring her skin not only to eye but the beast and the sharpened horn.

Even in her half-fleshed state Joyce was still a woman and all that sprang to Samuel's regard were curves and long sweeping lines. Cupped by gaze and mirror front and back nothing was hidden, an impossible figure wind-etched in bone. On display before him like any trinket you might purchase.

Rather predictably Samuel fled with his well-mannered ears burning brightly enough to guide Santa's sleigh.

Abandoned, Joyce's mischievous grin slipped as though about to drop off and smash on the tile. She faced the mirror, slowly covering herself up.

Nothing here but an ordinary town, right? Smack in the sandy middle of nowhere for her to stumble across. Coincidence? Not bloody likely.

Death was trying to come in at this place and more fool the fools for huddling behind their paintings and linen while veined wings trembled, boiled eyes stared blindly in at them from the other side of the pane. Patiently … stupidly? Surely death was stupid, the way it came dolloped out like thick cream. Stupidly it butted its senseless head against the glass for entry like a sick fly, not even looking for a way. Cunning was not needed because sooner or later sheer time would pull down all barriers.

With a soggy fingertip Joyce traced "please" on the mirror. Please don't make me hurt them. I don't want to let it in. But why else would she be here?

'Hurry up in there!'

'I am!' she bellowed back, fishing the nearest pants from the tiles. A cautious sniff-test pronounced them clean enough, and she began yanking them on.

Geoffrey's wake was held out in the parking lot, under the burning sun. The trucks needed the steel-laced asphalt to avoid sinking under their own incredible weight—in fact a little rough excavation anywhere hereabouts would reveal the topsoil honeycombed with alloy. Samuel's first impression of the diner's lot as no more than a dustbowl had been dead wrong.

He was apparently also the only one brimming with questions. Such as: what massive excavations made this place? Who built it? Shrugs. No living memory recalled a truck getting bogged down so they at least must know the limits of the subterranean structure, but it had been in place long before the first townsfolk arrived.

So much for a passion for local colour: the wake's populace were both passion- and colourless. Although the entire town, whose houses huddled fearfully behind the diner, attended, their only shared quality seemed a cool indifference to what might be loitering beyond the wilful fog screening off the moments both before and after right now. An audience for his travelogue, Samuel suspected, was not to be found here.

The trucks, who knew more, said less. Like a steel wall they loomed in a loose circle about the squishy sapiens, observing through windscreens as big and blank as department store windows. Even the most corroding hulks had been scoured and polished diligently to bright shining glory, reflecting the unbearable sky. Here and there black silk fluttered forlornly, ribbon that the faithful trucks would wear long after the rust returned, until the last scraps of it bleached and rotted away.

People standing nearby simply let the massive vehicles dip into conversation as they pleased. Few laid claim to not having known the departed. Another time and it would have been Geoffrey himself zeroing in on any newcomers, drinks for them already in hand because the world according to Geoffrey would never let folk, especially strangers stand alone at a party. So in his memory the reluctant arms of the town enfolded Samuel and Joyce.

They joined the gathering close to Ben, sticking with what they knew although the red giant had little to offer. Ben seemed to shrivel in his metal shell as the afternoon progressed and people ventured singly or in pairs to offer condolences. Sad, for one who had spread his poetry and Geoffrey's laughter from one end of the highway to the other.

Even in sombre company Joyce and Samuel found themselves weirdly popular. The trucks had passed titbits of gossip like hors d'oeuvres until in the town's imagination the pair attained mythic proportion. Folk took Samuel's hand as though expecting blessings: everyone wanted to say they had spoken to him and had dared her, yanking their guests about as excitedly as children with a new toy to break. Samuel at least managed the onslaught effortlessly; Joyce stood ill at ease and itchy within her skin, making no one happy.

Luckily Mark, the tall biker who had reprieved Samuel and who wielded no little clout of his own, served as gatekeeper to the eager flood. *Be wary of Mark*, the schoolmarmish green truck had said privately to Samuel, away from the others. What she slipped him was more slander than history, but one can't choose their prophet.

According to her it had all happened ten-odd years ago, or perhaps not even so long. She remembered it well because she had been stranded in town having her tanks scraped out after picking up some clotted fuel at a very dubious corner-store pump out in the big red. She knew she ought to have held on and stretched out what she had but she had been sent on a lengthy detour around a town that turned out to not be there anymore anyhow. The tainting was her own silly fault for being overcautious but that was it, she found herself stuck until she could get the all-clear.

So one evening this fellow turns up at the diner having hitched in from the desert. A mean fellow, as the driver who had been fool enough to bring him took pains to go around cautioning. Folk quite rightly demanded what he was about bringing him here, but once the driver realised what an asp he had picked up it had been too dangerous to ditch him. He watches, the driver said, shuddering. Watches and waits with meanness flowing from him like some sick river.

So the town, it hunkered down to watch the fellow right back.

Maybe the scrutiny escalated matters some, who can say in hindsight. There was always a big empty circle around the fellow everywhere he went. Even in Mark's bar at the diner although the locals were too well dug in to let him shift their entrenchment altogether; they made space and carried on.

Still, the silent treatment must have puffed that fellow up right good, night after night. After some beers he gets that fat mouth of his firing, worse every time. Things that he is going to do to this shit-kicking little town and especially to the womenfolk if you get my meaning and never mind Mark's missus Mary is right there serving from the kitchen, eight months round and all. Awful, awful things that it might blight a developing babe just to hear. It *could* have been just talk from a sad little man, but won't do any good to prove any of that now.

Mark, well he had never been the sort to worry himself over divining consequence or regretting a lack of action, although he may well be a very different man now. In his bar he has always sat on the customer side with the boys and still does, just reaches over when he has to serve. When he had had enough of the filth spouting from this creep, Mark stood up off his stool, walked over and told the fellow this would be his only warning. Wasn't impressing nobody with his mouth.

At that the fellow just popped like he had been pushing for an excuse. Started screaming what does not bear repeating, wilder and wilder and stabbing his finger at Mark's wife in case he did not get the point. Mary herself was fading back against the wall with her eyes all horror and both hands on her belly.

At the time there had been this meter high wooden angel above the bar looking down on all of this; crudest-cut thing you ever seen with a solemn splintery face. Passed down from one of Mark's great-greats, who had had a penchant for chainsaws. Mark could still remember his own mother giving it to him and would recount it to anybody, although the woman herself had been in the ground before he hit seventeen. She had had cool grey eyes, always calm, and the earthiness of rolled cigarettes always brought her memory back to him.

Well Mark walked around behind the bar, probably the first time some folk had seen him back there. He lifted down the wooden angel like she weighed nothing. Then he walked back as ordinary as anything and swung, laddering up his hands with splinters. Whopped that nasty bugger right around the head. They say the angel impacted so hard that five teeth went spinning across the bar.

One hit was more than enough, but Mark stood over the mewling fellow with his face all blotched up, as hard as the icon he held. Breathing like an engine with legs braced, ready to bring the angel's grave smile bludgeoning down again. Nobody had seen the like: Mark intended that the broken thing on the floor never get up again.

This was when Geoffrey stepped in. If Geoffrey had shown any fear Mark might have put him down, too; but Geoffrey stood right there looking him full in the face and Mark backed down. Maybe he came back to himself, maybe it was for other reasons. Geoffrey was brave like that. Most of them are. He loathed the malicious stranger as much as anybody but when it came to the hard thing to do, the right thing that nobody really wanted, you could always count on Geoffrey.

Mark, he put the angel down on the bar with not so much as an edge on her serene face blunted. He sat back on his stool and picked up his beer in splinter-raddled hands as though nothing had happened; only the big blank circle was around him now. Chairs shifted away. Only Mary come up and put her arms around him.

It did not last long but to a fellow like Mark that isolated afternoon with only his wife cooing and picking timber out of his skin, one angel to the other, it must have seemed like the longest in all his life.

It was left up to Geoffrey and Ben to load that nasty piece of work all unconscious onto Ben's passenger seat, bloody drool leaking out his broken face. They set out at a run for the hospital but did not make it. Not even close. The fellow died about six hours out.

No great loss to the world should you ask me but Mark took it hard. He took his mother's carved angel that had watched over generations of his family out back of the diner with a bottle of brandy and burned her to ash on the sand. Paid to have Ben's upholstery changed too with really nice leather, nicer than what the boys had started with. Nothing is ever the same if a man bleeds out on it.

Of course, watching the lanky biker now by the glare of day gave the epic a taste of the ridiculous. Wrapped in leathers—did he even peel them off to sleep?—Mark gleamed like some strange oiled insect, nails a testimony to boot polish.

Nominally Samuel and Joyce were under a hostesses' wing as well: although Mark's wife, a roundish pretty little thing, had other disasters going. Out of the box her big incense cones which were supposed to be black, she had *ordered* black, sparkled with inappropriate Christmas cheer. On the hour Ben rather tiredly had to counter her dismay with assurances that Geoffrey would have loved the humour. Within the circle of trucks, lacy tendrils of sandalwood climbed over the gathering and twined with their fellows but ultimately failed to conquer the air's smothering grease, diesel and chrome.

Food being the great unifier, the majority of guests eddied about black-creped trestle tables. Elaborate finger sandwiches with the crust removed and sausage rolls cut into baby sized sausage rolls had been shrewdly distributed against the first wave of supplicants as they fled awkward conversation. There had originally been parsley until somebody mistook its decorative function. But the jewel of catering strategy was in the many meters betwixt alcohol and food, forcing folk to cross the intervening space and mingle. Largely successful, although several habitual cheats were stockpiling.

Completing the diner's little family were two young sons. Beneath envious eyes the boys scooted back and forth righting incense as it leaned over gradually in pots of gravel; Joyce was the only woman blind to another's good fortune. Every night the town's women lay bitter in the lonely dark beside partners who snored on. Consequently Mark's wife had been made a sort of pet by the rest of the women as they sought to expiate their secret spite by torturing themselves with her presence by day, while still burning up with it at night.

Both boys had knotted black ribbon everywhere they could find about themselves, even holding floppy hair from their brows. As Samuel watched them whip by he wondered with an indulgent, false nostalgia if he had ever been so small, or that fleet. 'You could hire those two out to a circus.'

'Gar we could, sure,' Mark chuckled. 'When Dave was born the missus had me all but convinced we ought to pack th' diner away an' take up farming.'

Gareth, the oldest boy, was as small as his mother and whip thin as his father. Flashing from pot to pot like a jet propelled weasel, the pure gold of his grin glimmered just below the surface: no crude ore but the wholesome yellow exuberance of ripening wheat, a radiant bloom of health. Donning the sober ribbon like the trucks had been his idea after Mark sat the boys down quietly to explain why Ben was very sad and they needed to be serious. Still, he could barely hold the life in himself back.

Young Dave on the other hand was a different kettle of fish, an absolute carthorse of a boy. He already towered over his older brother and shovel hands and feet attested that he may very well grow into a giant.

However, although the lad ducked his head shyly in passing Samuel caught a shrewd flicker of assessment cross that face. Boy scout would wager his fairly expensive teeth that although Gareth might be fair and friendly, life's little golden boy, younger Dave had been dealt more than enough smarts to make up.

He returned the boy's cautious smile. 'Every circus needs a strongman.' And a ringmaster.

'Hey, Mary?' Joyce's hand hovered about the elbow of Mark's vaguely pretty wife. 'Can I talk to you for a second?'

'Sure, hon.' There was not enough age difference between them for "hon" to sit right, but somehow the small blond in jeans managed to make Joyce feel like a looming tomboy straight out of school. 'Did you know your boyfriend keeps calling me "Becky"?'

'Sam's not my boyfriend.' Conveniently forgetting her revelation in the bathroom this morning, of course. Had she really blushed at meeting those cliché blue eyes? Must have been high on shower cleaner.

'I want to say something but the poor lad would be dreadfully embarrassed at getting it wrong. He's such a sweet kid.'

'He sure is.' Blandly. Mary sure was not grandmotherly enough to let that fly, either, but we all have our peccadilloes. 'Do you have any stuff, for … you know.' Joyce gestured crotch-ward, which did not seem to be helping. '*That time of the month.*'

'You've got your period?' It sounded like a megaphone announcement to Joyce; even in this day and age she could not help her eyes flicking about to see who heard. 'Oh pfft,' Mary flapped her hands chidingly. 'Don't be like that. Nobody here's so foolish as believes babies get dug up in the cabbage patch. And it's so like Mark not to leave anything for you in the guest rooms; I tell you, there's no marrying good help. Condoms he'll remember, sure, shovel them out by the bucket-load. Novelty assortment if he reads the situation and decides that you're really in for it. But come to the other side of the equation and the man's head's still dangling around his you know what.'

Mid-burble she unclipped her rather world weary handbag and began rummaging through. All day it had remained pinned firmly beneath her elbow, dispensing oddments like a magician's hat. 'What's your fancy? Only got light flow on me now but we can rustle up whatever you want, and drugs if you need 'em. Never been so bad myself but I had this friend back home who got it screaming bad: painkillers, off work, the lot.'

Looking up, Mary caught Joyce's eye with a twinkle. 'Why so astonished-looking? We aren't savages wadding up old rags out here hon, this is a trucking route. Who notices if a few crates go missing here and there?' She rattled the box. 'And I'll be damned if I'm paying GST on these.'

Joyce smiled weakly the way she always did when people got started on politics. Like the government was ever going to let a captive market pass them by. She slipped the little parcels into her pocket. Left to her own devices she would have probably steered clear of the leery leopard-print packaging, but beggars could not be choosers. She was also trying to remember ever noticing a giant bucket of novelty condoms in her room. 'Thanks.'

'Now don't you wander off; you just have to meet our academic. He's the most wonderful man.' Leaving the taller woman a little stunned Mary merged effortlessly back into the crowd. Apparently all blondie had needed to unleash a verbal avalanche was somebody to talk to, and any topic other than how lovely her children were. Mary knew her boys were lovely. She saw them every damned day.

Joyce looked around. For the moment Samuel was standing alone, awkwardly and despite herself she felt a rush of pity. The world according to Samuel required admirers on all sides to work, and this was a cynical diminishing world with less and less admirers to go around.

She sidled over. 'Hey, did you know that the first mummies got made just like this? Bodies popped into the desert and the sand sucked all the juice right out of them, made them eternal. An early Egyptian could be innocently spading the foundations for a new family home and up would pop great aunt Sobekemsat from a hundred years back.'

Samuel's mouth puckered as though he had bitten a big juicy chunk of lemon. 'Joyce, this is a wake. I suggest you refrain from sharing that little gem with Ben right now.'

Honestly, his incomprehensible fits of man-temper made her feel like throwing up her hands!

'Now isn't this so typical?' Mary resurfaced innocently, all gossip and light. 'Go looking for a body and he's right here. Our academic ...'

A man standing with his broad back to them turned, and Joyce found herself staring into the mildest eyes she had ever seen.

'Disher,' the stranger finished for Mary. As casually as he would shake hands with anybody he offered his grip to Joyce.

By God, this must be what love at first sight felt like! Part of Joyce turned its hopeful face to Disher like a sunflower to light, but it was a part that knew to whisper in case the rest of her heard and took umbrage. Luckily the heat covered for her: everybody was flushed and sweating like naked gay men at a rave.

She was frightened to take the academic's hand in case she did anything embarrassing, such as scream or pass out. But being polite was what people *did*, they clung to civilised little rituals while the world came down around them. Expecting a thunderclap she steeled herself, but his grasp was ordinary. Actually a little unpleasant and oily, oh prosaic reality, and she was glad to take her hand back. She breathed again.

The rest of the world faded back in without Joyce noticing its absence, like a talented supporting cast, and Disher smiled at her kindly. 'You must be the generous young lady who brought Geoffrey back to us.'

'Oh yeah, Joyce is a real peach.' Samuel had been roped into carrying a platter: mothers like Mary could smell such well-meaning suckers a mile off. "Come back with your shield or on it" Spartan mothers once instructed their sons and thousands of years later it was good to see the same philosophy galvanise the catering industry. 'Gets her orders direct.'

'Is this true? You hear voices, do you?'

Simmering with rage and shame Joyce mouthed at Samuel "You're going to get such a smack". Then she returned her attention to dealing with the academic, her eyes resolute to endure what was coming and shoulders squared back. Once again Samuel glimpsed what had been clear as she surfed joyously down the sand dune toward him: Joyce could be magnificent. 'Yeah. I'm not making it up.'

'What voice do you hear?' Disher prodded and his eyes shifted minutely as though they could read every flinch of her heart. 'What does it tell you?'

'That I'm supposed to end things.' The words that burned so potently in Joyce's gut stuttered out lamely on the air, but she had always known how unlikely it all sounded. With everybody staring she planted her feet mulishly and stuck by her truth. 'Machines.'

'Why?'

'Because people never saw how it was going to end up like this. Hemmed in by gadgets; cut off from each other. Every man an island. And as there were less and less people we just humanised the gizmos so that nobody felt lonely. No neighbours, only a talking fridge to keep you occupied, or a stupid dancing toaster.'

This old lament was not convincing anyone: Joyce could tell, hopelessly. Not in a town so small that everyone was married to somebody else's cousin. How could she convey the isolation; that for all their vast number humanity had become like a crowd in a city? No eye contact for all that they stood shoulder to shoulder. No smile on sunless, neon-blanched faces. They smiled at stock market wins, amusing emails, not at each other.

Everybody simply waited at the kerb for the lights to change so that they could go their unheeding ways, like frozen comets speeding by each other in the dark. Even if one of their number stepped blindly from the edge and was mown down not a finger would be lifted before, during or after. The crowd, that vast society-machine would merely pause politely while the pulp was scraped from the asphalt. Then they would continue on.

'Even now after the event nobody sees what's happened. I'm doing what humanity can't, to save themselves.'

Of all her listeners only Samuel had a thoughtful look, his baby blues scrunched comically as though trying to understand, mustering all scant resources to that end. 'What has happened?'

'The end of the world. Don't you see? It's been the end of the world.'

Now boy scout looked haughtily appalled: as though they were all at high tea and Joyce had just dropped a turd in the pianoforte. 'And you think some kind of deus-exinterventionous is going to bring us a new world? *That's* what you believe?'

"Belief" was a word that Disher could seize on: academic, he came from a world of words and their slippery blameful meanings. He briefly turned his mildness on Samuel. 'And what do you believe?'

That sure brought smarty pants up short. Belief was too mystic a word for the staunch rationalisations that rattled about Samuel's well formed head. 'Well … there probably is some higher force or purpose to life, I don't doubt that. But it doesn't mean we can go crying to it to be saved when things go wrong. We ought to save each other and ourselves—I think that a reward we earn for ourselves would be far nobler than some gift from a loving benefactor.'

Joyce sagged. It was so depressing, over and over this dragging out of her guts for the crows to squabble over. 'I don't think you'd want what we've earned for ourselves—it's exactly what we are all trying to escape from. Consequences.'

'And most of humanity gets saved, but not all. Should we be grateful? Are you going by Santa's naughty and nice list?'

Disher's laugh was a genteel patter. Not for the first time Joyce was starting to feel like the only foul raving lunatic at a benefit luncheon for foul raving lunatics. Brought in chains for their delectation, to drive donations up and inspire an appetite. It went a long way toward helping her natural truculence assert itself against the academic's mysterious pull. Disher was not finished: 'I'm afraid that I have to agree, humanity's task is as it has always been. To strive, keep faith, and perhaps be saved by hope.'

Not just to keep going at all cost? Now sunflowers bloomed expansively in Joyce's chest, fields of them blazing like fireworks. She locked her wobbling knees, afraid of pitching onto her face. What Disher was telling her was "You can stop". Rest. An entire wasted life lay behind her, desolate; but what ahead?

The sunflowers breathed warm agreement, nodding golden heads but they had such slender green necks. A promise no thicker than a word.

'Maybe the lady's an angel,' little Gareth piped up inspiring indulgent humour all around although the laughter withered when it reached Joyce. Angels again. A brief flicker of memory: colour and music; lent a twist to her full mouth.

Until Gareth spoke up nobody had noticed the kid creeping between Mary and the academic to seek his mother's hand. Mary took those twiglet fingers absently. "Little blessing" other women named him covetously, "little angel", stroking that golden hair, but Gareth was a blessing Mary was used to.

Despite leading the "isn't he adorable" laughing chorus, Disher also never looked at the boy. He seemed to find Joyce a more fascinating study.

'Perhaps the young lady would care to attend one of our sessions? Tea and a ginger biscuit is all we have to offer the body, but perhaps a little knowledge may bring comfort to your mind.'

'Oh yes,' Mary chimed in eagerly. 'Please come, Joyce.'

'I'm afraid I won't be up for it,' Samuel tossed in his two cents before anybody could ask him—modest as always, the thought never occurred that the offer might not be forthcoming. It had also not registered that he had not been introduced to Disher, that in fact Samuel the magnificent had temporarily taken a back seat—to Joyce of all people! 'I'm going to be, um ...' What? Washing his hair?

'Samuel's coming along with me to finish my run,' a sonorous voice completed for him.

Both Samuel and Joyce found themselves suddenly left

out as all the others stiffened, like wary cats just sighting each other. Disher's concern was particularly satisfying, it was good to see that real expression could exist on a face that otherwise suggested meadows of daisies and little lambs wriggling their tails.

In fact, it looked quite like fear.

Even Mark's habitually lazy eyes widened, quite a concession for him. 'Are you sure about that Ben? Well the fellow's no driver an' ... you know ...'

'I'm quite confident of Samuel's ability to handle himself,' the truck answered stiffly. Obscurely shocking news or not, it was good to hear Ben speak up finally, shake off his ennui. 'It isn't rocket science and I'll be doing all of the work. Besides, there's no one else in town to spare. My load's not going to shift itself you know.'

Joyce smothered a juvenile smile behind her hands. She failed to notice how very neatly the town had just separated her from Samuel.

'Whadda ya reckon, Gar?' Mark dispelled the mood, throwing a jolly façade over tension. 'Should we saddle up on my bike an' escort these two cowboys?'

'Don't you *dare* get on that thing!' Mary shrilled too loudly, fingers lacing tight as though Gareth might be snatched away any second.

'Dad's always promising a ride! When do I get to go?'

'Your daddy's not going anywhere hon. He's got his responsibilities right here.'

Disher slipped in a topic change before discussion could become dispute. 'That was a very moving poem you recited at Geoffrey's service, Ben.'

'It seemed appropriate.' Perfectly polite, yet perfectly shutting the academic down—although if Disher took offence it failed to show.

'Well I can only hope we'll prove sufficient to keep the young lady occupied until you both get back.' With a beatific smile Disher turned away, beckoning Mary into his wake.

Joyce's sore heart leaped: she wanted to cry "Don't go!" but so far as inappropriate outbursts went that would be a yowser.

It seemed that Joyce was not alone in her infatuation. As little as Mary had noticed Gareth's hand she now dropped it, following the academic as though drawn along by the moon. Poor little Gar stared down at his sneakers and swallowed hard, bravely hiding the slight—although not enough to conceal it from Mark. Luckily fathers have powers at their disposal far beyond loss and betrayal.

The biker lunged and swept Gareth up, poorly laced shoes flying, up his towering height above his head and into the burning sky with the hot air rushing too fast to breathe, upside down, with race car noises, aeroplane noises; joy, joy!

And then set him back on his feet as gently as you would handle a chick from the shell. The boy wobbled and giggled; for the moment every hurt in every wide world was gone.

Dave had snuck up on the group too. The youngest boy was too hefty to swing about but even while talking one of Mark's rough hands was scruffing up the lad's hair "to impress the fillies". Dave sniggered, never *quite* wriggling away.

Samuel popped a celery stick in his mouth, crunchy green wetness that seemed to drive back the desert. 'Odd to find a fellow of learning about these days.'

'If he is one,' Mark said darkly. The biker's fists clenched around whatever chain of thought he had struck on and suddenly Samuel *could* see the biker seizing a brute hunk of wood to bludgeon another man down. 'Seems to think he is. Disher appeared out of the sand just like you, about ten years back. Brought his own crate of textbooks so we thought it was like progress really, town gettin' bigger.'

'You don't get on with him then.'

Mark's next words came chosen very carefully, as there was not a single syllable that his boys did not drink in. 'You know, some people don't believe in themselves too much. It could be for all sorts o' reasons, but they find comfort following things that seem bigger, smarter or grander than themselves. They want t' be given answers rather than finding any out. Doesn't make them *bad*, but ... well. They can be led.'

Samuel nodded rather vaguely, it was a little above his head. He turned to offer Joyce a finger sandwich, snickering inwardly at the entendre but she had wandered off. Typical.

Well, let her go. Some kind of research club having a foothold in town did not inspire him with buckets of thrills, but she would likely have a grand old time. 'So Ben, what's this trucking business all about? Do I need to wear a special hat?'

While the rest of the crew were smiling affectionately at good daddy, Joyce had slipped out of the crowd's murmur and back into the empty diner. She could move that big frame with surprising delicacy upon occasion.

She wanted to get herself cleaned up, sorted out and back in control of things after a very confusing day. If life would only fire problems at her one at a time—instead, it was more like backing a tip-truck up and hitting dump. It seemed she had not snuck away subtly enough, though.

A pair of blunt fingered hands jerked Joyce about and flung her against the wall as though she weighed little more than a kid. The whole diner felt the impact and shuddered in sympathy; various anatomical hot spots shouted agony and bloomed great swaths of bruise, but she felt little inclined to listen right now.

Joyce was pinned by the force of Disher's blazing eyes. Any trace of mildness had been ripped down like gauze before the furnace. 'The Word *screams*, does it not?' Disher's hoarse whisper ejected high speed froth from the corners of his mouth and alone in the diner with him Joyce followed its flight with dull transfixed horror. One glistening blob zoomed by her head to darken the plaster wall, and the rest dropped in milky splatters down her shirt.

Some horrible fascination made her want to hear him croon *ssand* in that milky, drowning voice. His red tongue churned the cauldron of his mouth, in peril of those champing teeth while the oblivious world outside continued its calm burble.

'It screams.' Disher leaned his heavy forehead to hers and pressed home, driving her skull back against the wall. You did not need to be a phrenologist to trace cruelty in the thick bone of his brow, almost like a battering ram. She had to go cross eyed to keep him in view. 'Oh God does it scream.'

'Get …' Joyce's over-generous lips shaped breathlessly. She found it astounding that any part of her found the nerve to speak; although not that it should be her big fat mouth that went first.

It would not be getting much moral support from the rest of her: sheer horror had weakened her joints. The field of bright flowers that this man had called into being lay broken and trampled to the earth, sneering up at the rending sky.

Even while dead and cooling Geoffrey's mouth had been clear but Disher whiffed an awful sweetish stink against Joyce's cheek, panting like some feverish dog. She was going to shrivel away with revulsion on the spot although it would likely not afford any escape.

Only … when the rest had wilted away the bitter knuckle of self at Joyce's core remained. The little swear word at her centre which had always known this was coming. Hard and cruel and integral to her survival it came erupting forth in her hour of need, redeeming every minor pleasure it had ever ruined, spilling tentacles of angry strength everywhere. That breathless sigh became a snarl.

'Get … the hell … off me!'

The academic bit her nose chidingly and she would have flinched had there been anywhere to go. The plaster behind her creaked. This crazy man could take her entire face on his crazy whim, chew her right up. 'This town cannot be trusted, keep them from your heart. They have given their ears to the blasphemy of switches and circuits. The town conceals it from me but I will not stop looking. And now you come.'

Another playful nip, games on the cusp of shrieking pain. 'See me at my study hall. Reject the false mysticism, and knowledge will save you.'

Joyce had stored enough mini-gasps for another sentence and intended to make it a good one. 'I said, get the hell off me!'

Disher's wet mouth leered wide … and the diner's exterior door creaked open. Their stinking little universe of two was blown wide open.

A tentative voice slipped in to the diner. 'Disher? Are you here?' The door opened wider and now over her assailant's bulky shoulder Joyce made out Mary, standing blinking in the portal. Wounded disbelief stretched the little woman's eyes wide in her simple face. Joyce's first relieved thought was "oh good, I'm saved" which just goes to show how little she had learned from life.

Nobody gets saved. At least, not without putting in the hard yards themselves.

'Disher?' Mary asked again, her unsteadiness developing into horribly false cheer. Incredulously Joyce watched her do it: watched the little housewife decide that this could not possibly be happening, and therefore she would not see it. 'Disher, could you come outside a moment please?' So airily she might have surprised them sharing Ceylon tea and a crossword; what was nine letters down for "denial"? 'I'd very much like to talk to you in private … about that nice young man getting dragged off with Ben. Surely we ought to do something?'

Mary was trying to help, Joyce realised, although only so far. Should the town's precious academic set himself to throttling Joyce Mary would step back outside and shut the door. This was the crowded city intersection all over again, the people no more than blank mannequins for all the sympathy that passed between them. Here, in this quaint town where such things were not supposed to happen.

Smiling with only part of his mouth Disher gave Joyce's shoulders a final squeeze before turning to his disciple. Mildness dropped back into place like the tattered curtain at the end of an act.

'Of course Mary, I always have time for all your concerns. However do remember that if a grown man freely chooses an unsanctified path for himself there is little we can do to sway him.'

'But Samuel doesn't realise …'

Trembling hot and chill and slowly slumping to the floor, Joyce witnessed one final thing that afternoon. A sight to stick in the mind.

As Disher and Mary stepped out through the door in earnest conversation his hand rested familiarly on Mary's neck. A fleshy pink lobster nestling beneath golden curls. Like a blunt horn a forefinger extended and ever so tenderly caressed the lucky mother's jaw.

CHAPTER FIVE
AUTOMATONS

Ice Cold Chickies

It was a creepy quiet that reigned, a two am in the morgue sort of quiet. A taste of the day the town would finally turn up its toes and join the decline of civilisation. The revellers might have been struck deaf by their own racket, and greeted the dawn trembling on cold tiles.

Despite Mary's best efforts Geoffrey's wake the night before had deteriorated rapidly, with every radio cranked to Shaggy

Bob's Hard FM until the very steel in the tarmac danced.

By the time the seventh keg came rolling out to cheered incoherencies and a ragged attempt at a wave, even Mark's harried wife had to admit that all was pretty much lost. Not to be a bad sport she had flung the cumbersome hors d'oeuvre tray over one shoulder and, throwing back her blond curls, chugged a stinging draught directly from the tap. The sight of foamy beer streaming down her blouse drew delighted hoots from the crowd, although not even the drunkest would risk incoherencies with Mark standing by.

In the aftermath Samuel and Ben's departure slipped by like a forgotten birthday.

Dressing before a mirror in the morning's devastated silence Samuel had to admit feeling just the teensiest bit deflated. Foolish, really: after all nobody here knew him. No reason then, he rationalised sullenly while yanking a shirt over his head, for them to bother turning out.

He had never had any trouble with friends in the past: there had been bucket loads of them, drifting in and out his door as they pleased. More often than not he would crawl from bed and through his doomsday hangover to find some random in their underpants making toast in his kitchen. There would be no toilet paper, and all the coffee had been drunk.

Not a single face among them he had needed to pay much mind to; always more around the corner, even madder and artier. It had been fantastic and oh so fantastically easy. But as his rather obsessive travelogue and, one had to admit, his age had advanced the clique had all just … fallen away.

No great send off for them either. One morning Samuel had simply rolled out of bed clear-headed and into quiet. He had an apartment stocked with loo paper and coffee beans but nary a never-been-to-bed grin or, his favourite, a bikini clad bottom in sight. Samuel knew the path that led from there to here, had walked every step of the way and could not claim surprise. He fluffed his fringe in the mirror. Strange how things came about. Perhaps as friends had never meant much to him, he would not miss them too much.

The lack of tickertape parade did not mean complete neglect, however. Ben's driver had been Uncle Geoffrey to a brace of mismatched boys before they could even crawl, let alone fly about a rowdy party like kites; he had been the bringer of fascinating toys, stories, and now the first intrusion of mortality into their childhood world. And so the morning of Samuel's departure Mark treated Geoffrey's would-be rescuer to a full cooked breakfast trucker-style.

It was awe inspiring. Gleaming scrambled eggs came mounded atop a chipped plate the diameter of one of Ben's massive headlights. With curls and ribbons of thick crunchy bacon, grilled tomatoes oozing seeds into the grease, avocado with lemon, mushrooms—and holy hell! Was ... could that be *blood sausage* in there?

Like exploring Tutankhamen's tomb, every treasure levered up exposed fresh wonders beneath and Samuel experienced some of the dizziness those lucky adventurers must have felt. Allegedly there was a base camp of toast sunk in there somewhere, doorstops of sourdough melting in butter, but he was damned if he knew how he would find it!

The artery clogging savour was only slightly marred by an acrid reek of martyrdom rolling in from the kitchen where at the sink Joyce still doggedly scrubbed and scraped for her board. Here they were, born into an era of hitherto unanticipated technological marvel ... well the tail end of one, anyway; but an era nonetheless of every convenience rabid consumerism had come to inspire. So how did she end up in the last kitchen on earth without a dishwasher?

But ha ha, *you're* the dishwasher Joycie. Hey, do you know why women have smaller feet than men? To stand closer to the sink of course!

She regularly broke off to shoot her old travelling chum sheer poison where he sat stuffing his face in the dining room. Assuming fatguts in there actually succeeded in clearing that enormous plate, there would be no prize for guessing who would be stuck scrubbing it.

Although he did not "do" breakfast himself, Mark lounged companionably at table with Samuel, as immune to the death rays of hate from the kitchen as he was to the heat belting in through the front window. The biker downed steaming short blacks one after the other while his guest ate, the entire coffee pot hauled to his elbow for convenience.

In concession to being indoors Mark had accessorised the obligatory leather pants with a faded yellow tee, "I ate the Thylacine" emblazoned across the chest in blue. Bare, blue veined feet wound about the chair legs. Untold years of motorcycle boots had done horrors to those toes, mysterious humped yellow peaks that were in no way helping Samuel hold down his meal.

But although the tall, lean biker looked supremely relaxed his teeth ground unhappily between sips as though there were dirt in his cup. Catching his table companion's curious eye Mark ducked his head guiltily, sucking up the rich dark coffee. 'Samuel …' he began, and trailed off again. Slurped gravely, considering.

Samuel could barely catch him over the dogged pulse of the fans, huge wicker paddles that churned overhead for effect more than relief. Mark may feel right at home but Samuel enjoyed no such thermal immunity: squeezed between the heat and the food he was beginning to entertain serious fears of having a heart attack. Greasy sweat oozed from his flushed hairline, colouring the air about the table.

The developing stench would not bother anybody, for this early the diner stood empty. Eyeing the forlorn tables and chewing grimly, Samuel pondered how the other men of the town must be spending their morning. His luckier brothers: they would be stirring sleepily beside girlfriend or wife, or boyfriend or husband for that matter: when the language was *lover* everybody spoke it. Hooking an arm about soft warm comfort or burrowing cold feet into the sanctity behind another's folded knees. Don't get up, Samuel wished them. Why hurry the day when you already had the world right there in your bed?

When Mark finally settled on what he wanted to say Samuel had to shake his head and physically drag his attention back. The gross food influx was making him scatty. 'Sorry, what was that?'

'I said; Ben didn't fill you in, then.'

Obviously not. 'On what?'

It did not help Samuel's mounting indigestion to see his grown companion literally squirm in his seat like an unhappy lad. 'He really ought to have said.' *Because,* Mark's eyes completed the sentence for him, *then it wouldn't be my problem.* 'The trouble is, Ben likes ya some, an' … you know it's hard when you've lost somebody. Real hard. Though you love them you hate them too for going. And you get left with this big old space t' fill an' it's easy to get caught up in quick attachments. Part of grieving and all.'

Eyes scooting uneasily, noting the empty chairs, the churning fans, and perhaps the empty nook over the bar where an angel once stood. The gap like a loose tooth. Which of them was he trying to convince? 'Don't get me wrong, I'm not judging or nothing; it's a damn sight better than giving up, an' Ben's got a lotta years ahead of him to get through without Geoffrey, a lotta years. Far more than you or I would have to endure. Can't imagine what it would be like. Like being in hell forever, maybe.'

Another slurp, the dainty cup dwarfed in heavy fingers. Mark handled it with exaggerated care as though leery of rough finger-pads against china, the cracked nails. Without looking at Samuel he helped himself to another refill. 'This trip you'll be helping on ain't huge and that Ben can go like th' red devil, but there's this, uh, harness, that the driver gets hisself strapped into on long hauls. Helps you go the extra so to speak, not black out under hard accel and such.'

Suddenly the biker clapped the little cup down hard enough to spatter the table. Instantly remorseful he snatched it up again, searching for fractures. 'My wife gave me this,' he berated under his breath. Not Mary but *my wife*. Perhaps saying it thickened the bond. Only once Mark was satisfied of no harm done did he lean in, holding Samuel in an oblique gaze. A dishonest gaze. Pretending he was looking him in the eye *mano a mano*, perhaps even believing that was what he did but failing to truly confront him all the same.

'I've never had the like on my ride and I've been far on that baby. Love my bike to bits, but made damn sure I was never turnin' her into a *person*.'

Mark's words had started to rush together and he hauled himself back with a deep gut breath, yellow tee rising and falling. 'Some folk, well … they can find Ben's harness a bit *personal*, you understand? It's part of him, see, not that he can help that …'

'I think I'm getting you.' Samuel had to put an end to it, it was just becoming too painful. Part of him wanted to snicker at the biker's earnest discomfort but the deadly serious face across the table suggested that humour would not go down. 'You're saying that this harness comes with what we might call some unusual "fittings".'

'Yeah … ish.'

Samuel beamed his goodwill to set Mark at ease and even shovelled down another forkful from the mega plate, although it felt like scrambled eggs might come bursting out his ears. 'Mark I'm ok with it. Really. Did something similar in deep diving suits once. Well—obviously it's not something I'd take up as a hobby, but I'm sure I'll manage.'

'Well …' Swishing coffee from cheek to cheek Mark managed to look simultaneously relieved and doubtful. He had also finished the entire pot in one sitting: it was a mercy his pancreas had not dropped out, or whatever horrible thing it was that caffeine did to you.

Landing on a decision the biker swallowed and deliberately sparked up the mood. 'But hey, here's a thing. Be sure to ask Ben about this freight you're hauling. The town does well off this route, but this is th' first load we've never been tempted to dip into.'

'Do …' Samuel coughed and shifted breakfast out of his lungs to speak. 'Do tell?'

'Naw.' Mark waved his free hand dismissively, battered wedding band glinting. It had done hard yards, that smidgin of gold dented in around the digit. It was almost as worn and warped as his toes. 'I'll sure let Ben field that one, he tells it better. And it will give you two something to, uh, while the time away.'

'Field what?'

Both men looked up with a jerk of surprise. Joyce stood inquisitively at their table with suds pattering from her waterlogged fingers. The two had been sitting with their heads together for so long that she had been unable to resist the aura of secret men's business.

'The great mystery,' boy scout answered with bombast, playing it up. Leaning back with a groan he laced his hands behind his head and pondered whether it would be crass to unbutton his pants and allow his swelling belly free reign. Crass, he decided regretfully. 'The mystery of what Ben and I are going to be hauling across the world's biggest sandbox.'

With a humph Joyce crossed bony arms, leaning one hip on the table. 'Why does Ben need you along, anyhow?'

'The Union.' Since they were all looking so chummy and relaxed Mark rocked back on his chair too: a mantis reposed. Leather groaned softly. 'There were all those protests years back about th' smart trucks not needing any drivers. At the worst of it you had whole loads an' sometimes the vehicles themselves getting torched n' dumped in the desert—gone, once you done that. The sand just licked its lips an' asked for more.

'It was losin' that consignment of vaccine for the big new flu that made folk really sit up 'cause so many suffered for it, not just the transport companies. Protests, huh; more like riots. But a rotten means to a good end if you ask me: finally folk tryin' to *prevent* job loss t' automation. They got things fixed. Now it's hardwired into every truck's brain that th' driver can drive or sit like a lump as he pleases, but without a warm body in that seat th' truck can't so much as stir from the parking lot.'

Joyce scowled. 'In Ben's brain, huh? That's "fixed" things? What the hell's he supposed to do if there are no people around? What if …' *they had to go to the hospital?* '… there was some kind of emergency?'

Samuel blinked but apparently Mark had missed that weird lag in her sentence, the dragging feet of something almost said. He fixed his stare on her, intense noon sky blue. 'Come on Joyce, that doesn't make sense. If there were no people the freight wouldn't need hauling anyway.'

'So Ben gets to spend eternity sitting and watching his ass rust off?' Her voice was rising and so was she, physically coming up on her toes as the two men sat looking up at her. Panting quick and light so that her breasts danced to her distress.

With a situation brewing Mark lazily rocked his chair back down again. 'Don't see why you're getting' so riled on abstracts. It's not like we're in line to follow the dodo or anything.'

'Oh! Sweet! Lord!' Joyce raged, each word snapped off. She flung a hand at the door; 'Have you tuned in to reality lately? Go on, just take a look at the state of things out there and *then* tell me we're not on the decline. Look at it! You reckon that the people in charge, the government or whatever would let the highway get this bad if everything were just hunky dory? Well it's only a major transport route! And there are already fewer trucks making it through I'll bet. Have yourself a good long look at that road Mark because that's the future, *our* future that we've built right there.'

Consciously or subconsciously this could not be news to Mark but the truth had never been stomped home so callously. The biker managed a tight, bloodless smile but with only one half of his mouth. The other half trembled like a shot bird trying to rise.

He creaked to his feet, a long way toward the ceiling and the frail cup he had taken such care with was left spilled and abandoned. In towering over Joyce he seemed to regain some lost ground. Still wearing that horrible half-smile. 'If you kids'll excuse me, I believe it's just turned smoke o'clock.'

Would Joyce's sweet charm never end? 'There was no need to be rude,' Samuel mumbled reproachfully.

'Actually Sam, there is.' She glared after the tall biker as he clapped open the screen door and disappeared into brilliance. During the moment of confrontation Joyce was sure that the desire to deal her a vicious blow had burned bright in Mark's eyes, the threat exhilarating and infuriating her all at once. He was a man all blocked up somehow. 'There really is. Also, didn't your mother ever tell you not to eat with your mouth full? I mean, talk?'

'Mm, the old bat said a lot of things. I've spent a lot of life un-learning them piece by piece.'

Joyce resumed her table side pose, mentally resettling the hairs which had sprung erect all over her body. 'How long does Mark intend to go on pretending everything's peachy? The man's wandering the streets in fantasy land and if he doesn't look up he'll never see the bus that's about to hit him.'

'Bus?'

'Oh for crying out loud Sam, it's a metaphorical bus! We've gone and manufactured all these things like Ben to run our world—nothing so grand as "creation", just rolled 'em off the production line like God was a factory and surprise, surprise: we've let them down so they let us down and now everything's falling to bits.'

'I can't imagine Mark likes hearing that's the world we've built for his kids.'

'Well I don't like hearing my ass is like a carriage car, but you can't halt progress.' She shrugged herself off the table.

'Wait—aren't you going to run tearfully alongside the truck waving a lace hanky?'

Had he gone barmy? 'What?'

Samuel's mouth quirked. 'Where's my passionate goodbye?'

To his astonishment—he fully expected Joyce's reply to begin with an "F" and end in "off"—she spared only a brief troubled grimace before hurrying from the table. Almost as thought she were fleeing. And … was that *blushing*?

'Where's my goodbye?' he called before she gained the kitchen's safety; 'I want to see tears!'

Joyce rallied enough to return a popular if rather guttersnipe hand gesture. 'You're coming straight back, aren't you? Then that makes this all the drama you're ever likely to get.'

Samuel found Mark out by the highway. He stayed upwind of the suspiciously herbaceous smoke that roiled from the taller man's nostrils and teeth: having dated a girl who smoked rollies once he was no fan. Used to find foul bits and curls of brown stuff all over the place: in the bed, the food, even in the shower! What type of person smokes in the shower for Chrissake!

The thin man stood smoking his cigarette and staring vacantly out over melting tarmac, his body slung at ease even on its feet. He seemed as quietly indifferent to the molten sand under boot-gnarled toes as he was to the musky heat baking off leather. His balls must be broiling.

'Don't mind Joyce. She comes straight from the school of "if God falls in the desert when she's not around, nothing can possibly have actually happened".'

'Is that what you reckon?' the ghostly murmur came back. 'You think God's fallen out here?'

'What? No, Mark I didn't say that. Come on, it was just a joke. Light verbal pun.'

Not so much as a blink.

Following the biker's gaze Samuel found highway and more highway, rolling out to the watering eye in an impossibly eternal line. It was not without its finery. Sunlight came back in small gleams where the asphalt's reinforcing had been unearthed, like surgical pins in a wound. The latest in a series of tiny rifts ended its snaking course by Mark's left foot and the man's squint gradually slid down from the giant ruin to this smaller offspring at his feet, a scale more easily understood. He kicked a shower of sand into the gap.

'So.' Samuel shifted his battered shoe and sent a second cascade down after Mark's. 'I'm heading out now.'

Mark seemed mesmerised by the gritty red sand that they had sent racing through the break in the highway. Toppling grains pulled more of their neighbours from the edge until it was a miniature landslide in motion, silica tinking off hidden metal below. So deep. It was only a small crack, but it seemed as though the entire desert could be poured inside and never be filled.

'Yep. I'm heading on out.'

'I ought to get some pitch mixed.' When the biker finally spoke it was not the farewell and good luck that Samuel was fishing for. 'See if I can't neaten this out some. Maybe get th' town involved, like a community project. Our doorstep shouldn't look so bad. People built this. We ought to be able t' fix it.'

Slowly Mark's eyes rose from the innocent, hungry little crack to the wider heat distorted desolation of the highway which stretched away to the left and right as uncompromisingly as a raised fist. The diner was a fleck by the wayside. He was measuring a few soft hands against a fallen godhead.

With an abrupt snap of the wrist Mark flicked his cigarette down into the crack and headed back to the relative cool of the diner, giving the clenched line of his back to the world. Instead of a farewell the door clapped shut behind him.

To salvage Samuel's ego, Ben at least stood fuelled and waiting for him. The truck was so gloriously polished that the glare from his paintwork was painful to see. The assault sent the eye to those fluttering, crisped-looking scraps of mourning which he still wore, the silk already limp and a little tawdry by daylight.

In ascending to the cab Samuel made damned sure to keep to the rubber handgrips. The radiant heat off chrome was enough to cook with and he quite fancied his palm skin right where it was. As he climbed he grinned: the sight of the intimate little cab in Ben's gargantuan head tickled him. It reminded him off the old theories about the dinosaurs, that they had taken the extinction dive due to teeny brains in great big bodies. He padded the ladder affectionately. Benosaurous. Hopefully not the last of his kind.

Unfortunately one individual had turned out to see them off.

'Ben! Samuel!' a voice hailed before Samuel had reached the summit.

'Oh bloody hell,' Ben groaned quietly through internal speakers for Samuel's ears only; who was inclined to agree. Disher jogged up to join them. It was patronage they could do without.

It was the absolute icing on the cake that the academic had kitted himself out in cream safari linen. There were even flares, swishing about his ankles like languid white wings. Priceless. However in spite of its glow the fabric failed to impart the intended sense of purity. It hung crumpled and limp at the junctures of elbows and knees, a crazed starburst radiating from his groin as though to draw particular attention to the area.

At first Samuel thought that Disher was lugging some kind of large carmine handkerchief and his eyes began to well: between Ben and the sand he did not really need more red. But as the pale figure trotted to a halt he saw that it was actually some ridiculous flower that lolled in the cradling arms.

'Is that thing for real?'

'The bloom?' Disher held it up and actually laughed for pleasure like a child, the corners of his eyes crinkling to match the suit. 'As real as you or I. To the Lord I'm sure the humble thistle stands equal to the mighty ash, but I must confess a weakness for beautiful flowers. A man might be forgiven for failing to love indiscriminately, I think.'

He offered it up and Samuel took the thing gingerly. "Beautiful" was certainly not the first word to spring to *his* mind. The blossom felt strangely fleshy, with large petals so lax they might drop off any second; the whole thing threatening to disintegrate in his hands under Disher's infatuated gaze.

Being both smarter and less rational than his head, Samuel's gut seized on the word bloom: yes that was exactly it, like some horrible fungal bloom in deep water. The sort that creeps its long fingers into a village well and leaves every person blighted. Creeps into their mouths to leave them kicking and guttural on the floor.

'The plant is my own hybrid.' The way Disher was carrying on he might have been clucking over a bouncing baby. 'Unique in the world, these flowers. Totally new in life's grand plan. They will be my gift to the people who come after—that's my immortality you're holding, right there.'

Samuel fervently hoped that his travelogue would make a better legacy than that. Dragging on his shoulders, his pack full of notes, monologue and trail lore felt reassuringly heavy, like a promise. When the young man on the ladder offered no more than a bemused smile Disher clicked his tongue, stepping back to survey Ben's long line of trailers.

'Ah, and this must be the infamous cargo. There's only one point the gossip hasn't been clear on, though: where's it all off to, then? Who could possibly want it?'

'The hospital,' Ben supplied promptly as though he had been dying to say it and Disher's good ol' boy affability dropped so suddenly the truck might have slapped it away.

'I ... I do wish I'd known that earlier. Samuel, I might have persuaded you against going to that place.' *That place* came spat out as though something nasty to be expelled.

Samuel's first instinct at seeing another fellow's composure so shattered would have been to sooth, to steer the conversation back to safer waters but Ben was prey to no such lenience. 'The hospital is where the consignment needs to go. And that's all.'

'Ah.' Disher sniffed and squared his shoulders. It was fascinating to watch, you could actually see the mental gears crunch as he became a man coming to terms with circumstance. A man with his mind racing. 'Take my flower with you, then. Who knows?' An ironic shrug of those heavy shoulders. His bodybuilder's physique bunched and loomed. 'Perhaps it may protect you. But take a piece of advice as well.'

With the academic leaning up toward him Samuel was struck by the unsettled feeling that he was nothing more than some treed critter. Trapped on his perch, staring down pop-eyed at the slope shouldered hyena whose slavering grin reached up to drag him down. Drag him down screaming.

'I'd stay snug as a bug in the cab if I were you.' A predatory smile, the childish words spilling between jaws that could crush bone. 'Stay out of the hospital. Don't even look at it. It's no place for people to be.'

'Yes, thank you,' Ben returned condescendingly. Teeth had yet to be invented that could rend him; were Disher to try he would likely find himself with a smashed mouth.

Quite unlike Samuel who was so scared he had stopped sweating, and was pretty sure that his balls had lodged in his anus.

'Now if you will excuse us we had better get rolling. Time moves on and all that.' Disher nodded solemnly like that was an acceptable formula, a password, and with Ben's intervention the prey was released to climb to safety. For now.

Frowning, Samuel barely had time to scramble into the cab before Ben slammed the door and rolled the window up firmly.

'Fond of him are you Ben?'

'Geoffrey didn't like that so-called academic,' the truck growled blackly, 'And he wasn't one to take against folk, even the rotten kind. He used to say ...' A stumbling block of life-goes-on, realising that he had already begun to speak of his dearly departed in the past tense, '... say how everybody has a mean side, given the wrong circumstance and that's just life. Ain't none of us angels. But with Disher ... Geoff could just never pick much to dislike. That was the whole problem.'

'Come again?'

'All the years Disher's been in town nobody has ever seen him lose his temper. He hasn't got drunk and cried his heart out, or thrown a punch, or anything. Geoff reckoned that the man's mean streak must be pretty black for him to keep it buried down so deep.'

'So ... by that logic, parading around being jerk de la jour puts people like Joyce on the moral high ground?'

'After a fashion. At least with your young lady nobody's ever worried that she's hiding something.'

Samuel laughed. 'Too right. All the crazy's right out in the open for us all to enjoy.'

As it rumbled into life Ben's engine sounded like a chuckle of agreement. The indicator clicked, a line of little orange lights winking all down the road train, and they began to pull ponderously out onto the highway.

Disher still stood waving, framed perfectly in one of the wing mirrors. The fellow looked so damned ordinary that Samuel had trouble crediting his paranoid panic of only a few moments ago, except that he had never shown tendency to be flighty. The academic was just some guy. A little heavy across the shoulders, sure but he likely worked out to stave off middle age. He seemed completely at ease as canyons of tyre tread slid by his shoulder, although the least careless twitch on Ben's part would rub him out against the sand.

Keeping his feet politely off the pedals Samuel stowed his pack and slid into the driver's seat. He deposited the crude blossom beside him where it flattened out like a sleeper taking the least line of resistance.

'Giving me the flower was a little odd.'

More air through the vents, unmistakably a snort. 'Disher hands them out like candy to everybody he can catch leaving town. Geoff and I used to slip away secret-like at all hours: it drove him wild. Well, not so as you could see but we knew.' A chuckle that slid way before fruition, becoming dark and fragmented. 'Geoff even tried rolling one up and smoking it once as a joke.'

Samuel could not even imagine wanting one of the nasty things anywhere near his mouth. 'What happened?'

'Scary stuff. I tell you what: Geoff's familiarity with recreational substances was no passing thing but that damned flower had him puking up scarlet for hours. Massive great gouts of it. It wasn't blood: looked like blood, all over him but I don't know what it was. Never been so terrified in all my long days as watching him heaving, sweating red all over like he was dying and still insisting that he didn't need the hospital, didn't want to go there.'

Ben's voice that Samuel had first heard bellowing out across the night time desert was very small now. 'I loved him, you know.' Almost inaudible, this whispered confession in the booth of his own head and Samuel a priest who brought no release. 'I loved him so ridiculously much that I didn't know what to do with it all. I'd known him so long, you know, and it sort of snuck up on me; until one day I looked around and Geoffrey was a part of everything. Like being obsessed, but in a good way because you're not hurting anyone with it and least of all yourself; just feeling what you feel. But this must sound really stupid to you, I'm sure you get what I mean.'

'I'm not sure I've ever really been in love.'

'You'd know.'

Samuel had never taken himself for a sentimentalist but in the face of Ben's bland assertion he could not help but feel somewhat of a failure, depressed. Perhaps even the truck felt sorry for him, as the cab was quiet awhile.

Once they hit the highway proper it was deceptive how quickly they picked up speed. Although Samuel imagined he could feel the inertia of those massive trailers dragging at them when he glanced in the mirror the diner was already dwindling away.

It was such a raffish building, wearing its pink sign askew. The gateway to the entire town. Obscured by the boiling sand whipped up by the truck's passage, still it winked knowingly through the gaps. You'll be back Sammy boy, just wait and see. We've got your friend. Then it was gone.

Silence.

When Ben scrolled the driver side window down sound re-entered the cabin with a relieved rush. Samuel breathed easier; the atmosphere became heartier, more normal. The wind outside was already whining by, well on its way to a protesting shriek and Ben had to raise his voice to compete.

'Right. Disher can't see us anymore. Bung the damned thing out the window.'

'Don't you want it?'

'Do you?'

Hell no. Samuel had to sort of heft the floppy monstrosity rather than giving it the good shove it deserved, but once over the sill the slipstream whisked it gleefully from his grip. Disher's legacy was shredded in a burst of turbulence and churning sand. The bright scraps of those unique petals whirled high into the air, and then settled slowly to the highway in their wake like the confetti of a bridal train.

The window scrolled smoothly up restoring quiet to the cab but following their shared act of sabotage the silence was comfortable. Air filters hissed on the edge of hearing. Samuel could smell his sweat being soothed away by the air conditioning; it seemed to be settling in comfortably with the many lived-in layers of odour in the upholstery, making itself at home. A bubble of indigestion was forming in his belly.

'So. Mark said I should ask what this trip's all about.'

It took Ben a few heartbeats to reply and when he did he was cautious, perhaps distracted by their acceleration as labouring pistons bent their backs to the load. 'Did he? I don't know how much he told you …'

'Not a lot. Seemed to think I should hear it from you. He mentioned the harness, though.'

'He did, did he?' Openly bristling now. 'What exactly did he say?'

'Only that some folk find it a bit confronting.'

'Some like it, too!' Ben pulled himself up, confused. 'I'm sorry. That's irrelevant of course.'

Which made Samuel wonder at the sudden eagerness which the truck had flashed and concealed, like a player showing his hand too soon. 'Sure. look, I'm not fussed either way. I've had to take a catheter for the team before. I'm just here to help.'

Here to help. Did Ben feel bad? 'Pull those straps down from the panel behind your shoulder.'

It was a curious clanking tangle of buckles and industrial canvas webbing that resolved itself in Samuel's hands like a living thing. A conscious puzzle wanting to be solved.

'And, since you ask so nicely, we happen to be heading right out to the other side of the desert.'

'The end of the highway?'

A chuckle that Samuel could feel right through the seat. 'You make it sound like the end of the rainbow.'

'But that's just it. It's where I wanted to go, why I set out in the first place. I've always wanted to know where such a huge highway leads.'

'That's not such an easy one to pin down. When you've driven the highway as long as I have you come to learn that it's slippery. Can't be trusted like a normal road. Two trucks might strike out from the same spot on the same day, but lose sight of each other and end up in entirely different places.'

'But how can that be? It's just one road.'

'It's nothing you need to go worrying about on this trip. The highway's only tricky to those who don't know where they are going. You're with me, and I have our destination firmly in mind.'

'The hospital?'

'The hospital. Or to be more exact, the industrial-medical precinct. There are not a whole lot of people left there these days, or at least there weren't the last time I visited. Now, who knows? Perhaps none at all.'

'Why not?'

'They're not needed. Now those buckles you have hold of are a standard plug to socket combination. See? They are very loyal so don't worry about getting it wrong, each buckle will only go to its partner. Once you've got yourself all clipped in I can handle the rest.'

As the last clasp snapped into place the entire harness contracted with an eager jerk, tight and uncomfortable around Samuel's distended gut.

'Hey!'

'Everything's fine. Just relax, and I'll tell you about the hospital. Not many people, like I said but the technology they have there is the best in the world.' There was eerie reverence in Ben's voice; as huge and complex as he was, the truck stood in awe of those hospital machines. 'Not even the military have better and that's saying something: they always get the biggest slice of every pie.

'The hospital machines are a terrible old pack of gossips, too. They enjoy their own secrets well enough but woe betide should you be inclined to privacy yourself: they will just keep on at you until they get it. Think they know what is best for everyone, and to a large extent they do. If I'd been able to get Geoff there in time everything would have been ok. He would be sitting here right now instead of you.'

That did not sound too bad a trade to Samuel right now. Fine metal filaments were squirming their blind way from the harness that restrained him, tapping, groping forth like surfacing worms.

Still, this was obviously an emotional moment for the truck and Samuel tried to stay focussed on that. 'Ben, I asked around. Geoffrey wasn't just keeping secrets from you: *nobody* realised he had trouble with his heart. To race him to the hospital in time you would have had to know in advance yet he never said a peep, and you know what that says to me? That maybe he didn't want to be saved.'

It was a marvellously uplifting speech, humanists should be dabbing their eyes and such forth but, crawling with horrible wormy things the harness was getting persistently harder to ignore. 'Uh, Ben?'

'Why shouldn't he want to live?' And here were the raw edges, the sharp injustice of it all bursting from beneath forced acceptance. 'Why shouldn't he have stayed with me? Things are getting tireder in the world but I would never, ever have given up on him …'

'Ben what the hell are these things?' Stretching longer and more frenetic now, thin metal cilia whipping back and forth.

'Never mind those.' Responding to Samuel's alarm the truck assumed a soothing tone but was it a little sly as well? Cajoling, the way a mother might persuade her toddler to drink medicine that she knew was nasty and would be greeted by tears. The way the troll beneath the bridge wet his lips and pressed the stray child to accept a sweetie. Go on. You'll like it.

'Never mind be damned!' Samuel was no child and pretty bloody far from feeling soothed. Clamped rigid and unable to escape his flesh shrank back from the crawling steel.

'Nobody's hurting you. Just chill out a bit and let me tell you about the hospital at the end of the highway. The hospital, and chickens.'

'Chickens?' Now that was pretty bizarre.

'Sure, chickens. What do you think we're hauling?'

With difficulty Samuel bent his thoughts from his predicament to the long line of trailers streaming behind them. Towering cargo containers, unforgiving perfect oblongs, sealed and sterile. They loomed with the obduracy of old standing stones so that it seemed it was the sky that raced behind them.

Although no expert on a great many topics, Samuel knew chickens. His mad hippy mother had kept a hobby farm, favouring fluffy footed bantams that lacerated knuckles with their sharp little beaks. "Everybody works" had been the house rule and young Samuel had been tasked with collecting eggs with sore cringing fingers, too timid to replicate his mother's laughing feat of bowling birds left and right across the yard. Never seemed to hurt the little buggers any: they would bounce to a stop on the grass and come scurrying back to the attack.

Samuel's entire unwilling experience of chickens came down to them being ridiculous nasty critters that nattered and shed and stank and crapped twenty four seven. You could identify a chicken truck by the biblical stench alone, let alone the blizzard of loose feathers that whirled off it for kilometres behind.

'Chickens my ass!'

'No live chickens,' Ben explained patiently. 'Frozen.'

'Frozen chickens my ass! Who needs that much chicken?' The mind boggled. Sure, some of the cities were huge but not one of them stood full anymore.

'I doubt you'd want to roast up one of these babies. They're going in for quarantined medical testing. The guys in charge didn't say too much about it to Geoff or I; no signs on the trailers to scare the natives en route which I'm pretty sure is illegal; but I got the story from a tractor who worked the source farm.

'Seems odd things had been going on there for a while. You see, all laying chickens are hens, right?'

'According to my understanding,' Samuel said dryly.

'But even so, people sitting down to breakfast started seeing little red blots springing up in their eggs. Samples pulled from the line all showed the same thing: it seemed the chickens weren't so keen on not being allowed to have babies, so they went and did it anyway ...'

A long pause. Don't say it Ben.

'… without the cocks.'

'Ben!'

'Sorry I couldn't help myself, it was too perfect. Anyhow this farm's little reproductive development was kept very hush-hush of course: could you imagine the hoo-ha it would kick up in the market? All those consumers expecting a nice sanitised breakfast; lord knows they don't want to think about where it's come squeezed from in the first place. And "plop!" look what's come tumbling from the shell! All sticky and bloody. That wouldn't do at all.'

Samuel's civilized stomach lurched, although not so far back into his hunter-gatherer ancestry it would have been like winning the lottery.

'Seeing themselves about to take a dive in a traditional if not lucrative market the farmers panicked and got the eggheads in. Eggheads, ha, that's good; I didn't even mean that one! Oh buck up Samuel, where's your sense of humour?'

I'm a damn sight more giggly when not strapped down, was the immediate rebuke but Samuel held his tongue.

'So then it all turned into a race, albeit a very silly one. At the hospital they say that all a gene wants is to be reborn as part of the next generation, even if it just sleeps there quietly, unexpressed: the future is all that matters. Those chickens' bodies must have been driving them pretty hard. The scientists would tinker to keep them producing conveniently pre-packaged food and then the birds would find some new way to push their genetic dream.

'Which left the eggheads digging deeper and deeper with their splicing viruses and lord knows what else. Humanity's best and brightest determined not to be outdone by a bunch of chickens gone clucky.'

'Ben, I swear I'll stop listening.'

'I promise that was the last one. So this one morning: one of those cool grey dawns, the type you can't get out here. Dew on the crops and such, and the radio said a chance of rain later which thrilled everybody because the desert's been spreading. Even way out on the farm belt they're starting to feel it.

'It was early in the morning because farmers stand by tradition no matter how automated things get: even these days you'll still see a farmer climb down to shut the gate themselves, and they're always tramping around at the crack of dawn to suss things out. Farmer Joe, or Arviramopoulos or whatever his name was, guessed that something wasn't right even before he cracked the barn door open.

'He hesitated, a hand on the latch and a low creeping starting in his gut. Normally the stupid birds who had given the farm so much trouble would be murmuring away to each other by now, warming through irritating to reach full blown annoying with the sun. Half an hour in the chicken barn was usually enough to bring on one of those stinging headaches that ruined his entire day.

'But now, silence. Only the occasional recorded rooster crow which the scientists had suggested might keep the hens happy—our farmer had his own views on those fine fellows and whether they knew in a blue hell what they were up to, but he would have given anything to have even one of them with him right now. Everything was so quiet, like the air itself was waiting. He pushed open the door ...'

And in that instant with Samuel's attention gone away to that deadly quiet barn and with Ben not knowing up until now if he really meant to deploy the whole thing—a billion animated threads of metal shot through Samuel's clothes and pierced his skin.

It was a mass invasion far finer than acupuncture: the lattice that spread through Samuel's flesh was too subtle to raise even the tiniest dribble of blood but Samuel could feel it *in* him, oh God it was crawling in him everywhere! Metal darted between hysterically trembling muscle fibres, curved around his wet eyeballs to caress the optic nerve beyond. More intimately it prised entry to his cock to divide and conquer there, and even slipped into his tender anus like an exploring finger. Before Samuel's virginal humanity could even howl its outrage he found himself paralysed. A too-mortal effigy strung up on a web of technology.

The harness' payload hit home.

Anticoagulants, tranquillisers and a whole pharmacopeia of other goodies that no honest chemist would own. The stinging cocktail stole the terror right out of his hands leaving them clutching and empty. The aftertaste of his farewell breakfast was metal.

Samuel could no longer close his ears to Ben's continuing narrative but it was a stimulus that rapidly lost all meaning as his mind blew its fuses one after the other, leaving him unplugged and drifting.

'The barn door creaked open and even through his rising anxiety our farmer set himself a mental note to oil those hinges.

'Inside his eyes had to adjust, and then his mind had to adjust because the whole thing was just a mess. A red and white Pro Hart mess smeared across the floor and right up the walls into shadow.

'It was the dawn light that helped him out, glancing in over his shoulder as another bogus rooster crow crackled over the speakers. It picked out gleams from a hundred thousand dull eyes. Lit a hard shine off all the beaks and scaly crooked legs jumbled in there.

'There wasn't a single bird left alive in the place.

'So being a savvy fellow our farmer slammed the creaky

door and ran like hell. Probably pissing himself all the way and praying that his sons weren't going to find him painted across the bedroom one of these mornings.

'At least he never had to oil those hinges: they burned the whole building to the ground, with quicklime and a curse for good measure. Just as none of the oh-so clever scientists knew how the chickens were breeding in the first place they could not put their finger on just how death had gotten in, either. The chickens just … died. Horribly.

'Which is where we come in. The carcasses have to be inspected by the hospital and this whole mess sorted out. Otherwise you might be the last man in history to eat scrambled eggs for breakfast.'

To Samuel it sounded like *breeeakfaast*. That well formed mouth of his retained the gape of shock even with his ability to feel anything drugged away. A thin streamer of drool depended from its corner, trembling in the air conditioning. His eyes flickered dully.

Ben's tale might have come echoing down the length of some incredible tunnel the words were so far away, but when they hit they impacted like stones against Samuel's abused body. Truckers' white lightening etched his neurons in stark neon ice.

Time blew out and sagged. The vastness of the desert slipped from scale. With Samuel clutched in his guilty embrace Ben raced through the day and out the other side of morning, dawn and dusk flickering at epileptic speed and yet he was merely a grain of metal amidst the sand, going nowhere.

Irrespective of the hopes and betrayal of such travellers, night came to the desert and under cover of sleep dreams settled like dew on its scorched and salted mindscape.

In her room at the diner Joyce twitched and frowned on sweaty sheets. Her nightmares were production-line clones, always the same and yet there was no getting used to them. They were eternal in their ability to clutch her brutally in despair.

She was standing alone watching a procession of bright colours and joy march away over the low horizon. They were already out of reach and she cruelly naked in the cold, stripped of even her bravado. And once the bright company were gone, once they had abandoned this old world it would be nothing but a clot of dry, sterile sand.

They had somewhere to go, a whole new world for everyone to rejoice in. But while Joyce did not want to be left behind she knew that she did not belong with those lovely, sparkling lives. She did not belong anywhere and was alone in the deadness.

Hugging herself for what comfort bony angles could give Joyce fell to her knees and without taking her eyes from the bringers began scooping great fistfuls of the desert into her ashen mouth. Seeking to stuff the empty space with anything. But the wadded sand dissolved like dust on her tongue and she shuddered awake on cheap linen in a nightmare of suffocation.

I am in a room, a space, she had to tell her heart and the tears that threatened to slip out. This unfamiliar place was only a hired room. Just a bed.

'Bastards!' Long repetition taught that anger was the quickest way to twist loneliness back into line. Anger as though it were their fault, the bright people. Brimming with bad dreams her bedding took a brief flight to crash against the far wall, where in the morning Mary would pick it up and wonder. Thin plaster trembled at the impact. They sure built 'em good at the judgment day diner.

'Stupid bloody bastards!' The thin pillow had migrated down the bed and Joyce treated it to a limp kick to the floor. 'Bollocks!'

Joyce's rebellion crept only a small way into the night before shrivelling under the immense weight of silence that leaned against the diner. Listening to it her skin shrank three sizes. What a crushingly lonely thing to wake afraid in the night and hear the world sleep on without you—even if you were used to it.

Suddenly the stifling oppression dissolved. Somebody was giggling outside her bedroom window! Quietly, with muffling hands over the mouth but unable-to-keep-silent humour, and all it took to banish the night's invisible fear was one human voice.

'Hey!' Joyce shot back the window to catch whoever it was in … whatever the act may be, although truth be told she was spooked enough to even welcome the bay city panty sniffer with open arms had he stood there. The free flowing air was an immediate relief.

Outside in the dark two small faces lifted, glowing with hilarity. 'You said th' b-word,' little Gareth confided through the flywire although it were the absolute news of the century. 'We heard you.'

'*Two* b-words!' Dave added, his grin glinting like shark's teeth in the night. There they were: both of Mark's kids sitting comfortably in the sand for all the world like David and Goliath gone on a midnight jaunt.

'What are you up to?' Joyce hissed, immune to the charms of youth. Expecting mischief she peered suspiciously into the dark but if there were other lurkers they stayed well hidden.

'Knocking.' Gareth's answer was well seasoned with undertones of "well dur". 'We thought you'd never wake up.'

'C'mon ma'am. Got something fabulous to show ya.'

Normally when a guy tried that line it was followed by the throaty snigger of a zipper but surely these imps were far too young. 'You want to show me something? Now?'

'Totally.' In unison.

'I see.' She tapped her teeth. 'And is this fabulous as in "the unicorn is a fabulous beast", or more along the tune that some marbles are more sparkly than others?'

That stumped golden boy but the younger brother had a keen sense of when adults were having a go. Dave asserted, 'Fabulous,' firmly, a hulking farm lad with only the gleam in his eye to betray him as anything more. 'Get out here.'

Joyce chewed her lip a moment but what the hell: she certainly was not getting any more sleep tonight.

'Alright, but I ain't climbing out the window. Wait there.'

She slid the glass closed on a volley of hushed mockery and chicken noises—they would have gone out the window, but on the other hand they were kids and still bendable. At least even in the glory of derision they had enough smarts to not risk waking their parents. It would not do to alert Joyce's kind hosts that she was sneaking around in the dark with their kids, it was unlikely to win her any breakfasts.

With the window shut anxiety descended again, thick and stifling. One bare foot rubbed the other's ankle indecisively, Move, Joycie. Get going. Quietly, though.

The hallway was even worse than her room. Joyce's skin trembled: if she moved too quickly, kicked up too much of a stink, the desert might simply roll over in its sleep and crush her. She had to force herself along with threats of dentistry and Italian love arias. Mary's loaned pyjamas with their jolly purple penguins did not promise much protection.

The front door rocked gently on its hinges and, intrepid

explorer, she ground to a helpless halt. A conflicting jumble of flee and freeze clogged her joints. The night beyond was impossibly dimensionless; yawning, unknown and horrible. Plunge in and she would be lost, a mere speck in the void.

But the bloody kids were still out there, ghosts laughing in creepy piping voices in the dark. Joyce bit the flesh of her large lower lip and slipped from safety.

Not so bad once she was out here. Surprisingly simple, almost like letting go. To tip off the edge of a cliff must be wonderful, Joyce mused. Falling with only one direction to travel and all the important decisions already made.

Grains of sand spilled over her questing toes like foam. From up ahead came the yeasty reek of boy-feet released from shoes: she could track them by nose rather than eye.

And then by ear. 'Word is it you've been invited to one of Disher's dos.' Dave capped the statement with a charming snort and there was the splat of a thick nose-goblin hitting the sand.

'Word is, huh?'

'Ought to take him up on it.' Unabashed childhood cunning without any adult gloss.

'Ah, gee, you know. Swell as the invite sounds and all I'd rather eat my own feet.'

'Gross!' Gareth piped up admiringly; Dave shushed him.

'We got a trade for ya.'

'Go on.'

'We wanna know what the deal is with Swisher, right? An' you ... you want the town's secret.'

'Secret?' Joyce's blood thrummed. This town. These people in their brave little castle with its moat of sand, and death battering for entry like a fly at a window.

'We *know* it's what you came for. It's th' only thing here!'

'Huh.'

'Yeah, like anyone ever tramped the way out here for th' view.'

'Sam did.'

All three burst into sniggers, conspirators of a pragmatic world. Not for the first time Joyce was struck by how un-childlike these kids were, especially farm boy. Streetwise in a town with only one street.

'Why should you need the inside goss on Disher?' She had to struggle not to say Swisher now that she had heard them do it, and the uncomfortable feeling persisted that she was likely to drop it at some point in the future.

'He's bogus,' little Gareth answered bluntly. Up until now he had been happy to leave the conversational meat to his younger brother but when Dave fumbled he was not backward about coming forward.

Gareth's support gave Dave what he needed to continue and in Dave's lower, ugly tone Joyce glimpsed the man that he might become: was this a poisonous inheritance, or one of the sour gifts of experience? 'That Swisher is up to something and it's our Mum he's messing with. So we help you and you got to help us.'

Tough guy, eh? Joyce crossed her arms. 'And just how do you reckon you can help me?' *Help* echoed a hopeless voice, raising cobweb fine hairs down her spine; *the hospital* … but she shut it down. There would never be help for those voices.

'You want th' secret. He even told us to bring you, so come on.' Verbally beckoning her into the blackness behind the diner while the world slept on. 'You'll see.'

See? Even a hand in front of her face was nothing. Flitting ahead Joyce's guides seemed blessed with the vision of owlets but she moved slowly with shuffling uncertain step and both arms stretched out in front.

No stars peeped out to aid her. There was no moon. A conviction that had lodged long ago in her heart, watered by paranoia, put out dark leaves—the clockwork of the natural world was running down. Nothing was immune. One day having sagged exhaustedly below the horizon the sun would fail to return. The last such pathetic scraps as herself would wake to a day without a dawn, cast adrift in a void just like this.

'New,' Joyce whispered to herself like an absent lover's promise repeated years later on cold sheets. A watery sniff, a squaring of the shoulders. 'I can do this.' Putting her trembling hands back out in front she groped ahead to whatever might be waiting.

'Come on.' Faint and thin as though they had fled far away, abandoning her. 'You'll see. C'mon ma'am. Down here.'

Down here?

Both hands hit a corrugated wall, jarring Joyce to a halt. She had run up against a flimsy shed, a cube barely two meters in diameter.

Sand had scoured the outside but bending to the low entrance she found rough oxidisation flourishing within. Grinding against her touch it released a stinging coppery smell, an arterial reek that gushed into the air. She was immediately, desperately thirsty.

Her tongue felt thick and heavy, and … well well, what was this?

Hesitant new organs of sight, Joyce's seeking palms slid over a ceramic manhole cover heaved aside on the floor. A nest of pipes and the smooth rungs of a ladder leading down—rungs that bounced with the kids' eager feet. All smooth stainless alloy this, unlike the cheap shed thrown up around it.

So. An underground something or other. Buried in this hick town, in desert and obscurity. *Sand* indeed!

Conscious conjecture held garrotte tight around a welter of unease. Since daring the desert Joyce felt that she had come to know sand's nature, its way of swallowing in and smothering. Anything committed to it might well be lost forever: preserved, sure, but unreachable and therefore good to nobody.

You always heard rumours of old shipwrecks on the beach: the lovely flank of a figurehead revealed after a storm but vanished when you returned with camera and shovel the next day. Only myth left behind for generations of tourists to dig for, and a legacy of shopfronts and cafes named Our Lady of the Ocean. Nobody would ever know her real name, where she had sailed from or what she was seeking. Why she died. Bury and forget.

And the kids had gone down there. Into the desert's sightless guts where something throbbed like a living organ.

Joyce's elbow hit the shed's doorframe with a crack, bringing her back to the prosaic reality of banged bones and other discomforts. She put a hand, stinging with pins and needles on the frame to steady herself. She had been shaking her head unconsciously she realised, and cringing back on long coltish legs with a comic thirty centimetres of ankle protruding beyond the cuff.

She had also bitten down hard enough to taste the good old red stuff even through the gagging rust. A sneer thinned her mouth: scared, Joycie? Well tough, because you're going in anyhow.

Quick as a snake for all her size, quick before her nerve caught up with her Joyce slithered down the hole.

And immediately broke out in a lukewarm oily sweat. Following her claustrophobic progress a red mist came drifting down the pipe, clogging her up like a nasty case of the super flu. Overzealous bouncers, her abused sinuses refused to let air through, her heart laboured and worst of all was the low lub-lub everywhere. Half heard and half felt through her vestigial monkey tailbone.

Surely it was some kind of engine although not even Joyce's imagination could summon up a machine big enough to own such a rumble. Or did it have an organic note? She was getting confused: the rush and jumble of her own overheated body was building and as she descended it was difficult to listen through a rising panic.

Even the pied piper voices that had lured her thus far fell silent. It finally came to Joyce, too late of course, that she had stuck her stupid head in a trap. A damn hole in the forgetting sand.

'Fuuuck,' she groaned on a breath sour with fear, flat and dead within the pipe. Her chest was bursting for air, impregnated with rust. Her elbows scraped the sides of the prison, skull knocked it from behind.

'Ma'am?' Came an innocent chirrup from below. 'You swearin' again in there?'

'None of your business,' Joyce snapped, lurching down the ladder as fast as shaking muscles would go. A brace of fingernails split painfully in the rush but she would likely have let the fingers go too if it meant getting out of there.

Out of the pounding clamour she thought *stuff it* and dropped the last meter out a hatch and into an open space stuffed with darkness and quiet, twisting her ankle a good one in the landing. Nice one Joycie, she panted to herself in the delirious rush of relief. Graceful. Elegant. A veritable gazelle in flight.

The first thing that struck her was that although it was too dark to see, the air about her was shockingly wet. Following the austerity of the desert it felt positively indecent against parched skin and tasted even better: nary a puff of rust. Her mad desire for water eased into a thing which could be told to wait.

Mark's kids stood waiting for her, the torch in Dave's hand an intimate little comfort in the dark.

'Oh, like you couldn't have used that outside.'

'The light?' Dave rolled it between his palms and their shadows flipped and twisted. 'Too risky. Swisher's been looking for this place since he got here.'

'The man needs better hobbies.'

The kids just looked at her gravely. 'You don't wanna know about his hobbies.'

'So why do you two come down here? A bit out of the way for hopscotch don't you think?'

'What's hopscotch?' Gareth queried, making her feel incredibly old but Dave waved it off.

'We come for stories. Good ones. Stories that don't try an' make stuff seem dumber.' He crossed his arms. 'Stories ain't what Disher's after, though.'

'Dave watches Swisher,' Gareth rushed in breathlessly; 'He hates him …'

'Shut up dickcheese!'

'.. and he's scared.'

'I said, shut up!' The torch swung up to blind Gareth but golden boy had the bit. He stood defiantly with eyes squinted shut, washed and drowned in the glare.

'It's true! You're not scared of anything but Swisher scares you!' It was undermining the bedrock of Gareth's world, this failing in his smarter, stronger, invincible little brother. Tears began to spill, heedless that he would likely be ribbed for them later. 'And he's got Mum, she's out there now and we haveta tell someone Dave, somebody has to know!'

With his nose running now along with the eyes poor Gareth looked very much like what he was: a child. Very small in the face of the world and shunted aside the way children were these days, while those who should raise them strode on with more important business.

Unable to pierce the torch's dazzle about his brother he turned to the tall woman and got even less there. Compared to the blaze she made a dark indistinct shape offering neither comfort nor hope.

'Do something! Please; Disher's bad, he's a bad man up there growing freaky flowers an' putting voodoo on people and nobody sees, nobody knows but us! Someone has to do something!' The kid's thin voice was rising into the overtaxed scream of hysteria. His wits were buckling: how could any little kid bear safeguarding his own parents? Dismayed, Dave tried to shush him.

'Now you settle down there Gar,' a stranger's voice soothed from the darkness beyond their light. 'The story gets pretty scary from here in. I can't well tell you the rest 'less you're gonna be brave now, can I?'

Joyce heaved an impatient sigh. She was getting pretty bloody sick of mysterious voices from the dark. As though in response to her bad grace a handful of fairy lights glimmered to life about their bare feet.

Two sets of stinky tanned boy feet and her own long pale ones with their knobbled ankles. The lights in the floor nibbled for a moment like curious tadpoles before darting excitedly away. They jostled and multiplied, shimmying up the walls and along the ceiling until the long oblong room was all lit in moving pinpricks of yellow, green and blue.

No more need for the torch, Dave clicked it off and set it on the floor.

'And welcome to you, dear Lady Joyce,' the voice continued jovially in a room revealed to be empty aside from themselves. He employed the same vocal smoothness on her that he had used to sooth the kid but with an edge to it now, grim humour at his prowess, mocking her as well as himself. His voice was the ultimate vocal tool, wielded with cynical precision.

Ignoring her interlocutor for the moment, with an undignified groaning of joints Joyce crouched to tap her fingernails on the smooth Perspex floor. Their dancing sprites were a liquid crystal display sealed away from the moisture.

Fingers came back damp. Resisting the urge to pop them in her mouth she rubbed the pads together thoughtfully as their mystery host went on.

'I've been so looking forward to your visit, ever since these lads told me of your somewhat dramastic arrival.' He dipped a couple of octaves toward sly. 'Love the jammies by the way. Penguins are so in.'

'They're borrowed.' Creaking upright Joyce pivoted on one heel to survey the room. Skin squeaked on the smooth wet floor and the lights spun out around her like an unfolding galaxy, a pinwheel. The impatient geometry of one woman translated into light.

Slick, in the modern sense. There were no cameras in the room so far as she could tell. No screens, sensors, buttons, switches, knobs, dials, meters, toggles, circuits or cables visible—not even a mouse powering a wheel. Merely serene smoothness and bibbles of light that twiddled and bounced off each other.

A blank room empty of function. The shadow cast by an architect with no vision, no dream, no future. How uninspiring. Nonetheless, without knowing what the voice did Joyce harboured no doubts as to what he *was*. 'Built into the walls, are you?'

The machine—of course, what else?—chuckled and the lights mirrored his mirth in a higher visual register. 'If you like; should you look at things from that perspective.'

'Super. What do you do, walls?'

'I am merely a child in gross terms, much like these two young 'uns. I like children. You always see them asking the right questions, poking around where they shouldn't be, seeking that all important *why*. Wish there were more of them. You might consider popping a few out yourself, you know—it would do a lot more for humanity than your current pastime.'

Joyce's jaws ground up tightly but not being much of a verbal fencer she refused the bait. 'Shows what you know.'

'I actually know a great deal when it comes to your good self. Word gets around you know, word does indeed get around. Every one of us has debated the whys and wherefores of your actions, whole essays have been composed. You can do a degree in Joyce these days, just be sure to finish before she finishes you. But my query is: do *you* know what you are?'

An angry toss of the head. 'I don't need to know me. I don't matter. Only the things I do matter.'

'Well reasoned, if you ignore the fact that one gives rise to the other. Deny the first and watch the second wither of meaning. Where is your meaning, lady Joyce? What is the truth in what you do?' Lights rotated mockingly. Points to Joyce's nerves that she was not already queasy.

'Don't think you're so smart, bucko. Others bigger and uglier than you have gone poking holes in my philosophy, and you know what? I'm still here.'

'Ah yes, the splash of cold reality to knock all intellectual maundering on the head: Yet Here I Am. Others may quibble and debate but never you. The only one to never ask why.'

'I find "what" more interesting, and I'm getting pretty tired of putting it to you politely.'

'Oh my, that was politely? Well, as to the what, I am in fact the beating heart of this town. The whole shebang started with its first building, being the diner of course, and every structure since has just run its pipes from there. I've been abandoned down here; the town has forgotten its roots. In fact if it weren't for these clever lads poking around I might have been lost until you came for me. Listening to my compatriots out in the big wide world falling silent one by one and wondering when I would be next.'

Pipes, huh? Joyce remembered the smooth feel of them swarming down the manhole. 'You're pumping the town's water.'

'Spot on and got it in one, pumping water I most certainly am. You cottoned on to that pretty quickly.' He became mock-serious, 'You lads didn't feed her any hints ..?'

A scornful chorus of "As if" and "We promised not" put paid to the suggestion, with an especially indignant, 'You said we wouldn't get the rest of the story if we told!'

'Indeed I did, I did indeed. Sorry to have doubted you. Well Lady Joyce, the point I was coming to is that it's a lonely ol' job keeping the dregs of civilisation alive, but somebody's got to do it.'

'These people don't need you.'

'Au contraire ma mere. The water table 'round these parts is so deep Jules Verne couldn't find it. Shut me down in your incomparable manner and the whole town will just dry up and blow away like a tumbleweed.'

'They don't need your like,' Joyce reiterated as though deaf to what the water pump said. 'If they have to, they'll make it on their own.' And not a bare second before that, she completed silently.

'Are you willing to bet their lives on it? Would you, say, unhook a patient from dialysis on the basis that she should be standing on her own two feet? But look who I'm talking to: of course you would. And you're here to do just that. I think I'm beginning to understand: who could like themselves, going around doing such things. Show me someone who can go home after a job like that and sleep the night.' There was genuine compassion in his voice; even tempered with the ever-present mockery it was intolerable.

'You know why I'm here. Why drag this out?'

The water pump's humour was unshakable. 'Dragging it out is all I've got. So why are you here? Go on, say it out loud. You'll get hair on your palms if you don't.'

'To unplug …'

'To *murder* me. Isn't that right?'

Mark's kids drew closer together and their eyes were huge but not a peep from them. They already knew. Why in hell would the water pump tell, and then have them bring her anyway?

'In a sense,' Joyce conceded grimly. 'You can't really murder something that's not alive, but alright.'

'But of course. And God forfend the famous Lady Joyce should suffer a fit of mistaken identity, especially where her chosen work be concerned. How would you define yourself then?'

He was really beginning to get on her nerves. 'How can I get you to define what you're blathering on about?'

'I'm not the one you're here for.'

'No, really; my sides are splitting.'

'Just think on it. I know it's tough but indulge me a moment, use your brain.'

'Damn it, won't you ever just *say* something!'

'Certainly not if I can help it. Now, undoubtedly these clever pips will have brought you under some condition: an I-scratch-your-back-you-pat-mine sort of deal? I told them not to, I believe negotiation would be better handled higher up but, rather unusually for children, they've resolved to do whatever they think is right. How can I discourage that?'

Joyce glanced aside at the two kids, neither of whom evinced signs of such high morality and it all became clear. 'Disher,' she said flatly.

'Amen!' A blare of cheap recorded revival chorus made them jump.

'*People*,' stressing the word, 'Aren't my problem. Not even assholes like him.'

'Arguably they are everybody's problem. However in this case you'd be correct ... were I speaking about a person.'

Huh? 'Speak in my good ear?'

'That con is about as human as I.' A thoughtful pause. 'Quite a bit less, by most standards.'

'Oh bollocks!' Joyce burst out and there were no giggles from the kids this time. It was impossible to think things through the way that the water pump was pitching them: bang, bang; one nonsensical craziness after the other.

Her fingers itched to simply rip wires from their housing and have done with it, but the big bland room left her nothing to get her teeth into. 'Nobody in their right mind would make a machine shaped like a person! What would be the point?'

'I don't know about right-mindedness, but 't was those big 'uns at the hospital, the uber computers that cooked this one up. Or should I say cocked. Disher was their big idea of progeny, although I suppose we shouldn't be too harsh. Can you imagine them up there, enshrined in their pristine hospital with always less patients trickling in and then finally none. Those infinitely powerful minds gnawing away at their own frustration—Disher might be the least of our worries, who knows what kooky stuff they've come up with.'

'You, apparently, and all the way out here too! Machines come purpose made: form follows function. You want to drive around town you build it like a car; have a hankering to heat bread and it looks like a toaster. The only damned thing a machine shaped like a person would be good for would be to be a ...' her sentence trailed off sickly into the vista of a grotesque new future.

'A person.' The water pump sounded both smug and sad.

An awful queasy churn began in Joyce's guts, mastered only by the iron discipline of a thousand weathered hangovers. She wanted to smash things to let loose all of the terrified energy, to shriek in panic but instead stood very quietly with her arms by her sides and listened. Keeping it for later.

'There's your real threat, Lady Joyce. The so-called "academic". He's what you came for.'

'Suppose ...' her voice crumbled like old hope. She had to swallow and start again, conviction gradually firming. 'Suppose you're right and I buy your whole cuckoo story. Fine. Just dandy. I can flick *both* of you off like a faulty globe and call it a day. And I'm telling you now that I *will* sleep at night, qualm free.'

'Oh I don't doubt that you must sleep like an innocent widdle baby. And that's your day in a nutshell, is it? You're not at all tempted to wait for proof before rushing in and topping what might after all be a hapless, real live person? Just going to, uh, take my word for it. But what if I'm orchestrating revenge? Should you jam the knife in to the hilt and find red, red wine bubbling out would you finally deem yourself a killer?'

All of the lights flashed crimson and milled uneasily before returning to their dance. Joyce's heart thundered at the sudden theatrical flash of "Danger!" in the small room that had felt so safe. Would he ever stop mocking her?

'Face facts dear lady, you badly need a way to cut through the crap. Well ... not to cut it badly, but—anyhow, you get what I mean. You need what I know, and what I've got is the low-down on our bad guy. We practically rolled off the same production line: brothers, so to speak.'

'These kids tell me he's been sniffing around for hints that you're here. If you two are brothers, why is he after you?'

'Pfft, no mystery there: for the same reason all spoiled brats act out.'

'… Yes?'

'Don't you know anything about people? To spite Mummy and Daddy. The hospital machines are the ones Disher's hoping to get back at; but being too chickenshit to march up to their door he has taken it into his head to come at me instead. Funny thing, isn't it?—that you and he arrived from opposite ends of the same thought.'

Joyce ground her teeth in abject frustration, afflicted by jitters and flinches all over. This water pump was slick, too damned slick. He adored the sound of his own voice. There was something about the situation that she was failing to grasp as he rushed her along—but what else was new?

'Just to be clear, I don't trust you buddy. Not even so far as I could kick your rusty tin can ass.'

His snigger a burst of static. 'Shouldn't you say "Yo rusty azz"—and really hit that A, it's how all the colloquial toughs are doing it. Look, this isn't much of a clever dick on my part; I've no illusions as to how the conjunction of our respective tales pans out.

'In fact the tension, the *expectation* was so bad that I actually found myself relieved when you finally showed up in town. I have been reluctantly aware for a long, long time that out of you and Disher, one was bound to get me eventually.'

'And look who you picked, lucky ol' me. Should I be flattered?'

'At least in your case I have the chance to … shall we say negotiate, to bargain for a little more time to enjoy a final taste of life. But when it comes to Disher things would just be zip; game over.'

'What's the difference to you? Dead's dead.'

'You reckon? To have the chance to make a difference on your way out; and the choice between malice and empathy, however unwilling. Which would you choose?'

Joyce did not give a millimetre. 'I don't have to.'

'Given this night ten times over I would still be jumping on the Joyce bandwagon every time. At least you're not mad.'

She shuddered right through and braced herself even though the room had not tilted. How's *that* for psychosomatic, kiddies? 'And you claimed to know all about me.'

'I don't care if you argue soufflé recipes with Buddha: everyone's got license to be a little strange to get by these days, but the bare fact remains that you're not mad. Whereas Disher fell out of the crazy tree and broke every branch on the way down; he's genuine stark dribbling. Mad as a potato. Scares me. Get this: the fellow actually thinks he's human.'

'He what?!'

'Which really isn't going to make your job any easier. Disher's got things all ass-backwards: think's I'm the hospital's child and *he's* got to destroy *me* to save the future. Now if anything's going to wreck humanity's hope of a brighter tomorrow that nut-bar will, most effectively. He squats up there in his "study rooms" like some nasty black hole, sucking down their faith and giving nothing back—well he can't give them anything so real as what they're handing over, can he? He's just a machine.'

Joyce couldn't shake the feeling that the water pump was laughing at her threadbare philosophy, dancing verbal circles around her. Tired, Mark's two kids crouched together on the floor but Joyce kept herself stubbornly upright, standing over them as though they could be protected. 'Why drag the kids in?' she demanded.

'Disher is messing with their mother. We can't have that, these lads need her.'

'Cry me a damned river. Since when was that any of your beeswax?'

'I like the lads. I was lonely waiting down here in the dark until they came poking around.'

'Nobody programmed you to get lonely.'

'Nobody programmed me not to, either.'

'You lured them somehow, didn't you? Picked them because you could use their mother as leverage.'

'What a nasty little mind you've got! Firstly, they found their way down here off their own bat, as we all must in finding our way anywhere. And secondly if it's rationalisation you're hunting then have at it: there is a leverage point for everyone, nobody's exempt.

'The simple truth is that the lads and I found each other because we needed each other. The end. But of course you will go on believing as you like. I would have thought that of all people left on this big brown earth *you* would have an iota of sympathy for loneliness.'

'You'd be mistaken,' Joyce answered flatly.

'Surely? Such a sad old existence you've woven for yourself and you say you're not lonely?'

'I've never woven any damn thing! You think I wanted this, that it's my fault?'

'Tweaked a nerve, have I?' he gloated. 'You claim to have no life, yet you live. Can't deny it. You enjoy square meals when they come along—which isn't nearly enough from the look of you—you seek to be clean, rested and well just like all living things. And yet you've set yourself against peace with all the fierceness of that heart that you insist doesn't feel.

'Don't you see? *Nothing* stands in your way of having a rightful place in the future except you; and it's the one obstacle that you'll never shift. My dear Lady Joyce, your tenacity has become quite the legend. Always on and on when anyone else would have dropped by the wayside. Almost,' he added slyly, 'Like a machine.'

'You shut up right there!'

'Now, now, I wasn't really implying anything. Although it's not such a bad thought to entertain. If they dressed one of my kind in a skin suit then there may well be more of them. How could you know? Who could you trust? You don't even know how well made they are: one might be your lover, yet wrapped up in his arms at night you still couldn't tell.' His soothing voice like caramel, like silk. Lights rippled from wall to wall like the careless wave of a hand.

'I could of course go on like this all night but you wouldn't hear a peep. You've sealed yourself in there—look at you! I don't know whether to laugh or weep, I really don't. Yes I care what happens to these lads, requisite programming or none. I also care about you.'

'Shucks. If I'd known this was going to be a love-in I'd have worn my leather panties.'

'Merely "thankyou" would have sufficed.'

'I'm not thanking you for anything; I don't need the likes of you poking around in my life! It won't help. These kids won't be better for it, either.'

'Quit your fretting: I'm not meddling in their development even nearly so much as I have yours. I've simply told them a few bedtime stories, tales of the future. Parables and the like.'

Joyce's nose twitched suspiciously. 'The future?'

'The future interests me greatly. I had at one time hoped to be around to see it; and confess that even with you standing right here I still nurture a little spark. I had supposed that on seeing your face I might become resigned to cruel fate, perhaps there would be a tiny glimpse of the divine, but you know what? It's just an ordinary face. And I find that I'm not quite ready to roll over gracefully.

'Perhaps I'm just a coward, but I also see some good I might manage before the end and that's worth something. Oh, get that squint off your puss, if the wind changes you'll stay that way. If you can sort out the academic to your satisfaction come back and I promise we'll talk about me. Don't let the door hit your ass on the way out, though.'

At that, all of the fairy lights winked out. They were in the dark again, in a quiet space rich with the welling of water.

The torch clicked on. 'He won't talk now,' Dave supplied gravely. 'When th' lights go out the show's over. Come on.' He stood and hauled on his brother's arm.

Joyce sighed. 'What stories has the water pump been telling you?'

Tales were insidious things, they crept up on you. An underhand way of getting your ideas remembered long after you were bones for some archaeologist to fondle. The same little trick as Sammy was turning with his travelogue—although with those baby blues you would assume him to be more the type to sow wild oats than words.

Merely thinking of good old Sam made Joyce's brain hurt. Irritating as he could be he also carried with him this wonderful nostalgia of old-world normality. Bitter, but she could imagine how one would come back for it again and again. If Sam were here things would be more ... more ordinary. She certainly would not be hauling her sorry ass up and down ladders in the dead of night.

Joyce shook her head sharply: stupid, stupid! This was business, not the time to be mooning over a guy who if he *were* here would be driving her bonkers! Concentrate. Climb. Climbing ahead of her the kids were talking.

'It's just one story, really, that keeps on going. Better than Dad's.'

'Dave!' Gareth protested loyally.

'Well it is! Dad only reads to us about history stuff, not real things that are going to happen. And he never does it proper anyhow; always rushing like he's got to get somewhere else.'

'An' he tucks us in too tight so's we can't move our arms an' legs,' was Gareth's utterly pointless contribution.

'The story?' Joyce prompted before they wandered off entirely.

'Yeah, it's cool. About the future. The real future, not something made up.'

'And?' So much for ideas sticking dangerously in the mind!

But then the kids picked up the pace, fitting it into an eerie sing-song rhythm and Joyce's skin went cold.

'The story's about how folks' sins are s'posed to stay on the inside the way they are now: carried 'round like bad food in your gut t' remind you what you've done. But in the future there's gonna be this guy. Right from the day he's born he'll take stuff too much to heart, way too serious and he'll take so much bad stuff on board, all so feral an' sick that he'll find a way to puke it up, all burning an' horrible …'

'Like this!' Gareth supplied a round of gruesome sound effects to flesh out the story. The way they echoed in the hollow tube as they ascended was disgusting and funny all at once, like belching in a cathedral.

'… And out will come the bad stuff he'd been collecting. Bursting out like some monster but the weirdest part is he'll be ok. Totally freaked out; but won't seem to have hurt 'im at all.

'He'll be gaping at this thing that he's gone and choked out, 'bout the size of a small goat but pale, really pale, an' all threshing an' squealin' on the floor. And he'll run, just run like hell. It can be somebody else's problem now.'

'Asswipe,' Gareth chipped in pompously, having picked up on the best of the grownups' table conversations.

'Worst bit is how after this happens he's gonna go walking around like he's special or something. Looks all shiny without his sins in him anymore. And pretty soon all the other people start asking themselves why they should haveta lug their bad things around all the time, feelin' sick an' shamed. Soon enough everyone's doing it.

'They make a whole heap of monsters, monsters that don't stay goat size for long. Monsters that start getting nasty.'

'Ooh, I know this bit!' Gareth was so utterly thrilled to be contributing; it was easy to forget which was the older brother. 'It gets real risky for people to sick up their sins 'cause the big monsters always come to th' new one: they come, an' you can't get away from that many of 'em. They catch you, stick you through an' rip you up.' Consummate sound technician, Gareth let loose with a barrage of realistic "gaah!"s and "bleuch!"s.

'Even so, folk'll still want to look good so badly they slip off to do it secret-like. Way out in parks and reserves, hoping t' get it over with an' sneak right back into their lives— pretend they've been clean all along. Real dumb. In places like that there aren't even any neighbours to help when you scream. Loads and loads of folk sneaking away an' dying.

'Then there are so many monsters that they stop bein' shy of crowds. Enough of them to come right up to your doorstep, come right through th' window snorting hot steam while you sleep.

'So the shiny new people will build great big cities to hide in. Clever cities that roam around all the time so the monsters can't find 'em. They never stop bein' afraid of what's out there, beyond those walls. They will forget the sky. An' eventually the sky'll forget them too. An' the world will be left to the monsters.'

When Joyce finally stumbled from the shed, half drunk with exhaustion, it was like plunging into dark water. All that held her from collapse in the sand was the sure knowledge that prone, she would never get up again. The desert would swallow her. She was no night owl; or a morning person, or a people person for that matter; and they had come so far into the night that she had drifted into a kind of unconsciousness. A state where the only understanding was with her body's blind instinct, which had to be relied upon.

She reeled in place trying to feign sobriety as the kids bounded about: *their* fatigue had been banished by the prospect of action. Would the little bastards ever tire out?

Apparently not. 'We're going over to scope out Disher,' Dave announced proudly. Although neither boy had entirely tracked the tall woman's conversation with their friend they still vibrated like leashed terriers: done, done, something was finally getting done! Their joie de vivre made Joyce's brain hurt.

'You do that,' she groaned. The desire for *bed, bed* keened so heavily in her limbs that she might already be lying there on the covers, aching. She might never have gotten up at all.

Young Gareth had already mastered the art of the man-whisper, which although hoarse is not in any way quiet. As Joyce tottered away he "whispered" to his brother: 'Shouldn't she be sending us home or something?'

'Naw,' Dave answered confidently. 'That's what parents do. She isn't th' parent type.'

Darn tootin' she wasn't! Joyce finally achieved the diner, numb in every limb. She staggered between the upturned chairs of the dining room with combers of sleep crashing over her.

Everything felt so dark and quiet, like at the bottom of the ocean, that she pressed both palms over her ears to test if she could still hear. The air roared and was silent. Even the paddle fans lay still against the ceiling, although out of the corner of her eye a ghostly motion blur seemed to linger about them. The memory of spinning pulsed out a rhythm: *bed, bed*. But bed was so impossibly far away; how was she ever going to make it?

A maze of scattered tables. The faint pink smell of floor cleaner. And those big paddles overhead, just waiting in potentia. This entire queer isolated town had been rent into chunks and then tumbled back together so that nothing made sense. Machines made so cunningly like people that not only did the people fall for it but the machines mistook themselves for human. The pump beneath the sand, drawing up the desert's heart of water so that people could exist in this terrible place. This town. A rented room at the end of a suckingly lonely corridor. A blind insect head hammering a pane of glass.

The dissociation was so complete that when hands slid round Joyce's torso from behind they failed to inspire so much as a flicker of surprise.

Thick, rough finger pads explored her ribs under thin pyjamas, making jolly penguins caper. Joyce's nipples, weatherwise, tightened as painfully as when she went unprotected on a cold day … or when she was really, really scared. She took her own hands from her ears.

The room stood crowded with silently observing shades, impressions of everyone who had ever existed in the diner.

Strangers who had been just stopping in barely registered; the locals were stronger, and the long lean frame pressed to her spine was the most potent of all. He had been here the longest, breathed himself into the walls and floor. The paddles against the ceiling knew his name.

Joyce rubbed her temples—Mark, of course. Why shouldn't he be here? But surely he should not be *here*, his breath stirring the short strands of her hair. Dressed only in cotton boxers from the feel of him, with the richness of leather on his skin.

Unable to break Mark's enclosing arms Joyce turned in the circle of them to demand an explanation. The biker's towering height left his face a blank threat in the darkness, only the mouth was visible. Lips she would have expected to see parted were instead pressed bloodlessly together.

There was no motion in the man, no tenderness, no attempt to bring her closer. Ah: finally here was a language that Joyce could speak. One that she was faultlessly fluent in. Not desire's simple fleshy honesty but the modernised substitute that had grown up in its place, in vogue, perverted from the true.

Touch in the modern world amounted to little more than a barista's thumbprint on glass tilted against your mouth. Intimacies came as hard, fast and cleverly packaged as a low carb snack; they could not be stomached any other way.

The inhabitants of this society blindly accepted that their insides should be twisted by the intense pressure of its demands, the worst of them so distorted in soul that they could not even hate it. Living flattened as though at the bottom of the ocean, crumpled by the world's weight against the dark sea floor.

'Mark.'

Joyce dropped his name coldly and precisely into the dim

room. She stared upward to where she fancied his hidden eyes must be because the two of them needed to think instead of feel. Any natural warmth between them must die so that they could mechanically fuck and afterward remain just as isolated as before.

Each man is an island; more so a woman. An island shrinking without the resource to sustain its fauna. No help would ever come. Even if they screwed until their brains fell out nothing would ever get any better, they could not save each other. They could only further punish and warp the tectonics of their own private lives.

Joyce both pitied and hated the biker for being just like her. Here stood the real Mark, she had no doubt of it: the secret core of the man who stood at the bar, never behind it; the invincible father and stoic husband. Ravenous for touch and hating himself to pieces. Doubtless he despised Joyce in turn merely for inspiring desire.

Yet still, even looming above her the poor bastard looked simply male. Unshelled and vulnerable without his leathers. And really Mark was far worse off than she. Joyce could only hurt herself but Mark's entire family stood behind him. Their ghosts were strong in this room.

The grand sanctity of marriage was such a house of cards ready to go tumbling at the slightest breath—and perhaps that was what Mark really wanted from Joyce. Not to stick his dick in someplace but the act of tearing down his little world.

Then, finally, there could be no more pretending.

As though impatient with Joyce's conjectures the tall man opened his mouth; but in lieu of wisdom, 'Mary's pjs,' was what came out, which so far as explanations went was unlikely. Nobody in the same suburb as their right mind could mistake Joyce for Mary, front or back, regardless of what she was wearing. Might as well pop a giraffe into one of

Monroe's old frocks and have it bleat "Happy Birthday". Joyce shook her head severely.

Then Mark did a strange thing. Something which might have evoked tenderness in Joyce's overstrained heart had she any to spare. He leaned down and pushed his rather haggard face into the pyjama collar at her throat, inhaling roughly with closed eyes. Those big hands now pressed her urgently against him, her own nostrils full of cotton, skin and leather.

And then just as abruptly he shoved her away. Cruelly as though punishing them both for such indulgence.

'Sorry,' Mark grated stiffly, words forced through his teeth like nails; 'I won't … my wife ..' Although the stupendous erection that ravened in its white cotton restraint said otherwise—but Mark had the reigns, need being crammed back in its box. The smell of clean detergent. Did his wife wash those shorts and fold them lovingly, merely for them to end up here?

Joyce gaped at Mark, stunned and at first uncomprehending. Despite its exhaustion her body was in ascendance: she had briefly warmed in the biker's grasp as though trying to throw off fate, to reach toward life.

Of course that comfort was then snatched cruelly back. A lesson in reality that her stupid flesh should have learned long ago and failed for this happened and it only hurt and hurt again.

'It's fine,' pride choked out for her when nothing else could speak.

Mark might have said more. Joyce's face had bloomed warmly, briefly open; but now it froze back into chill immobility. His mouth could only return its silent shame.

If there were apologies Joyce certainly did not want them, she shoved past him. How quickly the electric excitement of being desired, wanted and real dulled into weary cynicism.

Sighing she turned back to face him.

'Really, it's fine.' A dead voice so at odds with how she had briefly glowed in his grasp. 'We can just … pretend like it never happened. What are you doing out of bed?'

'I was looking for them.' Mark gestured vaguely around the room. 'Th' teeth. They're somewhere here, waiting to bite, I know it. I have t' get them or my family won't be safe.'

Things that you could brush off as ludicrous by day sounded eerie at night and Joyce found herself eyeing the floor nervously as though the biker's delusion might come to life.

You're likely to need more than teeth to save your family, bucko.

'Right. Well … I'll leave you to it then.' Joyce left Mark standing alone in the dark with his failing hard on and whatever regrets he chose not to share.

CHAPTER SIX

AUTOMATONS

THE CLINGWRAP PLAYHOUSE

WELL, WELL; wasn't this something to tickle the interest and perhaps relax the colon. Voyeur of many a keyhole in her time Joyce stooped to this one avidly, striving for a peep.

One of the tantalisingly raised voices in there belonged to Captain Crazypants himself, the inimitable Swisher ... damn, *Disher*! Those kids were a terrible influence. And fair enough that Disher should be in what, for want of better terms, Joyce dubbed his study hall.

Even that was a little grand: the building was no more than a prefabricated cube, designed to be popped on trailers and hauled away. It was an aesthetic favoured in the education system for music, after school care and anything else readily pruned from the budget.

Took no architects to cough up such grim functionality: merely an extrusion factory and a relatively simple program. In the timeless tradition of its kind the step where Joyce lurked was redolent of cat piss and linoleum.

But that strident second voice pacing back and forth, ah, that was the kicker for it belonged to I-don't-need-help-to-keep-*my*-marbles-in-the-jar Mark. Here beneath Disher's very roof.

Joyce's skin tingled at the biker's coarse tones and she pressed eagerly against the door, although not without a self deprecatory grimace. Sad, Joycie, real sad. Somebody ought to come spray her with the garden hose.

Sad that even such a failed encounter was to be treasured by her starving, misguided heart.

'… If you're so happy to play daddy,' Disher was lecturing and Joyce winced; was the fool blind to the violent potential of Mark's hands? 'Then it's about time you learned to keep what you claim closer to home.'

'My boys thought they were looking for their mother,' Mark growled sullenly. 'They *thought*, you understand.'

'Ah, yes. Mary.' Disher could not help unveiling his gloating: just a peep but trashy, like a flash of petticoat at a funeral. 'Who was of course under the covers. Just as she should be.' So sly.

Deck him Joyce prayed with her fingertips white against ply: she desperately wanted to see the academic scattered out the door with his nose spouting red.

Surprisingly, Mark took refuge in a more democratic outrage. 'This is a small town! Bad enough my boys might've seen something, but might be more than them peepin' next time!'

'You must make things so dramatic. If you'd only give me what I need ...' for a moment a frustrated whine showed through; 'This ordeal would be over. For you, me, your white picket family, everyone.'

Mark chuckled blackly. 'Not this nonsense again. You just don't wanna hear it do ya? Nobody in this town has any secret maps, schematics, plans, or even a bill of sale for laying a single damned shingle. Read my bristly lips: nobody cares!'

'I want those plans, Mark. I want what's hiding here.'

'Ain't nothing hiding here! Why don't you just go on after whatever glitzy corporation paid for th' construction an' leave us the hell alone!'

'Do you think I'm playing?' Disher shrilled. 'Since we are discussing *want*, why don't you have a good long think over things you don't want young Dave finding out, huh?'

There was a long dangerous silence during which a frustrated Joyce tried desperately to see through the door.

'Are you hearing me Mark?'

'I hear.'

Joyce expected eruption but instead the tall man sounded soul-weary, a deep weight that he could not set down. Recognising its own kind her body responded more eloquently than words and flowered unseen.

'Save your threats Disher, since you can't seem t' keep anything else t' yourself. Dave's my boy, as much as Gar. Love made him mine. Nobody can change that now. It's love as makes sons, makes a man's legacy; not just a few miserable blots of jizzum. You, you got no more to give than a squirt of jizz an' a mouthful of lies.'

'Better than the other way around,' Disher quipped with surprising humour; however the grim biker was not laughing.

'If it's threats you want, I c'n speak your language right enough. I will never let on to Dave what I know, never break my boy's heart. Sooner break my own, and pull th' world down on top first. But. Should that choice be ever taken outta my hands you can set your goddamn watch by the moment I start breaking things offa you.'

No prize for guessing which appendage Mark would start with first.

'Yes. Hm.'

The academic sounded flippant but now Joyce thrilled to a different tune. She picked up the undertone of fear, the merest quaver that even Mark might miss.

She hoped, uncharitably, that it was killing Disher. Hoped that he woke trembling even on such nights as saw Mary's warm curls cast across the pillow. Hoped that he had to lock himself into the bathroom each dawn to gaze despairingly into the mirror, reconstructing his personality piece by piece.

Disher went on with the fear flickering and guttering beneath. 'Oh my dear Mark; but then what would happen to poor Mary? She was sinking when I came to this dustbowl town, sinking fast. Sinking with hubby right by her side, but as cold and distant as Pluto.'

'Mary …' Mark stumbled: he could not lay stake to her by *my wife*, not to this man. Nonetheless the name alone was an invocation.

Joyce was fascinated and unnerved. What had the diminutive blond been or done to inspire such acolytes? What might any woman be?

And deepest below where she kept the things she was not allowed was the sheer impossibility of what she herself might dare.

'Mary doesn't need you Disher, whatever you've got her convinced of. She'll come 'round to it, too; before the end.' Mark might have been pronouncing his wife's sentence. The room was quiet enough to hear leather creak. 'But for now my boys need their mother. An' I ain't about to see either of us ruin that.'

It looked like somebody's prayers were getting answered this week. Joyce flared with alarm as heavy boots came rapping toward the door, forcing her back in frantic foot-scrabbling retreat. Back out into burning light, half blind and squinting about for somewhere to hide.

She had to settle for cramming herself behind one of two tragically kitsch statues set up beside the doorway: scared-stiff beggars can't be choosers.

This statue she guessed was intended to depict biblical Mary at prayer, although which of the Marys was debatable. From certain angles the artist may even have had the hotly contested Mrs Judgment Day Diner in mind.

Although historical accuracy was no strong point of hers Joyce suspected that none of the woman implicated had actually tooled about all rouged up like some rent-boy during Mardi Gras, nor simpered straight into the burning sky accepting sure blindness into their gaze. Had the statue flinched beneath the sun's thrust, perhaps shielding its eyes in despair the bare nod to reality would have pleased her more.

Here he came, hurricane Mark. The door whammed in its frame. Checking that it was safely shut Joyce stepped out behind him.

'I've just been appreciating the art hereabouts: it's a bit out of bloody left field.'

The speed at which Mark resettled himself before turning was eerie, she would not have done so well—but after all, he did not *know* she had been eavesdropping. 'Disher's fault, those.'

'Really? He doesn't strike me as a patron of the chisel.'

'He got 'em off a circus some time back for a few bucks apiece.'

Among the last relics that the performers had to sell, from the look of them. The circus had already travelled some ways when their plank-sided vehicles groaned into town, shedding this thing and that as they went.

Mark as a person was gifted with a very basic belief in humanity, although one founded more on instinct than experience. He believed that people were like bramble: not glamorous, but with a deep rooted vitality which was hard to quench. Bash them down five times and they would spring up a dozen more.

But the world had been at these circus folk an awful long time: you could practically see the life flake from them, just the same as the paint did from their trucks.   Thank God they had no kids with 'em to pass this sour legacy to. Finding one day at a time that the tools of a trade they had little heart to practice were now only worth perhaps one last meal out of the world. Their horizons were suddenly, cruelly without audience.

'Money,' Mark snorted disgustedly. 'Th' damned academic couldn't even stretch hisself so far as to give them something they needed. I took on a few bits of jewellery an' fed them: a body for every seat in the diner. Tucked right up to the tables but the place never felt so empty.

'Opened th' bar up too but they never touched a drop.' Mark's guests had only chewed in exhausted silence. Every edible scrap. Here and there a sequin glinted in grey dust. Had even one of them licked their plate Mark believed he would have wept.

'This one woman.' Her face seamed so deeply it looked to be splitting open. 'She kept starin' right at this jar o' marshmallows that I kept next t' the espresso machine. Just starin', like she hadn't seen its sort in years. She wouldn't have taken if I'd just offered, so I traded th' jar for her to juggle for my boys.

'Didn't expect much. More remembered how when I was their age I'd begged to go to every damn circus in town. So she stands, clears this little space an' gets started. And well Dave and Gar, they'd never seen the like. It was all acrobats, lions and sawdust rolled into one, wonderful as any big top I ever went to.'

And the boys' eager cries of "Again-again!" had risen up and thrown back time. The juggler's face, that rumpled map of her life smoothed out and beamed, hands flickering faster to the rhythm of the cries. With a shock Mark had realised that she was not old at all! Rather in these dry times her life had sunk underground to wait, had been waiting all her days for just such a moment.

All of the chairs in the diner were pushed back silently to watch squarish fingers weaving nimble patterns in the air and Mark, as open-mouthed now as his boys, thought he glimpsed there all the mystery of our race's quickness of youth. He felt anew our desire to understand, to reach out and touch the universe. The balls flew like the movement of planets finally comprehended.

And his boys standing to ether side of him, little Dave's hand creeping unconsciously up his own. It was their wonder that made the juggler glorious. Mark's love swelled so immensely it made his ribs creak: secretly he believed that grown to men there was nothing they could not do. They might restore the world. So dreams the great pride of all parents, and so are they betrayed.

When the juggler finished and bowed, her face closing into immobility again it was left to Mark, Dave and Gar to applaud wildly. With a creaking of seats her people turned silently back to their meals.

Still her fingers tucked the balls away with new confidence and her three admirers were rewarded with a smile and a marshmallow each; Dave and Gar squabbling over the pink one until Mark swapped it for his own.

'She was good,' Mark managed simply. 'The circus might have stayed on. Some towns are funny about performers but generally only th' dregs make it out here, we ain't the picky type.

'But they all up an' made their beds before dawn. It was my wife's shift; I'd slept through as they'd packed themselves back into their rickety trucks. Didn't take breakfast, didn't take anything except well-wishes an' that with eyes that knew better.

'I asked after 'em as others came by but nobody's ever seen them again.' Nobody could say they had seen a woman with a young/old face and wise juggler's hands. No bones and sequins were ever reported out there on the sand. The world's upheaval had thrown these strange fish up on the town's shore, and then the desert had swallowed them away again.

What Mark chose not to recount to the curious Joyce was how often he dug through his wife's jewellery for those trinkets that had bought a meal. Mary refused to wear them, and in such a manner that Mark dare not ask again—not even in the bedroom where he had once dared anything.

He would pull the tawdry brilliance of the circus jewellery through rough fingers on the nights that the diner was empty, when his wife should be there and his strangling fury would not let him touch anything truly hers. Not for Mark to pine over the scent of Mary's possessions like a sick dog.

Joyce crossed her arms. 'You could just make Disher ditch these God-awful statues in the sand. He's terrified of you, you know.'

'With reason.' The biker knew that his mental landscape had become nothing to be proud of. His moods all felt the same: whatever the surface emotion, violence always bubbled hot and fresh beneath. 'I didn't hear they taught spying at finishing school these days.'

'Major A-Hole One-Oh-One.' Joyce barked a laugh although Mark did not get it.

'So did you find what you was looking for?'

'Yes, actually. Disher.'

Now Mark was surprised: 'You didn't follow me?'

'Oh sure,' Joyce drawled, deciding to knock this one on the head; 'I've been following you *all* over.'

Mark flushed, angry and embarrassed that the spindly woman was right on target: he *had* assumed it was all about him. Her bravado lacked finesse, though: it screamed nervousness far louder than honesty ever could. Had she been talking any tougher she would have been sucking on a cancer stick and glaring through a James Dean fringe.

'So how well do you know Disher?'

'Reckon you got a pretty good idea of that now.'

'Have you ever noticed anything …' she rummaged for euphemisms, came up empty handed, '… uh, weird about him?'

Mark burst out laughing. It was like a relief, 'Well aren't you just th' odd duck.'

'Ok, so not just "weirdo" weird; we can take that as written. But have you ever seen him do anything really out there, bristle the hair down your spine sort of stuff? Anything like … like he wasn't actually a person?'

'What, like aliens?'

'Of course aliens!' Joyce snapped. 'Obviously. What sane person could assume different?'

'Now you just need to settle right on down there an' bite into a big get over it sandwich.' Mark's humour glinted forth; Joyce's anger seemed to sooth his own. 'What is it you reckon Disher might be, if not a person?'

Joyce shrugged uncomfortably, looking away.

'Yeah, it would be great if it were that easy. Disown fellows like Disher, push th' lot of 'em out of "humanity" and we ain't ever have to admit what we've come to. Got to be an outside so we can have th' in.

'But if you ask me, Disher's all too human. Like somebody set out to exaggerate everything mean spirited about every man ever made. He's so human he makes me sick.' The mere thought returned Mark's anger to full blown.

Now Joyce's eyes were on him and she stepped closer, although putting herself in reach of the hard rage that surrounded Mark made her pulse hammer. 'Why are you letting Disher dick you around?'

Joyce's neck would be a twiglet in his grasp. But her eyes stayed on him, as severe as his own. 'T' ain't me he's dickin',' Mark growled. 'You don't get to comment on our private lives, ma'am. You aren't one of us.'

'I could be.'

The muscles in his jaw ground and he deliberately looked elsewhere. The cloying parable that men like him had been fed straight from the crib was that women were a prize to be won, but were they not a sort of punishment as well?

It was a conceit that lingered long after one's balls got nice and hairy: the boy lingering in the man and the boy believed in heroic endeavours, princesses to be rescued and women as reward. It was a role Mary had played so well.

And Joyce stood here the antithesis of all that: asking only to be claimed. Perhaps that devalued her. There may not be a man left in the modern age who could take up such an offer stripped of all the lies, excitement and pain.

Perhaps Mark's choices were not of love but conditioning. Perhaps he was merely addicted to the excruciating fiction of his wife, who knew? He could only follow the misguided staggering steps of his heart.

Joyce saw the decision in him; those chipped and cracked hands clenched until it looked like that was all they were meant for: brute hammers of meat. Hammers could not caress or toss a delighted child into the air.

'Don't.' The refusal strangled on its way out. He had to do it again. 'Don't. You're not Mary.'

Joyce's cold eyes hardened further and he saw scorn; why not, he deserved scorn. There was desire between them but no sympathy.

'I'm not,' Joyce agreed bitterly. 'But I doubt that even she is.'

'Who isn't what?' a third voice piped up cheerily.

It is a constant of the universe that if you are talking about somebody they will come and stand directly behind you. The hammers stuttered, dropped and became defenceless hands again.

Silly Joycie. She had been foolish once again and had nobody to blame for humiliation but herself. She had become so caught up that she mistook herself for one of these people with their vibrant passionate lives. For days she had seemed to wander in a maze of intense possibilities and it was only now watching these two that she was thrown back on herself: the outsider, the alien.

Painful, but she swallowed it. Who could deny their own nature? It was only by accident of being human that she wanted more.

Mark also took his medicine as given. 'You're going to see him?' A valid question. One would have thought blondie too ashamed to front up on Disher's doorstep the very morning after her children uncovered her nocturnal antics. It never pays, though, to underestimate people as here she stood front and centre. Consequences, schmonsequences; apparently there were none in the warmth of the academic's regard.

Mark's flensed eyes were swallowed up by wincing lines as Mary answered airily, 'Of course I am sweetheart. I've never missed a study session in years.' As though that were something to be proud of.

Mary noticed her husband all right. Every look she turned his way was tender with smiles, her eyes lambent: attitude and choices in cruelly insane conflict. No wonder the poor man could not rip himself free.

Mark's whole body yearned to his wife without moving. It was not even directed at Joyce but the exchange was so intense that she was left breathless as it brushed by, and flabbergasted when Mary turned casually to her.

'Will you be joining us today hon? I know Disher would love to have you, and I think you'll get a lot out of it.' Completely guileless.

'I'm, ah, thinking on it,' Joyce stuttered, caught off guard. Sudden contempt radiated from Mark in a tight arc.

However when the biker spoke it was unexpectedly jovial. 'Would you look at me, stood here with these two lovely ladies. How about you both ditch the boring duties for a day and come back to the diner with me for a proper breakfast? I'll do bacon, waffles; bacon-waffles, anything you like.'

'You will try.' On tiptoe Mary kissed his cheek. Only Joyce saw him tremble. 'I'm sure I wouldn't love you so if you didn't. I'll be along later. Joyce, I do hope to see you inside.'

So Mary went one way and Mark, without another glance at Joyce, the other.

Joyce supposed that she should not be shocked. The bonds Mark had set on himself had held thus far under incredible provocation; there was no reason to suspect he wouldn't hang miserably in there for further months or even years. The biker was no longer a man free to act but had become more like an insect crystallised in an amber bead, a decoration worn around the neck of the woman he loved.

Joyce spent her morning lurking in the shadows across the street; not patient by nature but patient enough to wait for a glimpse of Disher's "students", to see who was arrayed against her. Naturally she expected nutters. Although it was not at all politically correct to hate the mentally ill Joyce had known enough giggling, muttering, tittering old women in her time to have developed an overwhelming urge to chuck them down the stairs.

The town's fading blossoms who had fallen under the academic's influence arrived singly or in pairs. Average enough looking: nobody was obviously deranged or flinging their poo across the street. But what really boggled the grimly observing Joyce was the quality that every one of these dusty Eves shared.

They were in love. It had been a while but you could not mistake it. Every woman who filed between Disher's gruesome statues was sheltering the glow of one who hugs a delicious secret to her heart, transforming the everyday. A sixteen year old girl told *you're beautiful* for the first time would shine like that.

Swisher himself came out to greet each one with a smile and an embrace so fond it smacked of bombast. He might have been welcoming home long travelled children but in this piddly town nobody could have come from further than a street away. Flock finally safe inside the academic glanced up and down the street before closing the door, and Joyce drew further into the shadows. Looking for someone? When that door finally shut she sighed with relief.

Lord knows what the kids imagined her likely to do with this mess. Bust in there on horseback, probably; fry Disher with the white lightening of *right* before sweeping up their mother to whisk her back home—everything, in short, that Daddy had failed to do.

They did not yet understand life: how Joyce would fail to carry the day, how she would always fail. There are not any heroes to strike down wrongdoing and weave the fragments of your life back together; you cannot rely on rescue or even look to help others. Only yourself. Sometimes not even that.

Still the kids won a faint smile from her: good on them for being able to dream such adventures! Childhood may not be the magical realm beyond pain and grief so idolised by adults, but it was not without its powers.

Memory threw up their faces as the kids had looked during their sojourn underground. Wide-eyed and grim in the dark as somewhere cool water dripped, dripped. She imagined that as golden boy Gareth matured and took on Dad's lankiness he would retain his sweetness, but Dave …

Ah, Dave.

Mark was right. Best that farm boy should never know what dubious seed he sprang from. There had been such twisting hate in the boy when he spoke of the academic, hot and bright in this age of dusty resignation. Although younger, Dave already stood balanced on the last cusp of childhood:

each passing moment only saw him grow more inflexible and unforgiving.

Given a few months to mature, Dave's fantasy world might see Joyce crash into the hall to fry mother and academic together. And in not so many years, the growing up years where we set aside dreams in the way that we must relinquish all hope, thunderbolts and divine retribution would be entirely stripped away. Eventually farm boy would find his own justice with a kitchen knife in the dark.

Joyce stepped back out into the light, staggering a bit beneath the direct heat. Unfortunately she was no statue to stand unshielded beneath the sun; she seemed unable to catch the trick of living here. It were as though there were some secret inner desert to this town, beyond the ordinary perceptions of sight and smell; a state of mind at whose meaning outsiders could only guess.

Fleeing her thoughts Joyce slipped around the side of Disher's study hall and was blinded by a fantastic dazzle, retina yelping *ouch ouch!* Shocked she threw up an arm, finally assuming the position that she had wanted the statue to take.

Both pupils were stunned pinholes and she had to squint through her fingers. What was this horrible shiny thing? Some nasty bright lump, like a hernia extruded from the building's tired old ass. She would not have thought the study hall could get any uglier but the proof was in the pudding.

Joyce grimly managed to pry her fingers apart a smidgin more. Her jaw dropped. It was a greenhouse! What bloody, bloody idiot would build such a thing the way out here? What plants could possibly need it hotter? The greenhouse gleamed stickily like a colourless candy building, a trap for unwary children. She smirked. In the lost *once upon a time* such a lure might have snared a waif but if Mark's kids were anything to go by there was no chance.

Edging close Joyce snorted: the thing was not even glass. The dazzling skin yielded and clung to curious fingers: clingwrap if you could believe it. The same deal that school lunches came in, unless you hearkened back to the more classic era of waxed paper.

Here the clingwrap had been opportunistically stretched around the skeleton of some long defunct machine. The desert was hard on machinery: here some great iron thing had been brought to town and had died hopelessly, leaning up against the study hall, half-buried like a dinosaur in a tar pit. It might even have been one of the digging machines that had laid the arterial pipes of this town, placing the water pump at their centre. Hard to tell now. Sand had scoured away all hints of functionality until only this rusting hulk remained; bare metal bones that proclaimed not *I am* but *I was*.

Joyce had imagined Disher to be a builder, but here in his handiwork she saw that "scavenger" might be closer the mark. Sad. Like those greying men that you saw on grey suburban beaches; bending for bits of shell, twine or water-smooth glass to feather an already pointless nest. Men sunk too deeply in misplaced ideals to ever amount to much in the real world.

Deftly, working to avoid the hot springy stuff bonding to her fingers Joyce tore herself a hole in the side of Disher's greenhouse. Tore it bigger, reaching all the way to the ground. Why did idiot-features bother locking the front door when his building had a clingwrap ass?

Slipping inside Joyce stepped into another world. Into a jungle.

The interior was a confusion of potted plants heaped about. And hot, oppressively so, at least twice as steamy as outside. Already Joyce's head hung down and she began to pant in brief, hurt spasms, her heart labouring. All of her air was squeezeboxed out.

One hand thrust out to keep her from her knees squelched through nauseous plant gunk before finding purchase on a shelf. At her back she felt the thick air rush out through the rent in the greenhouse as though the desert outside had put its lips to the gap and sucked greedily. No change in the stifling atmosphere yet but the desert was patient.

Ugh! Finally registering what her hand was in Joyce snatched it back, staggering a little, wiping smears of clotted green on her pants with a grimace. The tender pink beneath her nails tingled and stung nastily, a burning that refused to be scrubbed off. What the hell was this?

Raising her head Joyce surveyed the greenhouse through swimming eyes.

Salvaged shelving zigged and zagged across the open space. It resembled a schizophrenic's reference library: neat aisles all fractured to chaos and nonsensical plant substituted instead of books.

The plants were something else; if any organism begged a slash and burn policy this was it. Green predominated but it was the plants' virulent blooms that caught the eye. Foul spineless things, vividly red against the thin watery green of slumped leaf and stem. It were as though the plants had risen up only once in their brief lives, pumping all they had into the red-raw bloom before slumping back, exhausted. All for the bare hope of propagation and nothing for themselves.

And there was so damn much of the slushy greenery. The colour of boiled cabbage, going translucent in the way of old stems in rancid water. It must have taken some devilish plant husbandry to arrest these things from their rot and press them back to life.

When people like Joyce said outdoors what they really meant was Outback. She had grown up in a landscape where between vast vacant tracts a moiling mess of woody scrub fought thorn and root for supremacy. Weeds throttled each other, encouraged fire to raze their foes; and above it all the occasional tree twisted long pale limbs into the sky like a Bacon painting in living wood, a Rubens. She had dreamed of touching such flesh.

By contrast she found the greenhouse's sickly occupants deeply abhorrent. Instead of reaching for the light Disher's plants sprawled, petals spread obscenely to the air. Or when they had run out of shelf they merely slumped to hang, exhausted, to the floor.

From the clingwrap sky a warm mist drifted down, straggling hair across Joyce's brow before boiling away with the force of her fever. She squinted up. A green and yellow snake of frayed garden hose sagged from the ceiling, water fizzing from pinpricks along its length. Its colour so very closely resembled the "Poison!" warnings of the reptile world.

At the start where the water meter went *click click* Disher had been meticulous in piercing the rubber and the cloying false rain drifted forth. But as the hose wound around the room his interest had petered out. Toward its end the snake bulged with its unreleased payload and the plants below had withered in on their despair.

It is typical that in disliking somebody you assume them to be crap at everything. How delightful when they affirm it to the full.

Joyce lashed out angrily at the shelf that had supported her. It teetered and toppled with a satisfying crash, spilling pots, plants and cascades of dry sand everywhere and ending up wedged firmly against the next shelf along.

Sand? The word rasped dryly in her throat and her fingers confirmed it: the pots contained no earth, only the same nutrient-poor silica as outside. No wonder the plants failed to thrive! What was Disher doing, trying to condition them to live in sand? If so sorry old chum: it was taking prodigious amounts of water merely to keep them clinging on.

And the greenhouse was an ecology Joyce had violated by tearing her way in here. Slowly but surely the boy in the bubble was getting a great honkin' dose of the great outdoors.

The thought filled Joyce with a rush of cruel exultation and she shoved the shelf again fiercely, kicked it. Finding its new position immovable, she attacked another and then laid into the plants lying helpless on the floor.

In the perversity of human nature there are many things deemed "disgusting" but which are great fun nonetheless. The saline glue of oysters was one. Much of Eurovision. Then for some it might be mainlining those little bowls of burning red stuff that they set out in Mexican restaurants, or walking in your socks in the rain.

It was with hot glee that Joyce discovered how profoundly the act of wreaking ruin on Disher's greenhouse really did it for her.

Raging up one aisle and down the next while plants exploded on impact, squishy grenades. A satisfying combination of pop and splat with each stamp at first and a wet veiny smell. Then as she progressed her shoes went pistoning in deeper mush making more of a "squoit!" sound. Varying her train of destruction left and right.

Soon Joyce's pants were painted febrile green and ochre right to the knee which was weird as the plants had no yellow about them. Clotted green spattered the toppled shelves which were beginning to resemble a forest of riot blockades. Her hair stood up in green rocker spines. She even flung fistfuls of mush at the shining ceiling but as was so true in life her efforts fell short. The glop rained back down.

Soaked, the heavy flopping fabric of Joyce's pants chafed her thin white ankles as she stamped about. At first the skin tingled, could have been the chafing. But then it began to sting: itchy like a leg full of spitfire quills.

Transported by rapture Joyce failed to perceive her danger until it was far too late.

The toxin's onset was not gentle. It rolled heavily in like that haunted time of the night when the alcohol turns against you: revelry curdles to revulsion and brings the return of all the bad old memories. Down Joyce went, onto the sodden floor with jelly legs pin wheeling in slow motion beneath her, lazy numb limbs that had lost interest in doing their job. She tingled with burning chills that ran up and down her extremities but it was damn well not from the excitement. The sensation swept up past her ears and then it was lazy head.

Things got confusing.

The cheap shelving shuddered and loomed up toward the clingwrap ceiling like monoliths, huge and forbidding. Through the ragged tear in the world the desert breathed its furnace sigh. Even the slovenly colours were wrong: a sick child's palette smeared together. The crowding shades of nausea, humiliation and a thick descending despair.

Pounding blood was pooling in Joyce's skull and the thick soupy atmosphere was awful; a world where false rain fell in drifts, stinking of rubber. Far above in the melting plastic sky the garden hose squirmed uneasily.

A spatter of half remembered laughter stabbed her already craven heart with fear, made her whip around. It was all well and good to stoke bravery with insolence but if you had been broken you could not fix that, no matter how hard you tried.

In a burst of determined sliding Joyce regained her feet. Her first, timidly hopeful thought was *the kids* but they were both back at the diner swallowing whatever just desserts daddy saw fit to dish out. Yet the laughter was hurtfully familiar. It came drifting from behind the shelving blockade as though *they* stood beyond.

Although Joyce squeezed her eyes tearfully shut she was unable to deny the bright people, the bringers of the new world. Behind those inert slabs of wood paced happiness and hope, the future. Her subconscious cringed. It could endure the prosaic ruined world but not what possibilities haunted her dreams.

For what had Joyce once laughed carelessly like those beyond the wall? Had it been the sight of a lit Ferris wheel; incandescent against the blood-setting clouds? Or perhaps tim tam slammers with friends around the coffee table at two in the morning, their endless nonsensical debates. Her days had once been full of small things that brought minor joy, a modest life.

Now she had proven herself a creature of the old world, the dead world, for the mere sound of laughter was frightening. It flickered forth again, foreshadowing a cramp which would reach right down to her heart.

All of this may have seemed like the end of sanity to Joyce but it would be well to remember that to the wider universe, our girl was just not that important. Outside the boiler of the greenhouse two of the ordinary townsfolk wandered by in bright sunlight; little more than moving blurs to Joyce through the clingwrap wall. Although they chatted softly she thought she caught the words "circumcised' and "cumquat". And they went on. How wonderful that out there folk could still continue on their merry way, separate from her trials. While in here poor Joyce stood trapped as though she deserved little else.

More laughter, getting closer and she scrabbled against the shelf like a hurt animal. Coward Joycie! She fished up a trembling sneer for herself. What she *ought* to do was to turn and fling herself bodily on the cruelty of the bringers, drag the hope from their eyes with her nails ... but which outcome did she fear more? To confront them finally? Or to turn and find herself in an empty room?

Aah, haah breathed the desert at her back. Disher's bright greenhouse swelled and contracted with it. Gelatinous drug-thick sweat was squeezing from beneath Joyce's nails. Ahead was an ugly utilitarian grey door into the academic's ugly study hall and she chose forward. It was as good as running away.

Sand. In her jerky flight to the door one shoulder clipped a shelf and she heard the plants rattle in their pots as though they too were terrified. Her head pounded. The heat pounded. Once she reached the door she clung to it gratefully for a moment; its hard surface was blessed in the manner of reality: ugly but dependable. Then she snatched the door open and snatched herself through.

Disher's students turned as one in their seats to gawp as Joyce burst in. Well right back at ya weirdos. There could be no graceful retreat on the cards for her now. Not after seeing this.

A yawing tape deck spewed chaos, age crippled guitars and synthpop beside an iron grate in which burned bunches of the red blooms, thickening the air. The floor was blackened and warped beneath from many such abuses.

Joyce clenched her jaw as beckoning hands reached out, not the least of them Disher who looked like the cat that got the cream.

'Lady Joyce.' The academic's greeting drifted, they all

drifted in here, swooping about like kites. His eyes were an inept fumbling at her breasts. 'Please join us. It's time for you to finally understand.' The hands pulled her into their midst.

While Disher, at the front of the room, continued whatever harangue of the faithful she had interrupted, Joyce's bony frame was settled on a bench between two ludicrously black robed figures. She blinked owlishly at them through the haze.

Beneath mistrustful buttocks her perch felt precariously wired together. To boot, both her eyes and nose were starting to run: she was a regular lady of the manor today. Trying to get a feel for the situation her groggy birdlike gaze traversed the room. Everybody was wearing the same quasi-gothic garb: black robes that for the most were no more than indifferently dyed bed linen with a hole cut out for the head. She brushed at her pants; how embarrassing to have arrived out of style.

'Joooyce. I'm sooo glad you've come.' The perspiring face to Joyce's right swam closer and she shied back in alarm. It was Mary. Mark's straying wife, pressed close against shoulder and thigh. Hers was the best dyed sheet of the lot, tending to true black rather than grey and tucked up beneath the collarbone it said JDD in neat embroidery. Ballsy to wear the diner's insignia here; bold, or something else.

Blondie's pupils were gaping black holes eating up her face. *I want to go home* Joyce thought forlornly, craning away from those starburst eyes but of course her spiteful side could not pass up a free kick. *What home?* it replied scornfully.

'Tell me who you love.' Mary's fingers bit excitedly into the fleshy part of Joyce's arm. Sick with shame Joyce could barely look at her: only that morning she had lusted after the woman's husband like some brainless beast in rut, wanting Mark's hard hands and mouth. And now here was his wife cuddling up like they were old chums.

I'm sorry, she wanted to grovel as though coveting alone had been enough to tear the little family apart. To want anything for herself was dangerously selfish, destructive to others. There could be no place in the new world for people like her.

'I knew you'd come.' Mary whispered, to slip beneath Disher's address to the room at large. 'You want to understand. Disher understood. He came out of the sand just like you and he saw that our love made us useless.

'Useless.' Savouring the word. Self-condemnation was so in vogue. 'All we could do in this world was to stand by and watch horrible things happen to our loved ones; couldn't do anything to protect them, just stand there watching and going quietly mad. Disher showed us how love could be powerful. How we could take control, lift all of our loved ones toward a new world. There are angels bringing it, coming to save us. I've dreamed them …'

At that Joyce gasped, rearing back and incidentally taking a good long toke of smoke as she went. Saturation point be damned. The flower toxin hit like a freight train.

Things came in bursts for a while after that, reality compressed into palatable sips. For a bit the creepy red flowers seemed to grow everywhere: blooming from the fire grate, winking cheerfully from various nooks and crannies. She twisted and Mary had acquired a blossom for a head. Cowled in the darkness of her sheet the flower nodded, nodded, smiled.

'The trick is to set the dye with salt,' flower Mary confided softly. Were they talking fashion now? 'Wear gloves because believe me you'll never get the black from under your nails. I can show you, don't worry. Everything looks impossible the first time.'

'Mark …' Joyce pleaded. The petit woman's warmth was too much—better that they hate each other decently.

'Mark,' Mary agreed tenderly. 'Mark suspects but he doesn't know. He *can't* know about all this, not until he understands. Otherwise he wouldn't be able to love me anymore.'

Then her voice hardened. In this new tone Joyce caught her first glimpse as to why Mary might be Mark's wife. 'It's all for him, and Dave, and Gar. Our family. This is the first time I've ever belonged anyplace, and I will not let the dust have them!'

Hints of the roused tigress. Her family. What Mary would not do to protect something worth keeping.

Joyce looked down at her crumpled hands. Time went splurt! like a paint tube squeezed. Ash tormented her nose. Jerking forward she sneezed twice, three times into cupped hands and vinegar bile warned that she had just upchucked a little although her palms were too numb to feel the wetness. Panicking she glanced about but everybody for the nonce was focussed intently on Swisher … damn, Disher! The robe overhanging the bench in front came in mighty handy. Its black wiped off on her palms.

'You!'

Mary jumped guiltily too, although it was Joyce that Disher was addressing. Funny and scary at the same time like being caught whispering in class. Joyce was halfway relieved to see Mary smother the same guilty giggle.

Disher raised his voice. 'Ah, Joyce. We are all so pleased to see you here. Why don't you come on up?'

Ah, well, Joyce thought resignedly. Here we go. Hands passed her up onto reluctant knees that clicked with the ascent. Time went splurt again as though in warning, but Mary's warm fingers gave her an encouraging squeeze on parting.

Joyce was handed up to the head of the room in front of everybody. That alone should have inspired fright only *that* train had already left the station and one big bastard of a locomotive it was to. A charging steel mountain that you could neither turn or halt, just as Ben had rushed from the diner taking Samuel with him. And what would boy scout say about all this? It would probably shake his rational universe up right good: a small trite reality that could be chalked up in that ridiculous travelogue of his.

Focus now, Joycie. She gave herself a little shake, finding that her fists were clenched. Now was not the time.

The academic received her, settled her by his side and—you would not credit it—settled one of his heavy arms about her shoulders. Tucked under his wing as though she could be safe there.

Interestingly his sheet also had JDD in those neat stitches which said far too much; no doubt dyed for him by his disciple's devoted hands.

'Whom do you love?' There came that ridiculous question again to both Joyce and the room at large and Disher held up a dimpled hand to forestall his followers shouting out the names of their family, their friends. His flock settled as docilely as pigeons, waiting for her.

It was easier to look at Disher than them. 'Myself,' Joyce grated.

'Ah,' Disher tutted, those false eyes so mild that they made her want to scream. 'Bravura, but I don't think so. In fact just between you and us chickens, I would say quite the opposite is true young lady.'

He got a mirthless snort for his efforts. 'You want me to say that mummy and daddy were never proud of me? Cry?'

'Who?' Disher pressed.

Joyce held out her arms. 'Oh, I get it. You want a hug.'

'Who do you love?' a demanding voice broke out from the peanut gallery, and then another, 'Tell us!' The pie eyed natives were restless. But it was the, 'What are you so scared of?' that really got Joyce's goat, lips peeling back from her teeth.

'Nothing, then.' Saying it she appeared to shrink into herself. 'Nobody.'

'And you seem to think that makes you tough. Don't you get it yet?' Paternalism did not suit the Disher that Joyce had seen, the man inside. The academic waved a hand at his breathless punters. 'When I asked the same of these good folk the name was already on their lips. Who they would save, given the chance. Who they would see spared.'

'Your point?' As rudely as she dared.

'How can you be a saviour of mankind yet be unable to point to a single person you'd see saved? This, *this* is why the machines couldn't spare us from their fate, and you've made yourself like one of them.'

Strident voices rang out to accuse her but Disher overrode them all, 'As did we all!' Defence from the unlikeliest corner.

Dismay sighed through the room but it was a polite, conditioned outrage. They groaned as obediently as Pavlov's dogs. Above their dusky sheets were a huddle of upturned faces with little comprehension beyond that they performed as expected. Pupils as huge and black as a gathering of weird anime characters.

Each had achieved the perfect surrender of responsibility along with their individuality; not one of them envied Joyce her place up front. Except perhaps Mary, who had stood there often. Here was a coherence based on polite anonymity and their pleasure was the bland peace of the herd. It occurred to Joyce that Disher may not comprehend how deep this conformist river ran in modern man when he tapped it for obedience. In which case, how tenacious his control.

If the wind blew fair it could be used against him.

Disher was still yapping. 'I hear that up north there is a community who have taken up in an airport. There they have become fearful, these strangers huddling in their terminal, always older and fewer. Seeking through flight charts for portents they strew duty free incense and tourist opals beneath the departure screens—and get nothing!'

The blare of his shout stirred the room again. 'For that is all the machines can give! I have known their empty promises, pretending to give with one hand while they take with the other. There is *nothing* any machine ever offered a man that we did not give to them first!' That at least Joyce could agree on, much as it smacked of humanity's vaunted egoism.

Disher actually shuddered, a lot of man flesh to quake and not putting it on either; moved by some deep loathing. If the water pump were right and Disher was merely aping a man he had the soul of the act down pat; for everything that a real person thinks, feels or does takes its root in the flesh. But for a machine there is no living, beating body, no pulse of instinct, perhaps no subconscious at all. Perhaps only a raving, terribly aware consciousness that goes on and on without surcease.

'There is another place. Theirs. The machines,' Disher spat, which Joyce's ear was treated to a slippery share of. 'Oh, it used to be ours; full of life but as the world empties ours becomes theirs. This place has become … terrible. The machines go out from it looking for people and when they find them, they tell them that they can save them.' There was an awful lot of that going around these days. 'They take them back to their home, where no sane person belongs. To the hospital!'

Joyce's ears pricked up. Excuse me? The hospital a la Samuel and Ben? A shiver started. Whatever the place and whatever Disher may be, he seemed genuinely terrified by it.

'I, *I* listened to their lies, as foolish as our entire race has been. Who doesn't crave salvation? I went with them to that place. What they stole from me ...' Furious hot tears springing beneath Disher's eyelids, his hand twisted brutally in Joyce's hair. 'THEY HAD NO RIGHT!'

'No right,' the refrain came back from the crowd, grief to his rage. The crowd's bovine docility seemed to quiet Disher and he released Joyce's scalp, bloodshot eyes roaming with satisfaction: complacent farmer surveying his well fattened stock.

'What we have to give ...' Disher's voice became a croon, 'Can only be given to each other.'

Ah. Now here finally was the crux of it. Joyce had thought the word "love" was being bandied about a little too freely in here, bless that pessimistic streak you could run peak hour traffic down.

Before the approving gaze of his congregation the academic's damp mitt slipped from Joyce's shoulders, thudding down the corrugations of her spine. An amorous flat-nailed finger slipped beneath the waistband of her pants. Knowing the trauma it had been through in recent times not even Joyce considered her ass to be a particularly erogenous area. Her nostrils were full of his sour excited smell.

These poor dispossessed men of the world. Denied success, fame, looks, all the hallmarks of a winner; and all the while the untouchable gamut of shiny cars, plum jobs and little skanks in bikinis were marched by under their noses, bright in high definition. When the lights went out they were left with only their crippling desire and the dark.

Just look at the tottering edifice of faith Disher had built! All the effort spent and people gulled, and for what? A desperate immature bid to have somebody fiddle his wang.

And now in meeting lust with revolted pity Joyce neatly pithed even that last desire, with more cruelty than even she had suspected of herself. She contemplated just letting Disher go ahead—how was that for crazy? But that was how little it meant. She might have if not for how recently a better man had reminded her body of what it was to burn.

Disher was still drivelling, the patter that had won him his little slice of heaven. '… the grace given our flesh … wisdom our minds forgot …' etc, etc. Grace, huh? His groping begged otherwise. And he had shown little wisdom in allowing her to step up front.

Joyce filled her lungs with the flat smoky air. 'Get your hands off me! Don't you ever touch me!'

It rang around the room. Disher fell back a step, his hand still describing her buttocks in the air. His congregation sat stunned in their seats, each too nervous to glance at their neighbour for the social cue they needed. Was it a joke? Were they expected to laugh?

Joyce steadied herself on Disher's podium, seeing its cheap finish peeling beneath her pale starfish hands. All fascinated eyes were on her and she felt a tremendous up-welling of power.

'This is what you've all come crawling around here for, this guy's big solution? Wow. Don't get me wrong, I'm sure if the sixties taught us anything it's that a world based on free love can be swell and I totally understand wanting to put your hands all over your neighbours consequence-free, but it isn't going to help. Can't you see? Not only aren't you saving anything, but you've gone and crapped all over what little you had left!'

Disher lunged at the shouting woman with everything that had lain hidden in his eyes blazing forth. He meant to kill her now and Joyce avoided him around the podium in a sort of drunken waltz. The manoeuvre brought back some serious high school flashbacks, although if caught now she faced something more serious than a twanging of her garters.

She was not finished.

'Smashing the evil computers and rutting like pigs isn't going to cut it—I know how nice the simple solutions sound, and I know that you don't want to but you have to *think* about it. There used to be countries out there with no machines, popping out brats ten a minute and they are every bit as empty now as this one. The thing with the kids is just another symptom of the real problem.'

Another skitter sideways. Joyce had always been a lousy dancer. 'If deep down you seriously think that one day you can march out there, tell your loved ones what you've been doing and have them *thank* you then please, be my guest. Prove me wrong.'

The only one to move was the academic and Joyce was out of places to hide but before his tentacles could tighten a low, almost subliminal rumble invaded the room. It warred sickly with the cheap brassy beats until some blessed person switched the tape deck off. Then the sound became clearer.

As one the congregation surged to the windows and door, peering out through shutters and exclaiming in overly bright, brittle voices. They imposed their milling bodies almost casually between Disher and Joyce, still foolishly posed on the podium in the stance of hero and villain.

Joyce was drawn out of danger although perversely she might have stayed, intrigued by the sick dismay that washed Disher's features as he too turned to the window. She had just dropped way down his priority list. Slow to catch on, she had to hear the exclamation 'Ben's back!' several times before the import really sank in.

Feeling the first stirrings of excitement herself Joyce was swept back and forth in the room like one of Disher's ridiculous flowers set adrift, until two small hands pushing determinedly in the small of her back steered her toward the exit. It was hard to tell in the confusion but there was something familiar in the voice that murmured, 'Go, hon. Quick!' Three staggering steps took Joyce across the building's antechamber and then she burst out the front doors into the blinding light and the clean hot air of normality.

Other people were coming from other doors, the town turning out for the red giant who came cruising into the parking lot, dust streaking his flanks like sweat. Even during the day little fairy lights stuttered around his front grill. No road train now and despite Ben's size he looked sadly reduced. There had been no shipment to come back this way.

A truck's arrival would not normally warrant such a crowd but Ben's plight had stung each of the town's inhabitants in their own secret personal dread. To be stranded out here, your loved one dying and nobody to help ... Everybody turned out with such relief that it were as though by returning home Ben had pushed back their fears.

In the excitement nobody noticed the green-smeared woman with shocked eyes who staggered out into the light. There was no one to see how desperately she craned to see inside Ben's cab but the light confounded her, flashing bright on her face. Her guts slithered uneasily and she popped out in rancid sweat all over.

Nobody saw Joyce and she slipped off into the diner and was gone. Creeping away to die alone like some sick dog under the house.

Had she stayed she would have been disappointed: Samuel did not look for her at all. She would not have been able to help forgiving him, though. When the cab door groaned open and boy scout descended he looked, if possible, even worse than her.

Pinpricks of red burned in Samuel's cheeks, one beneath each eye like obscure stigmata but the rest of his skin was like fine sifted flour. He seemed unaware of the crowding faces and hands that reached to help him down, moved in the company of ghosts.

Ben called after him unhappily but for once Samuel had nothing to spare for anybody but himself. He moved in a fugue state through the crowd, past Mark who had emerged to lean against the diner's door with his hands thrust into his armpits, grinding caffeine tainted teeth. Meeting no eyes Samuel went into the diner alone.

His buddy Joyce had already holed up in the bathroom; her old cowering spot. She always found such dignified places to die.

With a flannel clenched in one trembling hand she was down to the underwear, scrubbing away at clots of green before they hardened into concrete boogers. Small blocks of hotel soap were lined up along the sink like attendants. Thin green water ran everywhere.

She would far rather have ducked her entire self under icy runny water but, jests of dying in the toilet aside, it was all she needed to slip and be found with her brains leaking out over the tiles. It was a challenge just to stay upright.

Joyce scrunched the blessed flannel against her hot inflamed face. Her aforementioned brain felt like it was shrinking, pulling the fleshy moorings from her skull as it went.

There was a tap at the bathroom door.

'What!' she shrieked in answer and then stuffed the washcloth in her mouth, aghast. She had not meant to yell. The terror had just sort of leaped out of her mouth.

'Joyce?'

A small voice through the door. She spat out flannel. 'Sam?'

'Samuel.' It was him all right. And if Joyce had not been on the cusp of scattering across the floor she might have noticed how odd Samuel sounded, how … disconnected.

But people are always made more selfish by their own trouble. They have to be to ensure that they survive.

His tentative murmur again. 'Are you hungry?'

Hysterics almost splurted out—Joyce trapped them in the flannel. As a matter of fact she was not but that voice was so welcome that she would be on the bandwagon no matter what Samuel suggested. He was only on the other side of that door.

Please throw it open. Find me all huddled pathetically here on the tiles. Save me.

'I'll be right out,' Joyce managed through a gob-ful of damp fabric and her voice was admirably cool.

CHAPTER SEVEN

AUTOMATONS

RESURRECTION

EASING FROM its jam, the bathroom door disclosed a wildly suspicious eye. A bloodshot orb soon preceded the rest of Joyce, domestic clatter having finally lured her from her bolt hole.

Fashionista, our Joyce crept forth into the hallway dressed in threads from yesterday's hamper, skin by the school of scrub 'til it hurts. Even so, traces of lurid green still lingered beneath nails and tainted the exhausted pouches below her eyes, but a girl could only manage so much. She had somewhat reduced her resemblance to a hurricane evacuee and that would have to do.

Not being a fellow to ask twice Samuel had not returned; he was stirring noisily about the diner's kitchen. To set up the board that must put Mary still back at the people's democratic republic of nutsville, Mark out and about, and God only knew where the kids were lurking. Likely knocking about under the desert with their loquacious buddy.

Any of which could come bouncing through the front door any second. The prospect almost had Joyce shrinking back; *chicken* she berated herself but she had had quite enough of happy families for one lifetime. Indeed she might have served the remainder of her days cowering in the bathroom with her horns pulled in if not for the glorious siren aroma of frying garlic and onion. It was her intrepid nose alone that dragged her out.

Not including the kitchen among a few of Joyce's favourite things, mind. Not after the hard yards that she had spent there adding dishpan hands to her ever-expanding roll of complaint, Joyce's big bang of disgruntlement.

As Samuel stood working at the bench his back was to Joyce. She lingered shyly in the doorway, bare toes curling on linoleum. If the paraphernalia spread about were anything to go by, this would not be like their last rushed roadside throw-together; this meal the boy was inspired. She was unsure what half of those bits and bobs even did, the last she had seen their like was during a bracing pap smear.

So like any person off the beaten track of their own forte Joyce goggled in awe of a process that seemed both inscrutable and wonderful. Samuel's heavy knife was a blur across the chopping board and peering over his shoulder she drew closer, fascinated by those tanned hands with their funny flat man-nails and overlarge joints. There was no tremor to Samuel's hands. Joyce's frame might be a rickety advertisement of woe but even at his worst Samuel's sure movements broadcast only calm.

If she noticed how brightly he had the overhead neons burning with the blinds firmly shutting out the world right in the middle of the day it went unremarked. To run all of the lights was only a small strangeness, after all.

Despite the pace that Samuel worked at everything passed through his fingers so deliberately. Sliced to an exact angle, the finicky work of an alchemist. It were as though in that brief moment of possession the vegetable, or whatever, became the most treasured thing in his world. It passed near-worshiped through his grasp … and was then instantly discarded as he moved on to the next.

She could not help asking, 'Were you a chef?'

'Damnit Joyce!' It was finally Samuel's turn to jump, spooked: the worm had turned! A disappointing little squirt of movement though. It would have been so much more entertaining had he sliced something off.

But then as Samuel turned around Joyce received her own little fright, tit for tat. Absentees fade and with her fraying memory Joyce was more susceptible to the process than most; inside of a few weeks she had managed to completely forget what Sammy-boy looked like. His face was a shock, a revelation.

Just a big old slice of honesty cake, this stranger, this implausible man whom she pretended to know because in lonely places you need *some* touchstone, however prosaic. But how could he just stand there unafraid with it all hung out on the outside? Wasn't he ashamed?

It made Joyce want to raise her hard will between Samuel and the world, to protect him somehow and *that* made her angrier than ever because Samuel had no use for her slipshod chivalry. He merely stood facing her, terribly vulnerable yet maddeningly secure in the secret of his own life.

And he was the first to speak. 'You shouldn't sneak around like that!' Samuel waggled the knife half-chastisingly. 'Especially when your opponent's armed.'

He felt better already for seeing Joyce—and how crazy was *that*? It also felt damned good to be doing something. The familiar humdrum of cooking eased the devastation where Ben's clever needles had carved through his flesh opening up great freeways that ached hollowly for traffic. Occupy the hands, engage the heart; as some elderly and no doubt by now deceased family relic had once barked at him. Pat scrubbing brush and vinegar philosophy from an era before the uneasy marriage of technology and flesh.

Still, despite his dogged misery there was little enough of the modern narcissist in Samuel to notice how Joyce did not exactly look like she had attended any picnic in his absence. After all this time she remained stubbornly sallow, a feat impossible for anyone else living out here. There was no spying circumstance out from her eyes, too deeply sunk in greenish sockets but both hands were a faint tremor by her sides.

Far from being the sun blasted icon that he had first met surfing down a sand dune Joyce had been stripped back and exposed as being all too human. Good. That would make this easier.

Catching his glance down at her long pale feet she attempted to hide one beneath the other and glared through gathering brows. Samuel almost laughed which would have been a mistake: good old dependable Joyce. He could set a watch by her shifting mood.

'Where the damn hell have you been then? I had decided you weren't coming back!'

'Where?' Samuel echoed absently, his knife drooping to the board. Startling them both his chest heaved up a barking laugh. 'Why, wouldn't you know—I've been to the other side.'

'Is that like why did the man cross the road?' The tag end drifted by: *'cause his dick was stuck in the chicken*; and her mouth spasmed. Not appropriate, so not appropriate.

'The other side of the desert.' It must be all that newly sprouted hair, he decided. It framed Joyce's face, softening things somehow. A few tentative steps closer to woman, although her personality had not improved.

Joyce's eyes brightened eagerly at the news. 'Sam, your big trip! You can draw a massive map for your travelogue now, double page spread: Sam's great and glorious highway from start to finish …' but his lips all but disappeared into a mean little line and she limped to a halt.

What the hell had she done wrong now? He had not even bothered with "Don't call me Sam", a litany she had come to rely on. 'Can't help but notice you ain't exactly hopping with glee.'

Rather he leaned back against the bench and ground both sets of knuckles into his poor tired-looking eyes, so inhumanly blue in their reddish setting. It did not help matters that billows of garlic and onion still clung to the creases of those fingers.

Draw a map? That *had* been the idea hadn't it? A guide for grateful others to steer their leisure by, breadcrumbs through the future. But how could you stamp any chart "Here be Dragons" when the machines were everywhere?

'Samuel? Sam, what's happened?' Joyce's impulse was to step forward and touch him in some way: a hand on the arm or that most elementary of human gestures, a hug. It was an impulse easily squashed for being ridiculous; she would make herself look ridiculous. 'Sam …'

'Yeah.' He was breathing hard through his nose, eyes down. 'I'll try to explain. It felt like … have you ever been to a party where you didn't belong? Didn't know anybody there, not your sort of place—in fact well-meaning friends will have warned you off it. But because you have your own ideas about who and what you are you go anyhow.

'Right away you know you've made a mistake. Should the people there notice you at all it's only to wonder who brought you. All those half-imagined fantasies about being likeable, brilliant, the life of the party—all that is blown right out of the water.

'But it's still not enough for you. As though to prove a point you suck down the drink for occupation and wander the outskirts amid the cold perfect lights and the music, pretending to be absorbed by this or that. This party has made you a ghost. You say nothing. Speak to no one. Wonder what happened.

'Until even that knowledge becomes too much and you bull your way determinedly into a knot of people and start pitching some by-story as fast as you can. It's your best anecdote, has always won over the punters. Success, you're talking!

'But as your eyes wander between one smeared face and the next you realise with a nauseous twist that you are absolutely blotto. And guess what, it's still early. In that entire bright shining room you are the only one who is gone with the wind.

'And now it's like you can watch the disaster from outside in cringe-worthy slow motion. Grunting with your booze-thickened tongue. Waving your hands to be understood, tottering on your feet. Not even you get what you are on about. The icing on the humiliation-cake comes when you knock some innocent bystander's drink from their grasp.

'Always after that, after you have slept it off in your car and then slunk back home nothing will ever feel the same. Because you have never actually been what you thought you were. And you will always remember that your friends, well they warned you not to go. They already knew.'

To Joyce that feeling that Samuel so laboriously described was simply life but she pitied his dismay. Listening to boy scout's blinkers being removed was like seeing the world pluck some child's innocence: sorry kid but there is no Santa and what's more, you are entirely on your own.

She imagined that such things just did not happen in Samuelville; her own craziness might have invaded, cascaded down to bury him. But she lacked the language for sympathy. What came out instead sounded so sarcastic that even she cringed.

'So what—you went to some party?'

For an instant Samuel was terrified he might sob. How could he have imagined he would find comfort here? Thankfully the moment passed. How odd that at the end of everything one still struggled for social poise, fought against having the last rags of decency stripped away.

What came past his lips sounded steady enough. 'Ben, well he said ...'

Ah, yes.

Ben.

Ben who had had plenty to say, who had talked and talked across thousands of kilometres in long incomprehensible soliloquies of which only the shame and furtive pleasure had pierced Samuel's drugged fugue. It seemed that even for the best of us a foot off the path meant throwing it all away—

what harm we scatter when serving our own desires.

'Ben said that *they* wanted to speak to me.'

'Sam what are you ..?'

'At the hospital!' Samuel raged and Joyce flinched wide-eyed from the waving knife. 'Sorry.' He returned it shamefacedly to the bench although without ducking his head now, daring her to acknowledge his distress.

Which she did only partly. The rest of Joyce, connected to a short attention span was instead obsessing over whether Samuel's eyes had been so blue before. They were not like most eyes—most eyes sported speckles or shades of other colour to mitigate the impact but not these babies. Just big disconcerting circles of flawless blue like something manufactured in mockery of nature. Designer eyes.

Whoops, there was a conversation going on! Belatedly Joyce remembered that she had an end of it to hold up and little idea what Samuel had been saying. However, parroting with a blank look seemed to have served thus far so she stuck with it. 'The hospital?'

Samuel waved a hand dismissively. 'To hear Ben carry on it's supposed to be some whiz bang miracle factory but looked more like a cut price government housing project to me. We came rolling in from the great bright shout of the desert into this dim hopeless estate, like a grey coma. The sun never touched the ground anywhere.

'Casting about the headlights picked up grey block buildings with lots of machinery and ambulances abandoned all over. Nothing looked to be moving but us. Weeds were starting to spring up and take it all back.'

Samuel's gaze tuned out as he spoke; or in to something that Joyce could not see. His eyes became pretty blue zeroes. 'So much resource had been lavished on constructing it once upon a time. Such a sense of life having passed by—even though the highway led straight in. The whole complex come to nothing like two empty old hands.'

'You ought to have been a writer,' Joyce interrupted with an attempt at a diverting smile but Samuel was lost and staggered on as though stupefied by what he had seen.

'Even the taggers who had been at those grey walls must have been long dust by now. Ben lit up the graffiti as we passed: bored hormonal kids scratching at their own frustration, not yet integrated into the turning cogs of society. Kids desperate to put some mark on an indifferent world, to be acknowledged and remembered: misdirection of a drive that should have produced monuments or children. Real men build. Instead all that came of the urge was this insane, insane replication of spiky unreadable names, destructive, no more than dog piss on a wall. The hieroglyphs of civilisation's despair.

'Ben was right about one thing though. There weren't any people at the hospital anymore. It was only empty doors and shuttered windows. Without people the building had shed its functionality, become nonsense. With nobody to use it a hospital may as well be a rock or a banana.'

Then Samuel frowned and his spooky fixed gaze came part of the way back. 'Somebody was there, though. They had to have been. *Somebody* unloaded those chickens.'

'Chicken?' Joyce's ever-practical stomach rumbled. It was not her fault: the kitchen air was so thick and close and smelled so delicious. In fact everything around Samuel always seemed to smell good. It were as though his life was one long meander between civilised rooms like the kitchen and lounge, bowls of potpourri along the way. In Samuel's house such grim necessities as the toilet simply did not exist.

Joyce felt so intensely sullied by comparison. The sheer weight of her heart made her want to sink to the linoleum in this nice smelling kitchen and sleep forever.

Such was her disarray that she only twigged how close Samuel had approached when he dared to take her hand. Perversely curious she refrained, restrained the instant paranoid flutter of muscles and waited to see what he would do.

As boy scout spoke on he examined his spoils, the pale expanse of captured wrist and forearm. And with each exploratory stroke from elbow to wrist Joyce's alarm gentled a little. Touch was the only lingo that she could still hear; words were no good, words were where arguments got started. If she were a cat she would bristle every time somebody opened their trap but would roll about abandoned under caress.

'Somebody unloaded Ben's trailers,' Samuel continued telling two stories: one in hands for her body, and words for her useless brain. 'They were hard to see. I think it was the twilight … but they can't have been people.' Certainty firmed. 'I'm sure of it now. Not slinging those huge containers around like they did, like they weighed nothing. And the whole time they were chatting … no, *singing* to each other.'

Singing in weird high voices that had sizzled in the flat air like modems down a phone line. Bright phonemes that had drilled mercilessly into Samuel's ears until he felt that he could almost understand, nearly there—only he did not want to; he was bitterly afraid. Warm mammalian instinct shudderingly rejected anything that might take him closer to those figures flitting about the truck in the dimness out there.

'Their faces didn't move. The jaw just kind of hung loose like its tendons were cut and their mouths sort of, well, *glowed* from inside. Glowed even during the day.

'I really, really didn't like them. You know that creeping aversion that comes when you see something loathsome?'

Disher, Joyce thought instantly and then; his flowers!

'I don't think I could have stood one of them touching

me.' Samuel stuttered and laughed, a crooked sound that had never so much as shared a pillow with humour. 'When one shimmied up the side of the cab and opened the door I shrieked like a kid and tried to get into the passenger seat. It didn't come in, thank God; just waited there humming and moaning with that awful burning mouth hung open. And Ben said "It wants you to go with it".'

The rig had popped loose from Samuel with a nostalgic sound that few living would recognise anymore: a cork from a bottle. Ben released the man but studiously withheld the antidote used to scrub the driver's system neatly clean and hand control back. Calculatedly dangerous to let Samuel wander about groggy but sober he might never get back in the cab.

'I nearly fell out of the damned truck. Would have broken my neck; but the thing reached out to help and that got me under wraps real damn fast, barking out "No—no I'm fine" so fast it was one word. Thankfully it backed off and let me climb down under my own steam.'

Samuel omitted how he had fumbled for balance on legs that would not work, fumbled for certainty, for anything amid slow panic as Ben's drugs occluded a full understanding of what was happening.

The ladder was still hot and bright from the desert and a nice shiny blister pushing up through singed wrist hair was testimony to Samuel's inability to concentrate. The truck's paintwork had cooked flesh on contact.

And the thing that sang but could not speak had beckoned him on into the hospital. Through sliding glass doors and beneath red eye sensors that had watched for such company for decades.

'If you can believe it the hospital was even more depressing on the inside. Faultlessly clean but you could smell how bereft everything was, how long since the air had been used. And the hallways were all painted with this awful cartoon frieze. Dancing rodents in jodhpurs and the like; time had sucked out the primaries but it must have been nice and eye-bleeding when fresh. And not a soul left to be comforted by it anymore.'

'You were there.'

'There was I.' Samuel exhaled, a shuddering breath. 'I was a damn long way from being comforted.'

In fact Samuel had crept shivering through the hospital's corridors like some rat in a maze, following his singing guide and for the first time ever he had death on his mind. Not really his fault: the entire place felt dead, stripped of every joy and not even the most optimistic soul could duck it. Although he would not have been so susceptible were he not already maxed out on Ben's happy-twee driving cocktail.

You could tell that boy scout secretly fancied his first sip of darkness. A pity really, to see him spoiled and brought closer to Joyce. Especially as she would have given anything to enter his house instead.

'Finally we stopped outside a door with the hideous frieze continuing all around it and this big metal sign over the top. An antique sort of plaque that must have come from the original hospital before this pile went up on the site. An old-school hospital of human proportion with a chapel and doctors and suspiciously pretty nurses. It was likely that in comparison to the new hospital their witchdoctory couldn't cure a thing but patients would have trekked from far and wide for those nurses.'

'Sam.' She was unimpressed.

'The sign said Neonatal Care. My guide hummed encouragingly, sliding back at the same time to block the corridor in case I got it into my head to bolt; which was ridiculous. I didn't stand a rat's-ass chance of finding my way out—get lost and you'd die lost, end of saga. So in I went.'

And the hospital's cutting edge technology, that not even the military could beat, was waiting for him.

'And the machines?' Joyce put in eagerly. 'What did the machines look like?' Half eager and dreading that he was about to say people, the high end machines looked like people and there was no damned way to tell the difference. She waited, trembling; which Samuel would feel if he weren't so caught up in his own distress.

He shrugged. 'What was there to see? Hunks of equipment. I guess they must have been top of the line as they were all quite barbaric looking, enough to frighten the baby out of any woman; but unless you happen to be a surgeon they didn't look like anything.'

'Nothing?' Joyce was astounded.

'What are you looking for? The room was just a room full of junk, all dim, meant for newborns I guess. And the first thing the machines said to me was, "Thank God you're here", which was so unexpected that I laughed just to be doing something and said, "You have a God now?" because I'm used to hearing synthetic voices from speakers and still these gave me a turn.'

By way of reaction Joyce was down to raising her eyebrows.

'Well I was expecting more of that unearthly singing or maybe something terribly modern, some frontal lobe data injection—not women. Not cooing maternal voices that made me think of older women with their chicks all flown, ready to hug some new cause to their copious bosom.'

Joyce was not really surprised; and not only because everything was bosoms with Sam. So many machines out there sported silver tongues and for most of them it was likely their only defence to use our anthropomorphism against us. 'And then? What did they say then?'

'Don't worry. You won't have to struggle anymore.'

Now she was shocked; she could not have been more shocked if … if nothing, there was not anything worse, she was completely shocked out. 'What?'

'Don't shoot the messenger; that's what they told me, verbatim. That I didn't need to worry anymore. That if I let them they would take care of everything and it would all be ok for the rest of my life.'

'What did you say?' What could anyone say to that?

Samuel's thin lip curled. 'What do you think? Merry Christmas? I said no of course. What they had on offer was impossible! You can't offload responsibility like that, just stick it on another's shoulders and drop out of the flow. No one can! What makes me so special that I should get to stop while the world struggles on; there are people with worse lives than me, a hundred times worse.'

Joyce blinked, flabbergasted now. Of a sudden it was like she was really seeing Samuel for the first time. These precious lads, the darlings of the rational world; for whom the answer would always be of *course, obviously*.

Stoicism came easy to some but she could easily imagine another far more realistic type of person who would come to the hospital at the sunset of their day. Worn down and bleeding away through a thousand invisible hurts. Someone bound to falter; someone who would be grateful to lay down their load.

'The machines weren't about to let me go on being a grown up that easily. Well still no, and no again if it's all the same. At least my mistakes leave no one to blame but myself. Then they wanted to know if pride was so worth having, but I think anything that you gain for yourself is worth sticking to.

'After that they told me about the others who'd been to the hospital. Geoffrey; they played his voice and it was him all right, they must record everything. Made me wonder who might end up listening to our little chat years from now. They played me recordings of Geoffrey who said no. And Disher who said yes.

'Disher had arrived at the hospital all on his lonesome like some mutt nobody would pick up. Following technology's back-story, the word of this machine or that machine who pointed the way like it was the path to some enchanted fairy land. A magic place where all your burdens would be lifted.'

'They didn't lift the burden of his personality, that's for damned sure!'

'Been fraternising with the natives, have you?'

'Do. Not. Get me started.'

'Well the next bit of dear Disher's story, as the hospital anxiously recited it to me, came with security footage to round it out. Show don't tell, right? His surgery must not have turned out to be at all what he expected because he looked *pissed off*. I sat there and watched tape of Disher smashing the hell out of his room, wearing nothing but a shower curtain of a gown and screaming, screaming. I tell you that guy is *strong* as well as scary. He yanked this piece of metal railing right off the bed!

'Then the next shot came from a hallway camera, quite small and high up. There was Disher again with—thank God—his pants on this time. That gown flying open will haunt my nightmares. Disher sneaking into a store room. Sneaking, the idiot, like he didn't think that they could watch him anywhere he went.

'This was where the hospital finally intervened; they did not want Disher getting his hands on the contents of that room. One of the humming things was sent in. They were afraid he'd suicide which is what I might do if one of those damn things came after me.

'But Disher, he smashed the humming thing's head clean open with his trusty metal bar so that all of its light spilled out all over the place. That wasn't enough for crazy man: he started screeching with these big ropes of spit flying everywhere and stamping violently until every flicker was ground out.

'The academic left that storeroom with one hell of a heavy bag. He emptied the place of basically the entire supply of the drug that the hospital had been treating him with; far more than you'd need for one person. Enough to choke a whole town.'

'Well you can forget about warning *this* town. Shout 'til the sky falls in: they still won't hear anything that they don't want to.'

'Judge not: that may not be entirely their fault. The drug that Disher stocked up on makes you feel awfully suggestible and satisfied with your lot. It's a plant compound, originally came from some big gaudy flower that liked to trap things and dissolve them.'

'What the hell were they treating him for?'

'Too much life maybe? I gathered it wasn't the sort of thing you get better from.'

Joyce spent a generous few seconds mulling that one over in case any part of her felt sorry for the academic. Nope! Not even pessimism, her loudest, voice, was putting its hand up for that one.

'Still the whole drug thing sounds a bit convenient to me. Don't forget the population of this town chose to move out here in the first place: they're the sort who think distancing themselves from everything is a solution. But with them discounted what does the hospital expect *you* to do about Disher?'

Samuel skipped over Joyce's surely unconscious emphasis on *you*. 'Apparently our dear academic is to be bundled home to the hospital. According to them once you abdicate your life, you abdicate forever.'

'But how are *you* …' (there it was again!), '… supposed to manage it?'

'I dunno. A fireman's carry?'

She began to giggle through her nose, 'Cattle prod?'

'French techno pop?'

'No, we already did cattle prod—it's the same thing.' Giggles evolved into all-out throaty laugher; Joyce even forgot Samuel was holding her hand.

So of course what Samuel came out with next brought the whole multiverse of awkwardness crashing back.

With a wan smile of his own. 'It was pretty horrible going there, to the hospital—although obviously we can laugh about it now.' The smile flickered out: some could laugh more heartily than others it seemed. 'But it was bad. Joyce … I don't want to sleep alone.' Who does?

'It's the middle of the day!' Brilliant Joycie. Nice work. Upon reflection she could probably have stood to be more gracious … Actually, no. She probably could not.

Samuel flushed although the baby blues remained grave. 'You know what I meant.'

'You want ..?' This was how adults did it right? A sane, straightforward proposal. So why did she feel like a kid who had just found her Christmas gift empty?

'Now?' She took a half step back toward the door but he was not following.

Samuel smiled. Released her. 'Not *immediately* now. I refuse to do anything fun on an empty stomach.'

Thunderstruck. Utterly thunderstruck. 'Ah; what are you cooking?'

'I call it my mystery meal.' He beamed proudly.

'What's in it?'

'Can't tell you. It's a *mystery*.'

'You're a goon.' Despite herself the giggles started up again. It did not really matter what he made, she would never be able to eat—her stomach was a pinhole.

'Just trust me dear. I'm a proctologist.'

'Eew.' Still the stranglehold loosened. It is difficult to feel socially awkward when you have the giggles on. Uncharacteristically she offered: 'Is there anything I can help with?'

'You can stand there and entertain me?' Samuel suggested, mustering forces around the chopping board. 'And revel in the sheer glory of course.'

'Colour me revelled.'

Once again his hands were a blur and she marvelled at how many small talents for living Samuel had. Not much of anything on their own but seeming so vital and sure when enacted, somehow invincible. It were as though the boy could push back the apocalypse with one good meal.

Disoriented, Joyce somehow found herself standing in the warm kitchen chatting idly with this veritable stranger as he cooked. Talking over petty domestics such as the weather (too hot), drawing maps, travel, and finally whether either of them truly remembered how rain sounded. And for once the pleasantries fit comfortably in her mouth.

Even after watching Samuel in action Joyce would be unable to later relate what sort of meal he prepared. Each mouthful was like a precursor of what was to come. She ate slowly and found indiscreet little tangents dropping into conversation quite unexpectedly: such as how she had always wanted a crushed rock driveway in her dream house. She would have loved to open a window during a storm; feel cold mineral air gusting in. Listen to the sound of rain pattering from green leaves onto small stones.

This was crazy; like anybody cared what sort of driveway she would have chosen! Or what life. Talking at a civilised table and all the while knowing that he would soon be bare-ass naked—and probably she would be too.

Samuel was right on the money to ease Joyce gradually into the idea. Over a period of years she had forgotten the mechanics of desire, just one more thing lost to a wasteland of mendacity. It was a quality however that men never seemed to shed no matter the time between drinks: that essential link between body and imagination. A hermit alone in his cave for a hundred years could still be a lover.

Samuel led Joyce when she no longer knew the way.

She dressed for bed nervously, getting the wrong buttonhole twice and sniggering wryly at what a blushing flower she had become. Unsure of propriety she ended up donning several nightgowns one after the other and pyjama pants, as though the layers constituted some sort of shield. No one would be accusing her of wantonness.

Joyce was a straightforward, brusque lass and all of this courting put her out of ease. It would have been far simpler had Samuel just nailed her to the kitchen floor. Back in the sprawling bloom of her girlhood had any fellow been intrepid enough to ask her in for a post-date coffee there had better by thunder be coffee!—carnality should have been specified.

Surprise, surprise; boy scout himself seemed innocent of any evil. He briefly fingered her sleeve before settling; the nightdress was only cheap machine silk but skin warmed and interesting to touch. Just that sleepy caress of fabric and he snuggled right down.

It was his room that they chose from the mirror image options and here too Samuel had closed the blinds so that only brief tongues of light poked through. He had done far less to occupy his space than she; after all what was one more room to a tourist? Samuel would slip through the diner like a ghost.

Not so Joyce. When she stopped over anywhere it was hard to get the smell out.

The two of them slipped beneath judgment day diner sheets but unsurprisingly neither relaxed quickly, not in the hot embrace of the desert. For too long the closest either traveller came to oblivion was to lie stiffly, paralysed by the wide blind eyes of memory.

To Joyce Samuel seemed utterly serene but he had been the furthest flayed. Antidote administered the moment the diner was in sight Ben's rig had withdrawn almost painlessly, the sensation no worse than shaving and leaving less of a mark. But now his thoughts stood broken, baulking and twisting but ultimately returning to when the machine had been *in* him. Something vital had been scooped out, leaving his guts void.

Samuel lay on his side, sheet loose about a fuzzed torso that rose and fell evenly. Hints of a lost boyhood in that rack of ribs and the endearing knobbliness of his knees. One had lay lax outside the sheet and the other within, instinctively cupping his balls for comfort. Miniscule wires had slid beneath those flat nails, seeking every entry to his body.

With one ear resting about Joyce's collarbone he listened to the clockwork of her body through warm silk, her steady heart as relentless as any slow set engine. I am, it seemed to declare. I endure.

For her part Joyce felt her joints sinking heavily through the mattress, slipping down between springs like secrets seeking some private dark to rest in. Her hair still reeked of smoke. The red flower toxin exited via breath and nervous tremors: closing her eyes she could see its spread like an algae bloom down a river's tributaries. If the pulsation of the room's thin walls was anything to go by it was killing off more brain cells than an absinthe bender as it went.

Perhaps boy scout slept, perhaps like her he merely drifted. The slightly occluded rumble of his breathing gave nothing away. Looking for his secret Joyce gradually matched her own to his deeper, longer inhalation that seemed so peaceful. For a long time she drifted between the beams of light through the blinds and the afternoon was suspended in the unlikely shelter of his body. Her thoughts became loose things floating atop the dimness, warmth and comfort. Ssh, Samuel's skin murmured; for now let's pretend that the whole world was just a bad dream.

Gradually in the skewed manner of sleep logic Joyce became aware of their legs tangled carelessly beneath the sheet. Against one thigh she felt his erection rise, hardening in intimate little pulses. It provoked drowsy wonder. Was Samuel asleep, his body paying homage to dreams? The salute could not be for her, surely not for her.

As she grappled with the mystery they breathed slowly on together, dropping further toward non-being. Only his cock remained alert.

Then Samuel stirred, a small nestling movement such as one makes in their dreams. His face was at the hollow of her throat: slow and drowsy, scenting soap scrubbed skin. So pale, her skin, never meant for the desert. A caress of lips and cheek against pale smoothness, the comfort of his living pillow.

Joyce's eyes remained stubbornly shut, long limbs limp in Samuel's grasp. Next his lips were on her face, rasping a little. Feather light with warm breath issuing from between them. Exploring her placid features as though curious.

Who could pinpoint precisely when they both began to breathe faster? The admission was mutual, simultaneous, the jig was up. When Joyce finally turned her mouth to meet Samuel's it was with the most incredible relief.

Over a lifetime of refined technique our Joyce had come to police herself more cruelly than any moral authority could manage. Her internal censor was making a list and checking it twice; a mammoth, twenty-four-seven job. Lists of the things forbidden to say, places her eyes must not linger and above all her slippery treasonous thoughts were to be subdued. Ever fresh impulse twisted from the true.

When this clamp that she had sadistically tightened and tightened on herself finally let go an equal and opposite reaction was demanded—it was a wonder she did not catapult away through the ceiling!

Surely only seconds had passed yet already Samuel impetuously shifted his weight to lie atop her as he pursued the kiss, claiming territory with his body. In the dim light Joyce finally mustered the pluck to peek, hesitantly, and caught Samuel gazing gravely down at her face. His own eyes were dark and opened up all the way to inside. *Woman*, that gaze branded her and the answering jolt of arousal was so powerful that it seized Joyce up like an ocean.

To be fair Samuel had no way of seeing how she still battled weakly for the rational shore. Such an all-consuming desire, though lauded by ignorant romance stories was in fact destructive, obsessive. It was a drive that would burn down anything that stood between it and its selfish goal; be that career, family or happiness.

When Joyce returned no tart witticism, her mouth defused, Samuel took silence for consent enough and kissed her, he kissed her like one starved. As though he could tear her mouth from her face and swallow it.

His hands were still bashful though and her conflicted motivation moved one almost involuntarily to cup a breast where the nipple was more than ready for his fingers. Her heart hammered silently in its bone prison beneath.

There was no noise from either party now except for the increased pace of their breathing and a mundane gummy smacking noise that had no place in any decent company.

Patience suddenly gone Samuel tore at silk until it rent and he could get to the pale flesh beneath where his feasting mouth was cruel. Twisting and yanking as though he would rip the previously admired skin from its mooring. Punishing Joyce for her part in rabid desire—perhaps it was her half-yielding that sparked it.

Regardless he could do anything. By now the pain was only a goad, it satisfied what little of her that still wanted to hang back. The brick, or straw of Joyce's carefully constructed house scattered. She had laid each so deliberately over the years and thought them cemented securely in place, a bulwark yet there they flew away leaving only body, body.

The paranoid, difficult woman who had so self-consciously been "Joyce" was reduced to a body that raved mindlessly, jealously craved the taste of him. Should Samuel be cruel with fingers that alternately caressed and then dug in like talons she would rave still.

One hand grasped and explored his erection through cotton shorts—he immediately shoved them down and put into her palm a firmness over which the skin was velvet with an intimate supple texture. Not at all good enough though—Joyce's *hand* was not where he wanted it and her pyjamas were a feeble ploy. They sailed away into the dimness of the room.

Now prodded by a splash of icy modern fear her brain had a moment to cut in. Boy scout was not pausing for the nicety of a condom. Apparently he was of a "lust conquers all" type which would not do Joyce much good should he give her a hearty dose of the clap to remember him by. But Samuel was not about to be stopped by anything.

He guided himself home with rough fingers and rational doubt was ripped away by the guttural sounds that rose up in her throat. This was no longer her house. More like the dense forest that rose up behind the suburb, between home and the open black water. A thing that lurked in the trees, as huge and bestial as the desire that she had been snatched up in.

No longer herself. That terrible burden of individuality was stripped away in a fleshly forum that allowed her to transcend what she was, if only for a moment.

Joyce mewled under her breath, mindless little noises and Samuel groaned in response, the first and only sound of his eerily voiceless fucking as she felt him come. Pulses in that deep place that nothing else could reach.

All spicy sweat and overheated breath as he slumped down and then away, both of their skins cherry red from exertion. And as for Joyce, Joyce fizzed, shell-shocked, blown out like a bad globe. She was left utterly incapable of coping with anything. While Samuel slipped off toward sleep with all the serenity of the blameless.

Even now his influence might have drawn her along if not for the weight of her sea anchor heart dragging behind. As much as her battered only partly satiated body craved rest the closest she could manage was to lie there and look at him with hot dry eyes.

Samuel's own fluttered beneath purplish lids. Time which had been so obligingly sedate now leaped like a startled greyhound from the gates. Nonetheless Joyce had to admit that part of her wanted to play the sap. To simply stay and sleep enveloped in his sweat with the sheet tangled about them.

They would both wake in a golden dawn like a princess coming down off her bower. Smile, have coffee and perhaps breakfast, and build a white picket fence against the world. Except of course that she knew better; blessed or cursed with pragmatism such moments of false comfort would surely rip her apart.

Joyce ground her teeth. Fine. Foo-fucking-doo lah-lay. Then she would meet unpalatable reality in the same manner as she faced everything else—on her own terms.

She eased off the bed trying to keep the incriminating pinging of springs to a minimum. Her pyjama pants were there smack dead in a bar of sunlight like a spot-lit archaeological treasure. She retrieved them and lo and behold if they had not fallen across Samuel's pack of scribbles, now exposed to the glorifying light.

A woman less tied up with herself would have scooped them up and snooped through, casting surreptitious glances of wonder at the sleeping man on the bed at each revelation into his secret character. Joyce merely yanked her pyjamas back on.

Still she could not help pausing in the doorway. Samuel lay sprawled peacefully with both legs thrown across where she had lain, still shackled humorously at the ankle by his underpants. With the light between them his face was dark but it erupted on his chest, transforming wisps to burning red gold. The heavy mixed musk of their bodies hung everywhere in spinning motes of dust.

And damn if the soft insides of his elbows, even those ludicrously long feet did not beg for Joyce to return to the tumbled bed and put her mouth on them. And she hated feet! Had she recognised her final chance to really talk with Samuel she might have lingered … but probably not. Our Joyce was already too set in her ways. She slipped away.

Wincing and clutching her ravaged nightgown closed Joyce hobbled down the hall. No blinds closed out here and she squinted at a world streaming jauntily in. Surreal, surreal, surreal. Had she really just done that?

Even such a brief sojourn in Samuel's world had left her too raw for reality; the carpet bobbles were as rough as pebbles beneath her bare feet. And her poor legs were well out of the habit of being forced so wide; apparently it was nothing like riding a bike unless something were very wrong with your bike. Muscles that did not want a bar of activity had to be ordered to frogmarch her down the hall.

Discretion beat disorientation however. When a door slammed in the diner somewhere Joyce whisked herself into the bathroom quickly enough, latching the door behind.

Perched on the loo she had to bite her wrist to stifle a whimper: following the mauling Samuel had given her it was like pissing acid. However nothing in Joyce's life had ever outpaced endurance if she was determined. Rocking for comfort she glared fixedly at her upside down miniature reflected in the sink's bright faucet and waited dumbly for it to end. The air moving on her skin was chill, she was burning up. Wiping afterward was out of the question, instead she gingerly patted red and pink blots away.

Then into the shower. She reeked of cock, a chemical imprint that would be a few hours fading at the very least. She was not sure whether to feel irritated or amused. Surely anybody who stood close enough would realise what she had been up to.

The shower's frosted glass was scaly about the corners, all the diligent scrubbing in the world could only do so much for an old surface. Probably Mark, long suffering on his knees in yellow gloves, stinging bleach sending his eyes wrinkled shut.

For a moment the tall biker's whipcord frame was superimposed over the aftershocks that Joyce's body still trembled with, but no. The thin man was just as sealed away as she, every bit as alone. She would have come through an encounter with Mark with her protective fictions intact. Instead she had been shattered wide open.

There was nothing that anybody could do about that now. Joyce shook such thoughts out of her stupid head and spun the taps. Lukewarm water ran like flood rivers across her body. It diverted around fresh bruises, enormous and stark against pale skin, milder green fingerprints on her thighs. Revelation had not been gentle.

There was another reflected Joyce in the showerhead, tiny homunculus and she gave this one a lopsided grin. Just like the old days huh? It seemed that she was not *quite* past it all yet. The ventilation fan shuddered; poorly mounted, old and choked with old dust. Beneath its racket Joyce missed the surreptitious click of the locked bathroom door being tried.

She faced into the water's roar and sighed.

Samuel did not miss a thing of the intruder but it was not through any virtue of his own. By the time he finally dragged his lazy ass from sleep his erstwhile lover had well and truly flown the coop leaving little evidence. Perhaps … perhaps it had been a *very* perverse dream?

None such luck. A few strands of dark hair still clung to the pillow spelling out their glyph: *woman woman*.

Samuel inhaled, a deep breath that flushed straight through his forebrain delivering sweat, pussy and hard acrid anger. Joyce had definitely been here although she had left nothing else behind, deliberately erasing herself from his room as though it equated to never having been here in the first place.

Woman said the hair and Samuel had to agree. Just as crazy as the rest of them.

Who knows how long boy scout would have lazed about in bed if not for a knock at the door?

'Joyce?'

No answer but he sensed somebody waiting (shyly?) out in the corridor.

'Alright.' Samuel wiped his wet, now rather gluey crotch with the bedclothes and tossed them over the side of the bed for somebody else to worry about, pulling his shorts back up as he opened the door. 'Returned for round two? It's a bit late for polite knocking don't you think ..?'

The door was flung back against the wall. With blazing eyes Disher lunged to meet him.

CHAPTER EIGHT

AUTOMATONS

AND RELAPSE

'WHATEVER ARE you looking for hon?'

While Joyce stood frozen Mary merely flashed a faded rueful smile as though to catch their guest pawing through their belongings was merely another of life's trials.

It made the taller woman feel a right perve; on the money in this case although a little unfair, as aside from the booze Joyce's compulsions held far more tickle than slap. Small ordinary things were sacred to her: change tossed by the bedside, the paperback on the cistern. Tokens of an ordinary life.

And she had not originally broken into Mark and Mary's room to get her rocks off, stick a needle in her eye! But there had been such thick tobacco and leather, pungent masculine aromas to tweak all of the crude nodes in her sticky pink brain.

As though by deliberate visual contrast the room's décor was by Farmer Dreadful, the culmination of the same pastoral awfulness begun in the diner's paintings. A farmyard illusion that held right up until the moment you twitched aside plaid (plaid!) curtains and bore witness to the inferno without. No cows, chickens or crops, the desert had drunk them all away.

And should you dare nestle closer to the hot glass behind those heavy folds you would hear what you had been expecting all along. You would hear the patter of a blind carapace'd head on glass.

And that bed! It was huge, all crisp linen with hospital corners and extra, extra pillows. You could lose one another in a monster like that, drifting beneath sheets that failed to warm, lonely nautical miles away. Were Mary's husband a choice of *Joyce's* the poor lad would never even reach the damned bed, with the furnishings rubbed bare in all sorts of places.

Caught up in all of this Joyce had accomplished very little of her intended snooping; merely to the point of plunging her hand into a drawer so that her incrimination was nice and complete.

Like any odd fetishist finally caught out guilt was occluded by the most incredible sensation of flying free.

'You won't find salvation rummaging through my panties hon.'

'I'll say,' Joyce snorted nervously. 'It's like the damned Shroud of Turin in there.' Hair trailed lukewarm drops down her back; her skin felt too-tight and clammy.

The small blond advanced easily into the room, into her element as it were. Mary took down her jewellery box. 'Try here.'

Well of course, the *second* most obvious place that a woman would hide something! Men tended more toward beneath the mattress or floorboards, perhaps from all those years of hiding porn rather than secrets.

Eerily it was as though Mary could hear Joyce's scorn. 'Obvious spot, I know but I *want* Marky finding these. I like to know he's looking. Thinking about it. And he does: every time I step out, the top junk in here gets stirred about and the wood …' little pink nostrils flared. 'The wood smells of him.'

Joyce caught a whiff herself as Mary lifted the lid. Grinding frustration and a slow anger had soaked into the grain.

Inside the jewellery box Mary's "top junk" was all you would expect: filigree gold to make a dainty woman seem even daintier. All but for a handful of costume pieces which glowed like exotic strangers against the pilled velvet lining. Drop a proud Amazon into the munchkinland beauty pageant and you would have quite the same effect.

Joyce's magpie fascination itched to drip with their primitive violet fire like some jungle priestess, but wifey was already lifting out the top tray and contents to reveal the compartment that had been hidden with a complete lack of imagination beneath.

Mary proffered the contents eagerly but Joyce felt she had missed the punch line. 'Teeth?'

She initially mistook them for milk teeth as parents hang on to crap like that but these were huge chompers stained with every adult vice. Three of them rattling against fragrant wood. To Mary their dire import sprang from their origin in the jaw of a skulking fellow who had moved with malicious intent—but Joyce saw only teeth, threat pulled.

Her voice was an admirable instrument of distain. 'What are these to remind Mark of, exactly? Flossing?'

'Of being alive!' Mary hissed through clenched little teeth. Blondie was finally showing some corners. 'Of fighting for what he wants!' The bloody rapture in her face made Joyce slide back as though from some beastie that might bite. Not so long ago crowds howled in the colosseum and Mary's blood remembered it.

'Mark's forgotten to be alive, huh?' Could have fooled me, she thought saucily. Then ah to hell with it. 'Could have fooled me.'

'Don't go telling me it's not rotting in your nostrils too, this whole stinking town is merely someplace to die. I didn't want to come here! But Mark *always* has it his way and once he'd got us well and truly stranded he just … damned … stopped!'

There was nothing in that overwrought shriek off the blooming sixteen year old girl who would have gladly shut her eyes, clung to Mark and been dizzily swept along anywhere.

In their long-ago the biker had pursued that fresh young thing as though she were something precious, which was ridiculous as far as Mary was concerned but he was not a sort you said no to. Mark had stood firm as her family's collected childishness broke on him like a wave, like her shame, and all he did was smile. He had this smile back then where there was no need at all to come right out and say any of it.

That young girl crowned in gold in the sunlight had felt so reckless to be dashing down the front step hand in hand with such a man, swinging defiantly onto the back of his motorcycle and nearly choking on apprehension while her mother screamed '*Don't you dare get on that thing!*' without leaving the step, too riled to come any closer.

Might as well release a bird caged all its life and expect it to soar. And here was where daring had landed her: she was marooned in somebody else's dream.

'Well aren't you nice and ridiculous.' Like most women Joyce preferred to lash out with words; although of course pretty spoilt Mary would not be told. Nobody could ever be told. They either worked things out or did not and the river of their life flowed on regardless of how near happiness had been missed at the last turning. 'So what, the honeymoon was over and suddenly you weren't the centre of Mark's universe anymore, in fact hubby *dared* to have a whole life that wasn't you? That's terrible! How do you cope?'

Mary wanted to howl at the tall woman, maddened. Life came so easily to Joyce's type! She bet that Joyce's day-to-day was all action, dynamic and if not she simply re-wrote it so on the hoof; there was probably a twenty four hour swing band rocking out in that cropped head. *Joyce* had never stared into the smallness of each day. The ordinariness, the devastating quiet. Losing an hour, two, three but what did it matter because nothing happened anyway. Time passes.

Instead Mary rattled the teeth thoughtfully, reassessing. 'You're not here for these, are you?'

'Sorry *hon*. Got my own teeth.' Teeth that Joyce fervently hoped would lie quiescent in the dark following her own death and not continue about the world stirring this sort of trouble. The problem being that for all their labour nobody truly gets to choose what they leave behind, nor what its meaning will be to others. 'Listen Mary, little as you want my advice, you should toss those horrible things out. They aren't going to get you what you want.'

'But what then?' Mary's hand trembled so much that Joyce took the box away, maddened by the rattling. 'What are *you* looking for? It's nothing you'll find in this town.' Twisting sourness around her heart like payback.

'Same as the academic.' And humour suddenly smote Joyce, that they had both gone searching through Mary's knickers to find it.

However the disbelieving grin that bloomed across blondie's mouth did not bode well.

'You're kidding! Sure—and I see you're just as set to be all crazy over it.'

'That's the clever bit. If you knew about the town plans they would be in Disher's sweaty mitts by now. It's Mark who's been hiding them.'

'HA!' Burst out harsh and sarcastic. 'Mark's only damn plan is to sit and wait for his damned desert to swallow us!'

'The town ain't so bad Mum.'

Butting in, the third exhausted voice sounded sure but then what do kids know?

At the sight of her youngest Mary's petulance flew apart and she rushed to Dave with an anguished cry. The kid's shirt was all scabbing blots of tears and snot, and an ominous spatter on his shoe might once have been red. He stood inert in his mother's arms; no embrace could strike love from stone. Dave had finally thrown off the things that had so hindered his development and become what he had always the potential to be.

He turned his devastated face up to his mother, spoke in a flat affectless voice. 'Disher said that he's my Dad. My real Dad.'

Mary merely rocked her youngest child as though wishing too late that she had spent a little more time in her own house. And Dave dismissed her. You could actually see it happen, the same nullifying contempt that she had fled hearth and family on Mark's motorcycle to escape. There can be no haunting quite like a bloodline.

The kid shifted his regard to Joyce who was studiously pretending to be elsewhere while this family drama went down. For him the world's relationships were peeled back raw and Joyce at least temporarily had become the new pivot of his days. It would be on *her* choices that his river would turn one way or the other.

To Joyce Dave offered the rolled up documents that he clenched in his fist, the very plans that a lunatic had smashed his world apart for. Plans that offered ... well not answers, nobody was that naïve, but at least some recompense for the misery of the question.

However, he halted her greedy snatch for them. 'You can take these ma'am, an' do what you came for. But it doesn't have to happen how the pump said. What you *ought* t' do instead is get down to Disher's an' save your friend's life.'

What friend ... 'Samuel?' Just what the hell had been going on while she wasted her time here with Mary?

'Dad ...' Now the kid's resolution tattered; the within threatened to thrash loose and lay waste to the without; but Dave had learned restraint at Mark's leather-wrapped knee. The way in which he crushed emotion down would have done the biker proud.

Only, to see it Mark would of course not have been proud. He would have been devastated.

Dave backed up mentally and took another run at it. 'Gar and I was followin' Da ... Mark.' Determined to conform to this horrible new truth, and twisting it in his mother as he went with the extravagant cruelty of the young. 'I wanted t' go *with* him but Gar grabbed my arm, an' he looked all weird like he was gonna puke.'

In case of scepticism Dave rolled up his sleeve to display the evidence. Hard to believe that little Gareth had laid such stripes on his bulkier younger brother but the proof was in the pudding.

'Gar said we could only sneak along behind, just watch or else we wasn't going at all.'

It was a pity that Dave had failed to query his sibling's sudden fear or that compulsive grasping strength, but at the time the younger boy's attention had been all for the man that he had still considered his father. Things had felt weird enough as they were: Mark's hard stalking tension, the two boys creeping along behind. It felt like the day should have been dark and ominous, not bright prosaic sunlight.

Of course Mark was trekking to Disher's study hall, and if the boys had not twigged before that something was sour, they both knew it now. They hid and saw the biker's hard fist lash out, toppling one of the statues by the front door with a gruesome pop of knuckles. It was not a sound for an ordinary bright day, it made their guts twist.

Stepping over the fallen idol in pursuit made Dave queasy: face down in the sand like that it had looked too much like a real woman. Had he been alone he would have stopped to lift it but Mark strode on in and the mismatched brothers were drawn along behind.

'We go inside and they had your friend in th' study hall, tied up, you know?'

Joyce realised that she liked this kid's assumption: all that she and boy scout had needed was to arrive in close proximity and bang! They were friends.

'Tied upside-down on this … thing. He'd gone an' puked, too. Whole place stank.'

When Samuel's body had rejected the flowers that Disher's

cronies had stuffed him with the result had run into his hair so that an inverted halo of chunky dreadlocks scraped the floor.

Mark knelt by the semi-conscious man after a quick scan to see that they were alone—a glance that failed to find the hiding kids for all the sharpness of his eyes. You could not blame him for being distracted. Rope of a coarse russet fibre passed about Samuel's spare chest, neck and thighs. The bonds were shoddily hand-rolled and liable to disintegrate into fibrous red chaff that floated and stung the nose. Bizarrely, Samuel's tackle had been singled out for particular attention, gathered and roped around through his open fly. As he struggled weakly his tethered scrotum bobbed against his hairy inner thigh like a tethered balloon.

Mark's whispered, 'Bloody hell!' roused Samuel just enough to open bleary eyes and wonder why the room had been turned on its head. He sure as hell did not want consciousness; guts fisted up grimly but that brief glimpse of the biker's appalled face had lit some mighty big warning lights in the old memory bank.

'Sam!' Mark hissed, hard eyes flickering about for Disher's most likely entry point. 'Pull your shit together, we have t' get out of here!'

'Doon't,' the bound man groaned, breath like clotted grave dirt. The rope tightened and then dug in as he made his bid for freedom. 'Doon't call meee …'

Samuel's efforts came too late. Mark bared his teeth as Disher and his little bevy of scholars came trooping in right on cue. They must have been lurking in the wings right from the word go, tittering and shushing each other like the hidden guests at a surprise party just waiting to burst out.

'You lot stay where you stand.' Mark set himself between them and Samuel with the obduracy of a mountain but on the inside he was trembling. Not afraid for himself unless it be for his self-regard, what some people call the soul—rather that by coming here he risked the truce that had held his boys' entire world together.

In the furnace of his heart Mark silently cursed Samuel for being weak enough to be used as bait, double cursed a town where no bloody one else would stop an evil and these things always fell to him. But his third curse, the one for his wife flickered out ashamedly before it could be born.

'My dear Mark.' Disher's bonhomie bubbled, it overflowed like champagne. 'This, you see *this* is it! It will be my heart's desire today or nobody's you mark my words!'

Disher was not the only one flying high. His draped companions swayed perilously on their feet; as physical enforcers they were useless, entirely. Even as Mark watched one slid bonelessly down the wall to thump with such force that she was lucky not to punch right through the shoddy floor to end her nap in the dust and forgotten weeds below.

Even in merely recounting the memory Dave's lips peeled back in unconscious mimicry of Mark's own disgust, and the kid waved his hands. It was all too big and awful to be neatly parcelled into words.

'Then they argued.'

Gross understatement. In the face of the academic's gloating Mark turned an insolent shoulder, kneeling to free the captive before pooling blood made Samuel's poor brains burst. The move had him kneeling in the mess and he grimaced: how could so much vomity grossness have sprung from the one little fellow?

Disher ventured nearer and shriller. 'You look at me when I'm talking!' "You" scraped the cornice of high falsetto.

Mark shrugged and released Samuel to the floor as though washing his hands of him. Face down, Samuel's own liberated hands skittered either side of his head as though trying to raise him but they were not having much luck. Their paths traced little angels in the dead dust.

'If you wish to walk out safely with him give me what I need—or I'll take all on the board, Mark, just see if I don't!' The wave of sweet triumph lifted Disher into golden invincibility. He had never dared so much before and actually shook an admonishing finger in the other man's face!

Oh boy, Disher had rolled up heaven and smoked it. Toxic levels to anybody with less tolerance and even so he was sweating fit to pop, leaning in ever closer to Mr I'm So Scary Stupidpants.

'What will you do Disher?' Mark paced the line eagerly like a tiger, a restless light in his eyes. Disher's academics felt the excited heat baking from the biker and through their own befuddlement tried to catch Disher's arm but he had the bit and a hysteric's head of steam.

'I promise you that we will both see *my boy* Dave walk tall in my path; like father like son, eh? And I will make damned sure of turning mine against yours! I'll bring them both down.'

A miserable sob made both combatants stiffen.

In humanity's good old days laboratories used to ring with such pitiful cries, creatures pinned to medical corkboards that could only suffer and suffer.

This, though was the crucible of the world. It took only moments for young Dave's striving heart to split asunder.

'Ridiculous,' Samuel mumbled into the horrified silence.

Saliva pooled from loosened lips that felt as big as bananas. He managed to get both elbows beneath himself, which was a start but nobody paid him any mind. So he tried again, acid stinking fringe hanging in his eyes. 'Stop this. Mark ...'

But Samuel was no longer high on Mark's see-to list. Not now that Dave had stepped from hiding. Gareth too, towed along by a death grip on his younger brother's shirt.

All the wide desert was there in Dave's face. Dead sand blowing in the wind, everything that Mark had striven so hard to keep back and the biker stumbled with the sudden crushing agony of it. One hand clapped to his chest as he dropped to one knee, even as Samuel was rising and for the first and last time the two men were on a level.

The horror of seeing Mark going down before the monster was too much for little Gareth who shrieked, 'Daddy!' Forsaking Dave he flung himself forward and the impact near knocked Mark the rest of the way down.

Movement in the biker's void went slowly, without air or sound while the terrible unappeasable pain in his chest swelled with every beat. But strangely fortitude seemed to flow into him from the thin feverish arms that Gareth cinched about his neck, enough to keep him from the floor.

In his own extremis Mark still cupped a comforting hand to the back of Gareth's little skull, brutal fingers in cornsilk strands. He had witnessed both boys come smeared and squalling into this world; and although the births came years apart he had seized each babe from the midwife with the same impatience.

That blessed midwife! Mark could not even remember her name now but she had arrived right on schedule each time, unrolling the arcane star chart that she used to track births in what she called "her district". There had been trouble all through Mary's second pregnancy to the point where he had not wanted to wait; only Mary let him know in no uncertain terms that if he intended to carry on like a pork chop he was welcome to travel all the way out and sit in the hospital his damned self, because she sure as hell was not going.

Blown out by stress, Mark's mind wandered. With one hand he comforted his genetic child almost absently while the other reached out to Dave. Not a father's hands but a father's stark miserable eyes.

Right from day one the simple existence of his boys had contradicted the biker's inherit violence, fostered hope. How could such tiny things even be?

All those years back when Mark had first found out about Mary and Disher he had gone directly to wring the academic's neck, plain and simple. Not a word to his wife. It was a good plan but with hard fingers crushing Disher's adam's apple, not to mention the reek of a terrified soiling on the air the academic had still managed to set a barb in Mark's flesh that stayed him.

The biker could stand the slow degeneration of this awful world that two poor boys had to inherit ... but not this, not that on top of it all Dave might discover that the loathed academic was his father.

So began the long nights of cold jewellery burning Mark's fingers as he stood with his back to an empty bed; pressure that mounted without relief. And all that he could do was to pit his love for his boys against heedless reality and wait.

If Dave came to him now Mark would find the strength to rise and face the academic sanely, he knew it. They would all walk on out of here.

Without the boy he would be damned.

By reply Dave held out his own hand but his fingers were not open, clenched instead around some tiny treasure. His eyes never left Mark's. It seemed to take the boy forever to unbend those white knuckles and reveal what it was that he held: this first secret, Dave's first discovery which had led in time to this inevitable hardening of his soul.

When Dave had been quite small, back when instead of racing time had placidly swelled out like a creature breathing, he had found this thing wedged beneath the skirting of the diner. The tiniest trace of red at its entry, complicit in dust bunnies and filth. It took patience, fingernails and a fork to pry it free, Dave wide-eyed at this first taste of distrust, and as it balanced lightly on his palm it dawned on Dave that awful things had happened here, in his home.

They had happened. They could happen again. Violence could well rip its howling way back through the plaster walls at any second.

In gratitude and fear for that revelation Dave kept the thing with him from that moment to this: his talisman. It even nestled beneath his pillow where sleeping fingers could touch it in the dark, poisoning his dreams.

An interest in secrets brewed into obsession. He *had* to ferret them out: first his mother, then Disher, and then the water pump; ideally placed to do so, but each unmasking only added to the boy's frightened instability.

What Dave's reluctant fingers released was a lone stained tooth. The last lost seed of Mark's first violence. It pattered to the floor and spun to a halt near the biker's boot; and in a gesture of loathing Mark crushed it just as he had stamped out the man. A crisp porcelain crunch.

The boy's face deformed with the force of his loathing.

No Dave no! Inwardly Mark moaned. Although his hand was still extended all that moved within the boy's gaze was sand. Sterile rolling dunes of sand. Desolation blackened Dave's poor face. This man who was suddenly no longer his adored father, the super-dad who could fix anything and who knew the answer to everything; he had become only the stranger who had concealed this awful, awful secret.

It was far too much for Mark's straining soul to be blamed when he had fought so hard and for so long. He came up from the floor howling like a rabid thing.

Amongst animals that bloodlust cry would have sent other males fleeing with their balls shrivelled into their kidneys, the slowest ripped down mid-flight and torn to pieces. But Disher had no choice: in the confined space Mark came on too quickly to run.

Raised in the warm cradle of civilisation it was Samuel's hubris to blunder into the biker's maddened path, trying to prevent mayhem.

Drugged. Misguided. Perhaps Samuel even thought himself invincible, wonderfully sacred in the way of young men. Certainly no aspect of his pressed and starched existence could have prepared him for the fact that Mark was entirely gone, and the thing that remained needed only its hands to tear through anything to reach Disher.

The academic's congregation stampeded around him; and what did Samuel's sacrifice buy? A few spare seconds for a man that nobody else would piss on to save.

And in a surprising display of balls Disher sprang *forward*, snatching to himself what had been shoved aside. Perhaps the last remaining thing that might give the biker pause. It was a move that stopped Mark dead in his tracks. Samuel may well have been stopped dead as well: face down, he no longer moved. The blood spread.

Caught in Disher's pale hands Gareth might have threshed and screamed but this ultimate horror was beyond bearing. Hanging hopelessly without protest he turned his head dully to his horrified half-sibling and croaked: 'Run Dave.'

Dave ran, seeking not his mother but Joyce, revenge over comfort. Behind him Mark straightened to meet Disher and his hands took up their legacy.

Appalled and standing together Mary and Joyce listened to the kid's tale, united by their growing outrage. It seemed that they were always being left out of the action. And each woman's thoughts went racing with hard practicality down the same track: what can I salvage from this?

'Your friend …' Dave started up at Joyce again, acting the part of conscience but she was already snatching the pages from farm boy's grasp.

In her defence Joyce may have failed to take Dave seriously—what do kids know? Or perhaps just like Samuel she subscribed to that modern mythos that nothing fatal will ever happen to me and mine, a cant that leaves people so tragically unprepared for reality.

Just like Samuel. Of course Samuel. Despite the lure of Mark's blatant animalism it was aftershocks of Samuel's touch that cruised lazily about Joyce's skin in little shivers. Reconciling her attraction to both men was like trying to lie on both sides of an unfeasibly large bed.

Samuel's type was *sneaky*, that was the problem! Rather than storming the front door they slunk around your garden planting midnight roses. Carved your portrait into the fence post, left tiny exotic pastries in the post box. Until one day you woke to how cunningly you had been lured to live more outside of your house than in.

So don't dwell on things that will drive you batshit, Joyce counselled herself. Keep moving until you outdistance the worries, leave it all behind. Faster. Run!

Joyce unfolded the pages. The plans bared the entire town to her appalled eye like a whore sprawled on the slab.

The water pump was finally a disembodied voice no longer—oh it was corporate all right and nothing could have prepared her for the sheer physical reality of the buried thing. It was half again the size of the damned town!

Horror loosened her insides until she feared that she might drop her spleen or something equally embarrassing. The water pump was a monstrously large baby. Rolled over as though sleeping. Umbilical pipes rising up through the sand to a placental diner. Here finally she had found the man-machine and it was far worse than anything that paltry nightmare could have sicked up. The plans ticked off everything: diameter, welds, composition; everything except in the name of God *why?*

The shut down switch that she sought was there as well, the gun to its head. Humanity's paranoia so great that they had made damned sure that no machine could ever scuttle out from under the threat, even machines built by machines down to the nth descendent.

'Ma'am?' Dave called after Joyce's vanishing back but with no great hope. He retrieved the discarded plans from the floor, which were essentially worthless now that they had been read by one of the two parties seeking them. His bargaining chip was gone. Joyce had what she needed and there would be no more messing about with other people's futile desires, ideas and crazy conspiracy theories. What was Dave's tiny crumbling world to her?

Dear Joyce. Grim scarecrow woman stepping from the bottom rung of a deep reaching ladder, her physical recuperation already unravelling like dirty linen around her.

And so quickly inured to discomfort: once upon a time this strange worm-holing journey beneath the desert had scared the (pyjama) pants off her but now it seemed to get over a phobia, all you needed was a slightly bigger one to grab your attention.

A wet splat threatened to bring Joyce's whole operation crashing down as her feet shot out, only a panicky clutch at the ladder saved her. Ever-graceful. There was a lot more water down here than last time and such richness, a sanctity to the quiet cool air. It was the sort of room where she would like her dead bones to rest someday: hidden, washed by chill water and nibbled at by lights.

All the while the water pump worked stoically away in the background like a heartbeat, foiling life's exhausted retreat from the world and drawing it back from beneath the sand to the surface.

'So. You awake down here?'

Fey sparks twinkled to life, describing the cavern about her rather than illuminating it. They moved less joyously than last time, weighed down by some melancholy. Probably foreknowledge. 'As if I had the option. It's a pity I can't give sleep a go. It is said that great men have seen the truth in dreams and woke to action, but me? I have only reason to go by.'

'Yeah, and Freud dreamed of a world filled with lubricated bratwurst. Wishing for a subconscious is like wanting to have part of your brain snap frozen at childhood and locked up forever.'

'I'm sure that Sier Sigmund would find you a fascinating study. Do I detect a faint eau de semen on the air?'

Crassness was Joyce's meat and drink, she merely shrugged.

'And let me guess: you waited until the lucky fellow was asleep in his bower and then slunk away like a scaredy cat. Don't act all shocked: like you were ever going to do any damn thing else. Running like an emotional coward was stamped on that brow of yours the moment you were born.'

But Joyce's skin cried in protest. 'You can't know that. Nobody knows the future, not for themselves or anyone else.'

'True. Let's say that I deal in strong likelihood. And you, the great Lady Joyce. Hugging your bittersweet might-have-beens against mundane old reality. You will become a legend you know; while I and all that I have accomplished will be forgotten, the simple folk will sing your name for decades to come.'

'Mark had your plans all along.' Joyce cut through the water pump's bullshit like a hot knife through ... well. 'But of course you knew that, because Dave knew. Mark could hide documents from Disher, and from a wife who did not really want to know but kids weasel stuff out. That's their job, it's what they do, otherwise they'd never learn anything.'

'So you did get them before Disher. I ought to be pleased I suppose.'

'And while we are on the topic of you being an asshole, Disher is no more machine than I am!'

'Is that so?'

'Yes you rotten lying pail of rust! He's gotten himself a kid—your youngest protégée no less.'

'Well if you've unearthed all the evidence it must be so. And it's finally given you your way of telling A from Z.'

'No kids, huh? So you don't have it all bad ...'

'It's true, we can't make ourselves part of tomorrow like you can. That's why what happens now is so important to us—it's all we have. You lot took your spark from the gods and guarded it jealously like any petty thief, so now as each of you go out the rest of us are left with the dark. Not even some vague unconfirmed promise of heaven to believe in.'

'So cry me a river. I didn't make you.'

'You didn't. Working en mass, people seem to form a sort of amorphorous group morality that works so wonderfully that nobody is ever really to blame. I sometimes think that it must be society's greatest achievement.'

'Why tell me that Disher was yours?'

'To get you on the case of course. Feed you something you'd swallow.'

'Do you know who Disher really is then?'

'I thought that people weren't your problem.'

'Asshole.'

'Alright, alright. One last tale before bedtime. Disher showed up at the hospital one day having heard so *much* about it: where dreams come true, etcetera. What he wanted was plastic surgery.

'It was heartbreaking really. He brought along this male centrefold from some back issue magazine that he had been carrying in his wallet for years; the fold lines were all velvet and it practically fell to pieces when he smoothed it out on the counter. Make me look like *this*. Make me beautiful. Above all make me somebody other than me.

'He would have paid anything for it, signed in blood, but all the hospital machines wanted was a little semen to seal the deal. They had an IVF department all tricked out for donations, with rather embarrassing projected images to make the poor under-whelmed donor feel they were interacting with a flesh and blood person. Huge market for that sort of thing.

'Imagine the machines' consternation when the analysed their prize for quality control and found the malaise Disher was carrying. One of the bad old population killers, a shifter, never conquered by science although they'd swallow their tongue rather than admit so. For all their miracles the machines could not stamp this out even if they took Disher apart right down to the sticks and bones.

'Contagious in his fluids, his water. It had hunkered itself down and not a peep out of it for decades, while the host went about blithely infecting more poor souls. Anybody with average enough standards to sleep with Disher—bang! Their subsequent partners—bang! Bang! Kids, should they be unfortunate enough to have any … well you get the picture. And all this in a gene pool already shallow enough to wade in.'

'Dave.'

'I know.'

'That's really shit.'

'Yes it is.'

'Not Gareth? Or Mark?'

'Gareth was off the teat by the time the academic blew into town, he's hopefully clear. As for Mark … flip a coin and see which side comes down. I guess it will come down to how estranged the marital bed really is. Should hating his wife have saved his life, well then he will get to be around to nurse Dave right to the very end.'

'What's the point of all this been if the kid's going to die anyway!'

'Dave is going to die. He's not dead yet.'

'Hey I've got a pubic hair somewhere about, maybe you can split it for me.'

'Don't you ever listen? Disher has done this, brought this thing here, *his* legacy. I have been hoping for years that Mark might stave his fat selfish head in and do us all a favour.'

'Mark doesn't deserve to be lumped with your precious hospital's dirty work. Did you ever stop and think what it would do to him?' Never mind that Disher did not deserve such a neat clean escape either. 'They ought to've pulled the pin on Disher themselves when they had the chance.'

'When he was still an innocent? Disher could at least claim ignorance before strolling up to the hospital for his nose job; there's certainly no such luxury for him now. The hospital did what they did and they thought it would be enough but it really, really wasn't. Don't you understand how this could spread? What Disher has done here could happen everywhere, a thousand small towns that will just shrivel up and blow away on the wind.'

'Well you know what, people just aren't my problem. There'll be little of this town left anyhow when I throw this little switch—you *do* know what I've got my hand on, don't you?'

'Oh I wish that were innuendo.' The pump thought for a second. 'And that I had better last words to go out on.'

Joyce did not move. 'I've got time to let you think of some.'

A panel in the wall slid open and darkness ran out. Thick and rich like treacle; pattering to the floor it dosed the air with hard smelling minerals.

'A final toast then, if it's not too forward of me. Please lady Joyce, it's only water. Quite safe.'

Still unwilling to relinquish her hold on the switch in case this was his last trick, Joyce bent her mouth directly down. 'Freezing!' The water was wonderfully so, an icicle to the guts. It were as though she had never been cold before now.

'Straight from the darkest heart of the desert; few have tasted anything from so far down before. Who knows what wonders it will do. Think of it as a baptism of sorts. A baptism: yes, why not. You may well be the mother of all our futures.'

'Look, I am sorry about all this.' Joyce was beginning to feel that drawing things out might be more cruelty than kindness.

'Excuse me all to hell if that doesn't mean a great deal to me right now.'

'It does to me.'

Joyce flicked the switch hoping for a quick merciful end, without terror. But there was enough residual charge in the system to carry the pump's thin panicky screech: 'No, no, I'm not ready …'

While this was going on young Dave had taken it upon himself to stand guard above, outside the shed, crouching in the sand. He could not imagine anywhere else that he should go. The scant shade had shifted since Joyce had slid into the hole but he made no effort to pursue comfort—what was the point?

Dave just crouched in the hot sand, sifting it through his thick fingers. After a while he cocked a jaded ear as the regular throbbing of the pump began to stutter. It stuttered, and then stuttered out.

He shuddered. She had done it then. There was only the sound of the wind now, rustling, sweeping little grains of sand along. The smell of the shed's tin baking.

The lady certainly took her sweet-ass time returning. Perhaps she was drinking.

The first time that Dave had drunk the dark water it had twisted his guts so badly that he fell to the floor and all of the little lights flickered out. He thought he had gone blind.

Your system is adjusting to something extraordinary, the pump had answered the boy's alarm in that patient voice that was never raised or lowered. Don't screw yourself tighter by fretting. Try to relax. Like waves of sand, tumbling gradually down.

You had to be still and take your time to see the sand fall; by the scale of day-to-day it looked motionless. Watching for it had taught Dave patience. Each muscle gradually unfolded like flower petals drifting down through the floor and he had dozed down there in the dark, dreaming of the people to come in their great metal cities. Sealed into their hives in terror of the sky. The next thing he knew was Gareth's thin voice came crying down the ladder; what was he *doing* down there! Their Dad was gonna get after them soon.

Eventually Joyce put in her appearance, sweaty and tousled; hoisting hand over elbow to sprawl panting in the sand next to him. She was not much to look at: mania stretched over bones. But something had to be salvaged.

'Our Mum,' Dave said quietly.

'I don't know if there's anything I can do. We'll have to see,' was all he got back. Joyce and her awesome way with children; especially the trauma-brittled kind, those kids least in need of reality.

Although abused leg muscles moaned Joyce groaned to her feet and towered over Dave, up into the burning sky. The sand crust on her thighs broke up into continents. The boy squinted up at her, a hand shielding his eyes.

Joyce made a fearful goddess, as likely to strike down her allies as foe in irritation. Every bit as unreliable as any deity. But she leaned down out of that blue-blue sky and hauled young Dave to his feet.

What with all the hell else Joyce had done to this town the devastation that they found inside Disher's greenhouse was her fault as well. But did she feel sorry for this one? Not a damned bit.

Every plant within meters of the rent that she had made in their world had crisped, twisted in on itself like a charred spider. Remoter neighbours bubbled and warped like cheap Pyrex on the stove and the air stank of scorched polymers. Another failed experiment in the arena of evolution. Flowers tumbled and the desert's dry red blanket rolled in to cover all.

The sand had attempted to sanitise another disaster as well, one that was quite at home in here amidst the smashed pots and other debris. Were it not for diminutive Mary and the even more elfin Gareth kneeling to either side of him Joyce would have passed Samuel by.

This little tripartite on the floor: they had always been served up the best of life, the blessed, never having to reach for or earn anything. Look where it got them now. Being beautiful had taught only carelessness.

While in comparison Joyce and Dave stood over them and stared down, all hard faces and craving hearts. Not so pretty, nor so blessed; but at least when the drama finally concluded they were still on their feet.

Perfected disassociation only allowed Joyce's eyes to flicker across Samuel. Busy foot traffic in cities had once ignored the homeless or mad in the same way, applying the ruthless formula of finite resource allocation that dictated who was part of their concern and who was not. She addressed her question to Mary. 'A nice disaster you've got going on here. Where's your parasite of an academic slunk off to?'

Mary did not wish to tell but her flinch toward the building was betrayal enough.

'I know that voice.' Samuel struggled up on one elbow, peering at Joyce through his usable eye which was still so blue. With sand dusted everywhere the extent of his damage was debatable but when he tried to smile his teeth were horror. 'Fancy seeing you here. You missed all the excitement you know.'

'I know.' That did not seem enough. 'I could only pick one place to be.'

'He's awake!' Mary hissed at Gareth as though the kid lacked eyes in his head. 'Go get him some water—both you two.' Her first aid initiative left something to be desired.

Gareth obeyed slowly, stumbled vaguely and had to be shoved into his brother's arms, both boys thrust out of the greenhouse into the day on what Dave already knew was a fool's errand.

Why am I even going? he wondered in helpless frustration, looking first down at his clenched hand and then up at the sky. Taps'll just sputter out a few drops now, then air. The water pump is gone. Without even noticing he shook the slighter boy as he dragged him along.

'I thought th' monster died,' Gareth slurred up at Dave, pulling on fine blond hair as carelessly as he minded his steps. He did not look quite awake. 'I thought they poisoned it but th' monster was in Daddy. It was hiding in 'im the whole time.' He began to sob wretchedly into his hands.

'Gar? You gone loopy?'

'Sure; you wouldn't 'member.' Gareth sniffled and scrubbed at his splotchy face with balled up fists in the way that small children try to wipe away the reality of being lost, the cruel eyes in the wood. 'You were too little. I remember how I couldn't sleep but you were just a baby, didn't know we should be outside having fun.'

Gareth had already had all the places about town lined up that he wanted to show his new baby brother. No intimation now of how ridiculously that sibling would in time surpass him in bulk.

For the present the right-of-size allotted Gareth the prized top bunk while Dave was just a weird pink button in his crib. The boys had been put to bed unfairly early for two weeks running, and Gareth's perch afforded him the window's alluring vista. Through the open portal poured sunlight and the clean hot smell of freedom while he lay listlessly bored, itchy with it. The colour would darken to sandy in later years but for now the sunlight in his hair made pure albino feathers.

'Why were we in bed so early?'

'I hadn't *done* anything wrong. It was th' stray. The monster. There had been this great big stray stirrin' trouble 'round town.'

"Stirring" was how their mother had put it but Gareth had heard much tastier titbits fall from looser lips. 'It started with bins an' like, and I guess that was stirrin' right enough. Nobody really noticed; I think some was even leavin' food out 'cause I heard Dad telling them off. But then with th' bins sealed up tight, pet dogs started getting' ripped right off their leads.'

The savagery always happened at night to be discovered and discussed the next morning, which is when Gareth caught the forbidden crumbs from the adult table. His youthful affinity for the grotesque latched right on and he mentally replayed that throwaway horror during the long hours of early to bed tedium. Ripped right off their leads. Ripped. Many years later he could still recall the compelling phrase perfectly—it does not pay to put terrors in children.

'Just a dog.' Dave had never had the dread twisted into him, did not know what the fuss was about. Mark's streak of pragmatism ran in him all the way.

'It wasn't just a dog. It was a monster.'

The stray had been a massive dim lump, a melting pot of brutes abandoned and slashed free. Domestication had tempered the nobility of the wild animal away, going feral then peeled off the veneer of sociability. Ancient times would have seen such an unfettered gladiator hunting lions, or prisoners, and fed from golden plates. Sanitised modernity however had no place for such a thing.

In another three days from the moment young Gareth stared longingly out his window from the top bunk, the town would set bait that the stray's greed would seize on. A cunning gambit by Mr Packinghurst, the diner's neighbour to the west. In those days Packinghurst had both de factor and daughter, he had been more than a faded grey wisp in an unravelling dirty sweater, a fixture on one of Mark's bar stools so subdued that it was possible to close up shop and forget he was there.

Packinghurst's grand idea and his spaniel Boomer were one and the same. Plump, friendly and dumb as a short-sawn plank, Boomer shrieked horribly in the dark one night. Show ribbons and pedigree were no match for the stray and what the sullen moon had given it … just as the stray was no match for the rat bait that poor Boomer's flesh had been sown with.

They found the brute out by the highway in a crater of sand, dead eyes still staring to where the moon its mistress had been and for a while the diner was all congratulations, can I buy you a drink?

Unfortunately in his cleverness Packinghurst had neglected to consult with his family. He returned from the bar to find that his partner had packed their daughter into the car and gone. She even took the goldfish in case he found something to feed that to, too. Like so many who moved on from the town nobody ever saw them again. So Packinghurst turned around and trudged back to the diner. Where else was he going to go?

'I had been starin' out the window for ages a' fore I twigged th' b'stard was *right there*. Right in front of my eyes. Our backyard. And not even night time, like it knew the whole town was out runnin' around tryin' to catch it so it could poke around here much as it liked.'

The way the animal moved boldly through their yard had pealed ancient alarm bells in Gareth's small skull. Moments prior he had been daydreaming of being the one to find the stray, of somehow subduing it and being told by everyone but especially his father *Well done. We should never have sent you to bed.* But no longer the golden hero, pride of his parents, Gareth was suddenly just a tiny naked thing flung down from the trees struggling desperately to hide.

Many years later the sight of his father moving with that same lethal stalking would bring all of the bad old horror back so clearly that it physically hurt, and in reflexive terror Gareth's icy fingers would grind into his brother's meaty bicep hard enough to leave bruises.

'It was right there! I might have called it by thinking 'bout it too loud.' Dave did not scoff at the superstition, both boys knew how the world worked. And indeed the stray's great blunt skull had tracked back and forth as though searching for some hint, a whiff, the source of a summons.

Then it found the open window.

To little Gareth high on his bunk the world contracted horribly until it was scarce the width of the room. They had said that the monster only struck by night but this was all warm yellow afternoon that hid no detail of what was coming for him.

The stray put its head on the sill to look in, easily big enough to do so. Skin shifted loosely over that lumpy bone. Then it heaved both massive forepaws up with a sort of grunt, sand pattering down to the quiet sun warmed carpet.

There was no other sound. Gareth's lungs laboured but there was no air for him, only the decay streaming into the room from those cavernous nostrils. The boy twisted on his bunk in a stifled convulsion of terror. The light was bright and clear enough to see that the claws of one paw were jet, the other a mottled pink.

The blunt skull advanced across the sill, bristling shoulders following like ponderous mountains. Every gene in Gareth's body, reaching right down evolution's memory screamed at him: *Hide!*

'But somebody came't save us, right?'

'I couldn't … no one was coming …'

Dave pressed Gareth's shoulder, trying to squeeze fortitude into the birdlike limb and the older boy shuddered. His confession crawled out with all the shame of wet stinking sheets, of discovery.

'I screamed.'

Nobody was coming. Gareth's cry was not for help: his fear raddled world had shrunk too small to admit others; but nevertheless when his high voice split the air Mark came charging.

The biker thundered in like the apocalypse, the night light wrenched from the wall and hurled into the stray's snapping snarling face. The beast screamed with pain and fury at being thwarted, hind legs scrabbling the outside wall for purchase.

But Mark was not pausing, coming on right behind the lamp and the stray did not live to such a bulk by being stupid. It dropped gracelessly from the window, claws squealing on the sill.

Mary's firstborn thrashed on the bunk, temporarily insane with terror, blood lace flying from his bitten lip. He heard his father's roar and his jerking limbs slowed long enough to see the empty churned sand beneath the window. Mark lifted Dave from the cot, the baby's wail beginning.

Gareth burst into tears.

'My mouth tasted all blank, from the screaming I guess. I didn't want t' eat anything for ages an' got real skinny.' Flush with shame Gareth neglected to mention how their mother had had to change his sheets. And the next night, and the next like clockwork. Not a word from her but that somehow made it worse, her lips drawn with worry, eyes huge and spilling out love. Just his favourite train-print sheets washed and washed again.

And Mark brought those hugs, those wonderful enveloping hugs that seemed to barricade the world away. The window ledge had to be repainted but the biker did not stop there, he went over the whole outside wall as though to remove any trace of the stray's existence.

'I was on the top bunk, see. But you down there in your crib ... th' stray's nose was pointed right at you. I *wanted* it to come to me instead. If knew if I kicked up enough of a stink it'd have to come for me. It would come after me and you'd be safe.'

At first as the predatory shadow had descended Gareth had cowered as all young prey things have cowered since the beginning of time: doomed, quaking and afraid. The scream of *Hide!* was deafening.

But as the bestial head came on a new voice had spoken to Gareth. A modest voice; not nearly so primal as fear's clamour but its calm surety sliced his terror open. The word was no longer *survive* but *protect*.

Scrawnier and in no way as streetwise as his brother Gareth had nonetheless once shielded Dave from harm. And he was not finished. He looked up at his brother with haunted eyes.

'They said the monster was dead. But all this time it's been hiding—hiding in Dad.'

Dave was crying now himself, still just a kid. He gathered Gareth's shuddering misery into his arms and Disher's plan of pitting one boy against the other was broken forever.

Meanwhile back at casa del Disher, Samuel still clung conversationally to Joyce as though he had some claim on her time. Everything was red, always red. She longed for bitter air and ice crust on mud, a landscape of hints and subtlety.

'Thought you'd just sneak out without seeing me again, huh?'

'Um …' Mary interrupted them tentatively. She really could not help feeling that all this emotional acrimony rather failed to grasp the reality of the situation. 'Don't you think we should be getting Samuel some medical attention?'

To the astonishment of the others Joyce clamped both hands over her ears. The sad echoes, the cries for help were starting up again, always at the worst time. 'The hospital. Of course,' she muttered. It was like a haunted house: sooner or later everybody went there.

'But Disher says …'

'Was I muttering to you? And Mary, Disher says a lot of things, none of which have been particularly useful. A good Daddy'll often make up answers where none exist—it's more important to retain belief in his omnipotence than to be truthful.'

Furiously red in the face Mary struggled to her feet, mouth open, but it was Samuel who burst into inappropriate giggles. Trust him to miss a good scrag-fight brewing; what with all the hair pulling and thrashing about there was always the chance that the two women might, accidentally, kiss.

'Daddy?' he gasped incredulously. '*Disher*? Is that what all this' been about? He's about as likely to father kids as front for the National Ballet!'

The strength ran right out of Mary's legs. Chagrin is like that. 'No?' she husked, looking up at the other woman but this was as much news to Joyce, that all of this violence had been for nothing. No reason at all.

Samuel began a rank airless coughing but managed to squeeze words out between. 'That's what the hospital did to Disher, why he hates them so much. Instead of doing what he asked them they clipped his balls.'

Mary looked like she might faint and Joyce poked the ineffectual little blond with a foot. 'For Chrissake Mary; get him up and get him across to Ben.'

Breathing quick as a sparrow Disher watched Joyce push aside the strung curtain to the kitchenette. His final bolt hole was not much, little more than an alcove, the last shabby secret that his study hall had to offer. Here was where he had germinated his first precious seedling, watched its pale green head pushing blindly up from the pot. No matter; nothing would suffice. The town was Mark's in spite of all Disher had done. Everything belonged to the biker down to the last gritty bits of sand in his teeth and now there was nowhere left to flee.

Besides, Disher felt so horribly weary. It hung on him, hung over him as though he had never truly rested all his life. He felt he had been waiting forever for this moment but now it had finally arrived he could barely force his dreary eyelids apart.

These mood swings would be the raw death of him, he had

no energy left. Backing out of the hall he had been so terrified and the blond brat in his grasp likewise, blubbering and stumbling the more tightly he clung on. Backing and holding up the kid with all the confidence of opening an umbrella before a hurricane and all trace of the previous moment's exultation gone so he could hardly recall what the devil he had done to precipitate such horror, or why.

And all the while Mark had advanced to finally murder him. Both of the biker's hands had already been thick with gore after what he had done to the hostage, no bloody good as hostage now: fingers hidden in it, just cruel rams at the end of the biker's arm. The older kid had scarpered in terror but what did you expect: nobody would stick around to succour kin once they realised their own skins were to peel.

The Lady Joyce paused there in the doorframe, blinking as her vision acclimatised slowly. To enter she had to push her way past the huge faded bunches of flowers which hung head down from the ceiling as though in a witch's kitchen. The bouquets swung at her touch, silently losing themselves further to the fierce beams of light that stormed through cobwebby cracks in the walls. To advance through those knife thin beams and around the floral obstacles must be to be alternately dazzled and blinded. Dry petals and empty fly husks shifted soundlessly beneath her feet and gave up no discernible scent at all.

Disher had long wondered who might attend this last moment. His earliest imaginings had been of young Dave, and wouldn't that fuck Mark right up. But he could not have the dialogue that he wanted with some kid, not quite with Mary either. Discourse was not at all her forte. The fear had even begun to nag that perhaps nobody would come, this would be a grand gesture that he would never get to savour but once Joyce appeared it all just made such sense.

Poor misguided Joyce, sent to accomplish the task that he had already undertaken. Always in the wrong place making the wrong choices, pushed this way and that by events that she only heard described to her afterwards.

'Welcome.'

'Gee, thanks.' Surveying the kitchenette Joyce felt a hot rush of embarrassment for Disher. He sat alone, lording over his deserted domain at a cheap fold down table. And he had laboriously staged the pathetic scene with the same devastating hubris of every suicide since spite became a trendy way out.

When Disher twitched his hand glitzy foil rattled and flashed in the dim light. The packets were everywhere. A squeamish exit, then: using neat across the counter pills that were a boon when taken as recommended and frighteningly toxic beyond.

The stuff would already be corroding the academic away inside; a physical degradation to match the moral. Liver, kidneys, all sorts of juicy organs without which man cannot do, all cast smoking on the altar of his pettishness.

Disher's smile to Joyce across the table was that same beatific expression of what seemed so long ago now: fulfilment dropped over a lolling hyena grin. Ha—see, I got all of you good!

She seriously considered just turning on her heel and leaving him to stew in it. Which she would have done gladly were it not for Mary, and all of Disher's other little scholars scattered throughout the town. Disher's secret little death here would mean those poor dupes would never get to see what Joyce knew about him; lord knew they would not be told. Without knowing they would never get the chance to become more than what he had made of them. Instead they would sit in the sand and rot as faithfully as dogs dumped by the roadside.

It was not good enough. Joyce may not be one of them by a long shot but she had gotten herself too involved, to the extent of feeling that she ought to do something.

'How did you get away from Mark?' she ventured by way of distraction while drifting casually about the little space and ever-closer as though by chance, fingering the crisp dried flowers.

Disher lifted dreary eyes. He was propping his big head up with both hands. 'No one can have everything at once; and so we choose, and choose. Mark had to pick which he wanted first; me or the brat.' A pause. 'I did rather think it was to be me.'

Running her finger along a sill to gather the silky dust; 'And what about your grand plan?'

'Oh Mark will wish that he had given the plans to me now.' His voice was growing fainter. 'May he wish it in vain.'

'I found the water pump Disher. *I* turned it off.'

That snatched the academic's attention, rabid mania glittering through although the rest of him seemed to be beginning to slide away. His whole face had slumped, spilling forward off the front of his skull. 'You turned it off? Did it say anything? *Did it tell you who made it?*'

'Why do you care?' Joyce hedged, not giving up crumbs for free but it was a dodge Disher knew well for his face fell crafty.

'Everyone must answer for their works eventually you know.'

'That,' Joyce said grimly having worked her way around to stand close beside Disher. 'Is the first thing ever I think we can agree on.'

Her sunburned fist pistoned out and socked itself into his selfish gut.

Disher's drowsing eyes sprang wide and welling. This was not part of his set piece: he had envisaged calm dialogue, perhaps some wailing by the womenfolk toward the end but certainly not pain and humiliation! Not for him!

His throat bucked and disgorged a slop of wet strings across the scarred tabletop, as sickly and runny as he had suddenly become. The force of his expulsion grated the chair back through drifts of flies and flowers, stomach acid now a hearty offence to both eyes and nose.

Joyce shook what she would ever after refer to as her "punching hand". That really hurt. On the table white foam sizzled up around dissolving caplets in their paddling pools of bile. Disher slid from his chair and onto the floor, a smeared lump.

'No, no—upsy-daisy big fella. You have an appointment to keep.'

Slow as the going was they still managed to overtake Mary and Samuel. Mainly because although Sammy-boy made some manful effort to get his trembling legs under him and push, precious backpack clutched in his fingers and all, Disher was utterly useless. Joyce just dumped him exasperatedly to the ground and proceeded to drag the academic by his ankles. Even then his shirt racked up and gradually filled with sand, forming an annoying passive resistance parachute.

As they drew even the two very different women goggled at the spectacle of her fellow in each other's arms, as though they had attended some weird partner-swapping do. How wretched and dissatisfied the other looked with her lot; the grass being greener was obviously just so much crap.

Mary was never one to observe and reflect. Freeing herself from Samuel the little blond reached eagerly for the academic who had the bad grace to snarl incoherently at her like some sick mongrel that bites even the hand that feeds it. Mary in turn flinched at the raised stick of her master's voice but the day had already violated the bounds of their little arrangement.

'You promised!' Her protest came squeezed pinhole thin through tears that certainly looked genuine, although it was always tricky to tell on a woman in the habit of using crying eyes to get what she wants. She tugged pathetically at Disher's sleeve. 'You said I could save my family. You said you'd always be there.'

The ultimate indignity was that even with one foot already in unconsciousness Disher began to laugh. Weak hysterical laughter as his arms trailed in the sand behind him. 'Oh come on: you liked me because I made you feel like a princess. Well I hate to tell you, monarchy was abolished in this country years ago. I use you, you use me and we prop up each other's little egos.'

'Is that so? You know what she'll do with you, don't you. You know where she'll take you!'

'Disneyland?' Disher tried to roll his eyes up to focus on Joyce but instead they rolled all the way into his head.

'You just shut it,' Joyce hissed, showing Mary her punching fist for good measure.

It was not until they reached Ben's glowing flank that Joyce noticed, shuddering, how Disher's eyes remained rolled up to the whites. The academic had checked out.

She banged on Ben's door. 'Open up big boy!'

'I can't help but feel I've been missing out on one hell of a party.'

'For once can we *please* cut the funny? We've got an

emergency going on Ben, and I damn well hope that your shiny ass can fly.'

'Huh?' Ben said intelligently.

'It's high time we all took a fast trip to that place I've been hearing so much of.' Joyce glanced down, scuffed some sand at Disher. 'One way, for some of us but that's what they say in the song, you can never go back.'

'Huh?'

'H-o-s-p-i-t-a-l,' she mouthed and all of a sudden Ben's opening door froze up stubbornly.

'Nuh uh lady. Not Disher. I'll save Samuel, no worries, but not that sack of rubbish.'

'Come on now Benny, be reasonable.' Joyce's eyes darted about with nervous little drops running down her pale neck, expecting any moment to hear the ominous and decidedly un-erotic under the circumstances creak of leather. Any second now the tall biker with his hard murderous hands could burst from just about anywhere, even the hell of the open sand. The town was his place and they were totally exposed.

Mary obviously dreaded the same thing, she was sallow as an old candle. The last person to try and intervene in this domestic dispute was dying at her feet. Joyce shoved harder at the door; 'Ben, this idiot Disher's gone and tried to top himself ...'

'Good!'

'... and he will die if you don't help him. In fact he'll probably snuff it anyhow. By this stage it's not down to what sort of jerk he is but what we are. Where's your humanity?'

'Well isn't that rich as cake coming from you, you little ...'

'Please Ben,' Mary moaned, wringing her hands.

Joyce stared at the blond disbelievingly; even now she still supported Disher. Well there was no stupidity like unbroken habit. And even in desperation there was an art to Mary: wide eyed, dishevelled and tragically pretty. Joyce wanted to tell her that the O'Hara routine was wasted: a machine had no heartstrings to tug but something she was doing must have worked. Ben's door hesitated, and then swung sullenly loose in Joyce's hands.

'Fine. Put Samuel in the driver's seat then.'

'Nuh-uh.' Now it was boy scout who felt inspired to stick in the road like a damned mule. Joyce had thought he was asleep but an eyelid cracked and blue lashed out from his wan features, startlingly intense. 'Don't you dare put me in that thing.'

'Would you damn lot take this seriously!' Joyce all but shrieked, trembling. She could feel their time running away.

'Oh I'm dead serious,' Samuel insisted. 'I'm not getting back in the rig. Passenger seat, or you can bury me right here.'

'Sam it's not the same,' Ben pleaded. 'I can stabilise your condition, keep you safe 'til we get there …'

The eye closed tiredly. 'Bung Disher in if you're so keen to save somebody.'

'*He's* to survive when my Geoff didn't?'

You could not really blame Ben for his outrage but a sneer lifted Joyce's lip. 'That's just the world; that's how it's always been. What are you going to do, sit here and watch Disher die to make it right? Eat popcorn?' She pressed both hands to the door. 'Don't fear that you're doing him too much of a favour in seeing him safely there.'

'Quite the opposite, your tone would suggest?'

Mary bit her lip but Joyce gave a tight vindictive grin. 'Quite.'

'Samuel ..?' The truck tried one last appeal and got a hearty thumbs down for his trouble.

The two women were already moving on Ben's capitulation, propping boy scout against one massive tyre while they set about getting Disher loaded. But while other backs were turned Ben kept a critical eye on Samuel. He did not at all like what he saw.

The lad's closed eyelids were violet and the rest of his skin shading steadily greyer, as though that flare-up had been the final hurrah before ashes. The last time Ben had seen somebody slump over and turn that colour … well, things had not turned out so well. Let this be different, the truck prayed to the sparse grave where Geoffrey had been laid. Let things go differently this time.

Events would change if only the people could, too.

True to form even when semi-conscious Disher was tumbling about like a rag sack and generally making himself a royal pain in the colon to lift. However in this at least Mary proved an unexpected boon: able to lift many times her weight, while for all her flamboyance Joyce huffed and strained just trying to keep up.

Then it was one man loaded and one to go and both women heaving frantically, their fatigued arm muscles like spaghetti, spurred by the unmistakable snarl of a motorcycle engine approaching. Mary dropped back to the sand: the barest saving of face dictated that she should stay. At the same time Joyce barked her shin climbing aboard and then she was banging on the dash: 'Go Ben, go!'

They began rolling like one of those nightmares, like all the nightmares where the pursuit breathes hot on your neck and you are barely moving. Growling up his mountain of gears Ben swung ponderously out of the lot.

Mary failed to even slow Mark; short of flinging herself under his wheels there was nothing she could do. The motorcycle pulled alongside the cab. Joyce was glued to the window like some fascinated and terrified toddler at the zoo: Mark looked insane enough to fly right the hell off his bike and smash in through their windscreen. He was shouting something, and it probably wasn't "Happy Birthday".

The speedometer wavered uncertainly and Joyce's heart jumped. 'Don't pull over Ben!'

'But that's Mark.'

'Don't you do it! Whose blood do you reckon he has all over him? Wait—I'll give you a hint, it sure as hell isn't that time of the month. If you stop here you'll be helping Mark to become a murderer, and helping *this* fat head,' she poked Disher, 'To duck out of his responsibilities altogether. We don't want to help Disher do anything now, do we?'

That was enough for Ben, the needle began to climb. Mark screamed harder, a vein pulsing dangerously above his eye, rage lost in the general din.

'Mark?' Samuel tried to prop himself up to see; failed badly but at least he was making an effort to rally. Disher seemed to have renounced existence altogether. 'Did you say it was Mark? What's he doing, running alongside waving a hanky?'

Joyce had to clap a hand over an inappropriate giggle, atop her foremost impulse of the moment which was to burst into snivelling tears. She was all sorts of a mess today. Pull your shit together Joycie; no one else will do it for you.

Ben at least sounded unruffled. 'Want to biff Disher out the window? Might stop Mark chasing us.'

'Don't you damned well tempt me.' Joyce heaved a massive watery sigh.

Anybody reasonable would expect the biker to turn back once he realised that he could not halt them but it would seem that Mark was in anything but a reasonable mood. He stuck on their flank for hours, grimly unwavering even when his steed started to cough and gutter under him, the reserve tank dry. A body got tired of being on constant high alert: is he still there?—yep; still there?—yep.

Joyce mashed herself against the glass to see as Mark finally dropped back and was obliterated by their swirling wake of sand. It would be a dangerous roll to a stop on uneven ground, blind in the cloud, half choked by dust and entirely by rage as his prey roared away down the highway. And how long would it take to walk his bike back to town? A long sweaty walk wrapped in leather, canted diagonally against his steed's weight, grinding away at his frustrated grievance.

Not to mention that upon his return to town he would find an oasis robbed of water, cheated out of its buried mystery. The whole population would have to move on: scattering, losing themselves in the world. Only the buildings would be left. Broken windows, doors flapping loose like lost teeth, hallways filling with sand. Pastoral paintings bleached away to nothing.

Finally some distant day hundreds or perhaps thousands of years from now the dead water pump's corroding hulk would finally give way and its collapse would drop any remaining structures into the desert.

Mark dropped away, and that was the moment that the driving rig's probes slid into Disher's quivering flesh. The academic had only time for a final outraged squeal before the truck seized the reigns and his face dulled over, burbling.

From well over the other side of the cab Samuel observed the process with feverish intensity. That eye of blazing blue seemed the only colour left in him, the last of his decisiveness. When a filament waved coquettishly his way he shrank back and shivered.

Joyce touched Samuel's shoulder; she wanted something from him too, they all did, always. 'Sam,' she whispered. 'You've travelled. Seen things. You ever heard of machines built like people?'

'According to some that's all we are: stimulus-response systems so complex that we mistake it for free will. Travelling endlessly down the tired, worn out tracks that we were always to travel.'

'A machine,' she insisted.

'Something that you can switch off? Wouldn't that be just swell. Poor Joycie. If it looked like a person, how would you know the difference?'

'There has to be an us and a them ... we made them!'

'In our own image?'

'Would you tell me?' She crept nearer across the seat. 'If you were?'

'Leave off you ridiculous woman.' Samuel's eye closed wearily.

Joyce shook him; 'Hey, you can't go to sleep with a head injury. I saw that on television once, it must be true.'

But Samuel smiled, a classic youth, in love with his immortality. 'I'm just going to have a little nap, get my wind back. Then I'll get up, head back to town and kick Mark's ass for him. Then wrap up my grand travelogue, get dead famous, and marry some international grid-girl-slash-model. Have a bushel of itty bitty writer babies that I can teach about the wide world.'

'Don't sleep Samuel.'

He patted her arm. 'I'll just rest.'

'Don't you do it.' A head injury meant you could fall unconscious. Being unconscious was not at all like sleep: an unconscious person cannot protect their airway. They can die just because they are positioned oddly.

Wouldn't you know it, the smartass pulled her in against his shoulder. 'It will be ok. I promise. You rest too.'

And unbelievably Joyce did doze amongst the sweat, adrenaline and violent lurching of the truck. Tucked safely under Samuel's tender wing, sliding gradually down the upholstery until she fell through into slick darkness.

Familiar dreams where the bringers of the new world came after her, driving her ahead on their bow wave. Faster and faster until she was no longer preparing the way but fleeing, faster still until her feet were swept from under her, dopplering insanely into her own future where she could see everything. Every damn thing.

The past was bad enough, the past could be endured; but what might become of the life that she had made herself? 'I can't!' Joyce shrieked, tossed back on reality's bland shore.

Ben's air conditioning hissed. Dry stale air where she could smell the sleep-stink rolling off her, the sour fear. Joyce had to slowly re-orient herself with the here and the now using small details as her temporal bookmarks. She used Disher's blank eyes which stared blindly ahead through the smeared windscreen, the damned idiot catching no more view of the big picture than what grazed his nose.

Joyce used Samuel as well. Samuel's head bobbed bonelessly back and forth against the upholstery. No neat poise to him now, no more purpose.

This was how life went. While you exhausted yourself snatching at meaningless minutiae, companions and adversaries slipped unnoticed through your fingers. So went the dead's curse: to the living, the burden of life.

Joyce must have shouted or croaked stop, ordering Ben to the verge of that dark and ruined highway beneath the burning sky. She had no stored memory of her actions to go with the moment; just the blank of a good drunk only without the good.

Asphalt and travel-worn steel flooded into the cab as soon as the door was cracked as well as heat, heat, heat. Already Joyce missed Samuel's clean prim smell in this hostile stinging world. His inhuman calm.

'Samuel's dead, isn't he?' A simulated sigh from the air brakes. 'I'm sorry. If it helps, I doubt that you could have done anything.'

'Sometimes you just gotta say the right thing and shit on the truth, hey Ben?'

'It's considered polite.'

'I never figured a machine would go for being kind over being right.'

'You seem to have figured quite a lot of things ass-about backward, if you don't mind me saying.'

'None of us could have done any better than what we did. Isn't that just our problem: like little tin toys on tracks. Me, Mary, Mark … It wasn't anything more than being himself that got Samuel killed.'

'You figure that, do you?'

'Once the situation got rolling he was always going to try the shining armour on for size.'

'Well, I think that any one of you *could* have avoided putting yourselves there in the first place.'

'And if wishes were horses we'd never go hungry.' Joyce wrestled Samuel's body from the seat down onto the sand in a fine combination of practicality and gentleness. Her famed clumsiness was nowhere in sight now that her attention was finally all fixated on the one thing.

'So that's the plan now? I'm supposed to dump you out here with his dead body and just toddle off?'

'Your bit isn't quite finished. Disher's got some comeuppance heading his way.'

'And he is not going to be at all drugged when we arrive there; he will know full well what's happening. Really you ought to come along, enjoy the show.'

'I plan to sit right here on my ass and wait until the sand

gets cool enough for me to plant Sam.'

'Out here?'

'You never know, something might grow.'

'And then what, roll yourself in next to him?'

A rictus smile. 'I've still got my work to do. There's a glorious whole new world coming.'

'If there will be anybody left alive to enjoy it by then. Take Samuel's pack at least. You said yourself that nobody gets to just throw their hands up.'

She hooked it from the foot well. 'If only Sammy were a machine, hey?'

'I know I can't have heard that right!'

'If they had made some machine with blue eyes and a penchant for the moral high ground, then, well … he wouldn't be dead. Broken but not dead. He'd be spirited away to some secret chamber beneath the hospital where they'd pull out the solder or nanites, or whatever the hell they use …'

'And then Samuel would emerge like Lazarus, holding out his arms? All would be forgiven?'

'It only sounds dumb when you say it like that,' she muttered.

'And then you would switch him off like some faulty light globe and carry on your way doing your thing. We would all be exactly where we are now.'

'Go away Ben. Just go away.'

And he did. One of her wishes granted for a change.

Joyce, she sat in the sand and endured.

The greasy sun was sliding down its griddle before any other stimulus finally came to break the accusation inside her own head. It was the sound of an engine.

Joyce's first thought was that sentimental fool Ben was coming back to save her after all; which was nonsense. The truck would have gotten to the hospital, dear Disher would be scooped from the cab like meat from the shell (pissing himself and screaming if the universe had any justice) and then there Ben would have to stay. Stuck, the end of the line with nobody left to fill the driver's seat.

Besides, this engine was travelling in the wrong direction. *From* town. Go away, Joyce insisted with her head in her hands. She demanded it of the entire universe, fat lot of good that would do.

Rather than retreating the engine snarled ever louder and Joyce finally lifted her exasperated face in time to see Mark's motorcycle blast by.

The biker had his two kids on the back and panniers bursting with whatever it took to start over; other than sheer gumption, that is. A new life with no room for Mary in it.

Seeing Joyce both kids' heads swivelled, their helmets knocking comically together and they were banging on their father's back but Mark gunned the engine and they blasted on. Joyce was not for the likes of them. The hospital was not for the likes of them either, but there would be plenty beyond.

Sighing Joyce hitched Samuel's pack closer. Didn't old life just go on and on? Her fingers closed on the canteen, water in the desert, but they found something else in the bag as well. Something curious.

Paper—paper filled most of the space. Samuel's travelogue! Greedy thoughtless hands tore pages as they hauled the whole mass out. Samuel had poured his heart and soul into this project: his secrets, his discoveries, everything that he had witnessed in the big wide world. All tucked industriously away like a squirrel squirreling acorns, safe for a time when people would need such treasures.

'Can't hide from me now, smartass!' The sound of her own voice surprised Joyce. She had thought that she had only thought that. A malfunction of interior monologue. Perhaps it was a sign that she was finally, finally going crazy.

The sheets were covered with Samuel's handwriting: round bombastic letters. She had always pegged him for the sort to draw a girlish circle instead of a serviceable dot. But the script was in no characters that Joyce understood.

She leafed through ever more frantically, chunks of pages in her fists. This bit here, this might have been her name, and that there may be some numbers but the rest—the damn lot was unintelligible! Not even code. For the moment at least he had still eluded her. Joyce flung the paper, fluttering, at his body.

'I thought you were English! You spoke English!'

Samuel had no answers for her. A droning sand fly alit on his eye as it stared blankly up at the rose streaked heavens.

CHAPTER NINE

AUTOMATONS

LEGACY

Ben the hauler crouched on a spit of tarmac outside the hospital and brooded over the unchanging view. Extending like a finger of blackness into the red desert his perch could tentatively claim to be in better nick than the rest of the highway. As well as any spot, he supposed to watch the final days roll on by.

It was the truck's final resting place and a precarious one, for only a few meters to the left or the right would have spilled him through, the concrete splitting with a roar beneath smoking tyres. Down, down to end his long days as a rusting unwelcome intrusion in the subterranean plumbing. A curse, poisoning the supply. The hospital had sunk its pipes deep hereabouts, penetrating the landscape's guts to draw up dark mineral water with which to work their miracles.

Since that disturbed fellow Disher had been dragged off—and Joyce was correct, he had gone screaming—Ben had been left here grimly alone. Although melancholia was not to his nature the truck had plenty of whiles to get good at it, worrying at the past.

Ben's surface concern was of course how he had never wanted to leave Samuel's poor dead body with *that woman*, as internal monologue would have her. Just beneath was the shame of memory, to remember how Samuel had flung off the harness and fled him. As so often in life there had been no chance for reparation.

As his Geoff had died and left him so too went Samuel, slumped on the seat while beside him that useless woman had twisted and moaned in her dreams. Both had been men of bright warm humour, and now both dead.

The world was becoming more and more a place for Joyce's sort: the survivors who largely endured by being rather awful people. And what damn cheerless sort of future was that?

Some thousand years from now her knock-kneed descendents would roam solitary territories half-feral in rags and rage as her primeval ancestors had done long before this gracile hominid kind mounted stage. Tall, raw, beautiful people superbly equipped for everything in their lives but each other. Seldom used words like stones in their mouths.

In city graveyards they would use railing spears to stalk fat possums that chuffed at them from headstones worn to indistinguishable nubs by acid rain. Grave markers where the earth had heaved in cataclysm and jumbled everything up, all denominations finally mixed together.

The hospital had its own little boneyard which made up part of Ben's view. The machines had insisted on the cemetery being laid even before the groundwork of the buildings, despite protests that it sent a negative message to patients. The machines wanted a reminder of the mortality of their charges and the consequence of failure.

There had even been a plaque inscribed to that effect bolted right were Ben sat; the best vantage; but pollution had effaced its defiance of time leaving only a dull pitted mirror. It was likely for the best: flog yourself along with failure and were you to by some miracle succeed, it would be for all the wrong reasons.

Time passed. Such was its purpose.

Then a morning came that brought the Lady Joyce herself toiling into view on the horizon. The sight of that bent labouring figure wavering in and out of the heat haze afflicted Ben with a case of the superstitious creeps: it were as though his months of dwelling on the woman had conjured her forth, like bad luck.

The tall woman's trudging approach was hellish and burned up most of the day. Without wheels the world was an awfully big place. Not even she called the highway a mere "road" anymore, not after getting so up close and personal with it. At one point Joyce dropped Samuel's flaccid pack from slack fingers just to lean, although any rest was a risk. She ran a strong chance of not being able to get moving again.

Our girl had carried Samuel's extensive travelogue quite some way on the hope that the hospital machines might catch a thread somewhere and unravel it, all of his life. Well, why not? Cutting edge, weren't they? The best that money could not buy; you had to be born into the right place at the right time, a relatively stable country whose successive governments had built their people's healthcare brick by brick.

Otherwise there was the option of an entire extended family passing the hat to fly their afflicted one here for yet another miracle, often somebody who had never left their local village before. The networks would make a featurette screening between six-thirty and seven that we could all feel good about, the curtain drawing before the recipient of the cure had to fly back and face their impoverished family. The viewer's guilt absolved over having been born here and not there.

But as her condition gradually made itself undeniable, Joyce had let the travelogue slip page by page. Paper chasing itself playfully away across the sand. There would be no trail of breadcrumbs to find her way home, no return.

As it turned out Samuel's cavalier approach to contraceptives had left his lady with far more than a solid dose of the clap to worry about. It was the vomiting that finally clued Joyce in; not that vomiting was an exciting new experience for her. Gestation burned through her scant reserves, mental as well as physical, at a frightening rate and it was amazing how the ordered world according to Joyce just crumbled away. The tall woman was not made for life, was not prepared. Eventually she found herself wandering the direction that she had originally set in a vague stunned state.

As Joyce passed, Ben's cab door shifted and creaked in the wind but it was noise without volition or purpose. What could either of them have to say to each other: I did exactly as expected? The truck remained inert, turned inward on his thoughts, a steel monolith. And thus he remained for the rest of his days.

The hospital received the tall woman as she had know it would. Its efficiency was undulled by waiting: a blast of air conditioning on her tight sore face that brought instant nausea, disorientation. A wheelchair hastening to sweep her off her abused feet.

Time ground on. It was many hours later that Ben saw Joyce emerge again, pale and sweating, her overstretched belly now slack. So she had given her child over to those who could not make one of their own, a gift from the woman who should not. Surrendered him to a taut womb of synthetic chemicals and hoses.

He would be a gift to raise, but not to keep—Joyce had seen to that. The mechanised care came with an expiry date: there would come a day when her child would be able to do without the machines, having grown beyond all that they could give. That day the machines would run their shut-down sequence, and the child would be set loose in the world to make of things what he could.

There was then a faint chance that these were not the last days that Ben had been given to witness but the first. At least there was a dim curiosity for him to wait and find out.

Joyce had also abandoned Samuel's pack at the hospital, kicked to a corner of the nursery facility like a shed skin. She had not seen Disher inside the facility. She had not asked.

Joyce turned wearily from the hospital and let the hammer blows of heat drive her out into the unmapped desert. Unburdened, she intended to pursue her shadow across the uncertain sand until finally she could find the path behind her and confront the bringers, those who sang as they followed her, unrolling the new world as they went.

Whether it was hatred or hope that lightened her step remained to be seen. Effacing Joyce's tracks, the sand sighed behind her.

CHAPTER TEN

AUTOMATONS

SOMETHING FOR EVERYTHING

THE OCCASIONAL season came when clouds roiled overhead, shedding brief droplets over the hospital. They pinged as steam off hot chrome where Ben sat, a silent sentinel.

Eventually another woman came to the hospital, seeking. She came laden with provisions: the desert was not cruel or kind, it simply was and the unwary could vanish into it like a stone into the ocean.

What this woman had lost had been taken from her rather than given away. She came doggedly following the trail of hearth and love, drawn along behind as helplessly as a balloon on a string. By the time she reached the hospital she was only just beginning to realise that she would never catch up with them.

A woman who was as unlike Joyce as sunlight to despair. Who nonetheless was quite passionate enough to damn herself just as thoroughly.

The neon of the hospital lobby glinted an unnatural green in the woman's shining blond hair as the machines welcomed her home.

If you enjoyed this, please read on for a special bonus chapter from Something for Everything: Automatons Book Two.

BOOK TWO

SOMETHING FOR EVERYTHING

OLD SKIPPING RHYME

Walk and jump and skip and run
The Blessed are coming, under the sun
Run and climb and get real high
The Blessed are coming, bye bye bye
Climb and jump, stay at the top
The Blessed are coming, smell of rot
Jump and run and don't look back
The Blessed are coming, all is black.

WITHIN THE LATEX BUBBLE

JOHN'S ADULT LIFE was passing in a series of incomprehensible bursts.

Sporadically he clawed at the blurred dioramas speeding past, trying to make sense of them. Branded across the forehead with the invisible mark of a hero. Luckily everybody talked to the mark, not the gravel-rash eyes.

There had been this grizzled fellow who approached him in a bar, back when he would morosely still visit such places. Back when he'd still been fooling himself.

'Excuse me, Surgeon? Sir?' Shyly fumbling for all that stolid girth. The chipped physique of a tradesman, which demanded its own respect. His body language broadcast on a wide frequency how badly he wished to grasp John's thin arm in the hearty way of his tribe, assert physical reality, with a mitt that would go right 'round the bicep. Knowing full well it would be the last thing he would ever do, touching a Surgeon. Calamity for them both.

Clammy from taking even this mild risk of approaching. Good on him. The other patrons were clustered right up the other end of the bar.

'Oh, hell.' Shifting restlessly from foot to foot. 'One of you Surgeons saved my boy. Of course, they won't ever tell me *who*, but I ... just wanted the chance to say thanks to one of yeh. He's a good boy, my boy.'

Real men would brusquely shake hands. Stupid John didn't even think to buy the grateful sod a drink.

He simply stood there like an idiot and his withered fingers in their latex casing padded sadly at his leather palms. Stood there, wishing he was drunk and verbose. Stood until the mystified fellow shook his head angrily and stalked away.

John was a Surgeon, and Surgeons were heroes. Or at least his fucking hands were.

Often in dreams his hands would separate from the wrist entirely, finally conceding he was no part of them and their grandiose future. Severed appendages that freed themselves in the deep wallow of night when his raw eyes finally closed.

Then they would come creeping up his bedclothes, groping their way blindly along his spindly hirsute body. Yellowed nails scratching through the coarse greying hair of his chest. No—Go away! What do you want?

Still, fear didn't prevent folk gathering to peer curiously from a murky distance, as though through aquarium glass. To witness him drowning in public idolatry, cheer his submersion with their idiot applause.

That's right, he asserted within the grim privacy of his

long skull. Clenched his teeth into it and refused to let go. *I save them. It's what I do. It's all they need me to do.*

Curious eyes poked at him, hungry for a piece they could nibble off and take home. Shoulders back, he had to remind himself, chin high.

A woman at a café giggled, her colour high. She had a napkin clenched in hand, smeared with her fashionable lipstick.

'Surgeon,' she tittered, holding it out. Streaks on her teeth. 'Would you kiss this for me?' Friends at the table egging her on, the bold spear-tip of their social wedge. They laughed because they were scared, and it was a high.

Kiss me, kiss me by proxy. Everybody loved to be desired. And what lust burned greater than that ever-denied?

Overtaken by a sort of addiction they jittered. Would take to their beds afterward and gulp water as their brains melted in a gooey rush. *Look at my body, Surgeon, let me pretend you're touching me. Ooh, let me be your nursie nurse?* The flush on them so strong, an aggregate of grasping hands and wet lipstick mouths, it was difficult for John to even see them as people.

He finally abandoned the warm noisy hubs of life. He'd no right to go messing with ordinary folk, he was ruining everyone's night. Surgeons must not be touched. Not outside the mysterious act of surgery. And surgery was only safe because the patient's mind became untethered, lost to the world. Just insensate meat slammed on a gurney.

Comfort, reassurance, *contact*; that precious warmth the human animal can't remain sane and functioning without. It was a heinous crime for a Surgeon, with swift and pitiless punishment. Awareness of this peeped just below consciousness, and by great exhausting effort John kept it there.

The days when things made sense seemed long ago. Snippets of impossible nostalgia, steeped in a rosy haze. He'd had the friend along all that time, he supposed, flapping and dangling at his coattails. But even she wasn't entirely sane anymore.

A morning happened.

Probably the same as most mornings.

John jerked awake with teeth sunk in his forearm to bite back a scream, leery of the neighbours even as he slopped out from the thick waters of slumber. Without thinking he raked the bedclothes down in a panic. The horrible, creeping, severed hands would be bundled in them and flung from him.

Of course the disembodied appendages were not there, he was trying to throw away his own hands. Any thickhead would know that.

His sheets, John realised, were flooded.

This was not the way a hero would sleep. He lay in a rapidly chilling sweat and piss bath, rank enough to peel paint right off the walls. Quaking, unable to even be disgusted until he'd calmed, he rolled to the dry side like a man washed from a shipwreck. His fists were clenched lest they dare touch anything.

It was the beginning of a brand new day.

CHAPTER ONE

TACTILE

'So, A FEW NURSES from the census came by mine.'

The friend was a blur, scarcely understandable. Shaking and blue to the gills because the city's heat cycled down at night. It was no time to be wandering about with fever on the brain.

'Asked if they could take a quick poke about my ladybits. You know, to check if there's any issue. Because there hasn't been. Any issue. And they laughed like drains, like they hadn't trotted out *that* old chestnut at every house.'

Even through the vibration you could sort of guess she'd squandered a striking youth, but ah, that face. Already sagging off its bone scaffold, circus pavilion coming down.

The friend and the city, both.

John winced at the telling, knotted fingers until latex squealed. He was vastly happier to imagine her *sans* bits, but to mention so was a rookie error. He'd get twice the earful. 'Did you tell them to take themselves on a long walk, or what?'

'Ha. It's amazing where, "Fuck off, my mate's a Surgeon," gets you. You seem to have an effect on people, Johnny. When your brain's in gear, that is.'

At three in the morning he ought to be rehearsing surgery, or dead to the world. Instead, bursting in, she'd caught him staring apathetically through the wall, his behaviour hung like a cheap toy.

Didn't she fall on her ass cackling at the sight. Annoying, but hyperactivity was typical of the city's mounting hysteria; if he wanted to condemn her, he'd have to shriek it to the streets. A wave of thundering panic built and he alone of the masses became lethargic and depressed. Perhaps he'd started off lower.

The friend, however, was clearly getting worse and he was running out of blind eyes to turn. Thoughtlessly bare toes waterlogged on plush carpet. Ought to feel lucky she'd remembered pants. He'd seen his own fingers appear just as dead and white any number of times, peeled from imprisoning gloves with the nails all spongy.

Only music should stir on the streets in the wee hours, especially around here in *The Cutters* surgical district. They got tinkling music, from frost rimed speakers. Ethereal confections of piano and flute playing to themselves in the bitter concrete night.

Out this way, for your sanity in the grey breaths before dawn you closed your eyes tight beneath bedclothes. Those sweet chimes acted fine on punk vandals and kids, but they wouldn't dissuade the downstairs folk from creeping about.

If the downstairs people were real. Nobody John knew had ever been brave enough to look.

Silent, they were, in case you stirred. In case you betrayed yourself as awake and listening, in which case something would have to be done, dear, wouldn't it?

Their music erased thought. It was the crash and thunder of vast stamping pistons; cogs the size of buildings that rolled ponderously, filling all of creation. A chorus of overwrought machinery crying out for relief, for a moment's rest that would never come.

From the moment of her launch their city, *A New Life*, had been in flight. Her very purpose for being. Fleeing mindlessly, like all the cities, from something only the downstairs folk could claim any contact with.

The friend's teeth clattered audibly as John ushered her into the lounge with little sweeps of his arms, snapping on a fresh pair of gloves from the steel dispenser by the door. He no longer noticed when he sent a dusting of talcum in silent rain, and tracked it about everywhere he went.

A crown of dreadlocks piled atop his head, secured by string. It gave the impression his attached body ought to be of the robust, caber-tossing variety; but in reality that great ginger noggin sat more like a lollypop on a stick. Most people had eaten meals with more meat on them than John.

'Johnny,' she chattered dazedly, still in the throes of what had driven her from her safe home, driven her to bring it *here*. 'I don't know if the visitors triggered it, I was so *angry*, but it happened again. It happened while I was yelling at them, I'm sorry. I was asleep … or awake … or—I don't know, I don't know what! I woke up suddenly and it was dark, and the nurses were gone!'

Probably out of there like their wimples were on fire.

Tranced is what she would have been. Every man and his dog were *au fait* with the symptoms. Everybody knew to flee.

Some trancers returned to bed, seeking comfort on autopilot, but most stood as the friend had, wherever they'd been hit. Staring off into infinity, probably drooling. Breaking out in jelly sweat as their temperatures shot up and up. It would end in seizures, if that went on too long.

For something to do John busied himself topping up the kettle, water hammering on copper. She rubbed gooseflesh on her wobbly white arms. Night had trailed her in, with its marrow-cracking chill, a damp tang that was slow dispersing.

'I remember thinking I had to calm the hell down. I was still in my house, after all. Still in the city and nothing could get me here. Not here.'

Not here. Only out there.

The world rolling by with all its wonders remained a shunned void, the antithesis of bustling life within the walls. The majority of citizens had never glimpsed the natural sky. Only the comforting embrace of a solid grey ceiling. Sane and credulous by day, but the lights couldn't stay on all the time.

When you closed your eyes all bets were off, your mind could wander anywhere. Grim legend held that if the monsters out there, the Blessed, seized you in their great square teeth before you could wake yourself up ... Something had to explain the waves of sleep-death that swept the population, defying all analysis.

But these day-trances, this thing happening to the friend, anyone could be prone to it. There were those who tranced and tranced helplessly, every day. Growing haggard and bony, sheets stained yellow. If the neighbours caught you stuffing that linen in a dustbin you'd be shunned; disposal had to be secret, it could take months.

Made up of dark hints and rumours to the uninitiated, there was even a terminal stage. Vague legends of the underbelly, down there where the downstairs people crawled. An unvoiced suggestion that there might be a way, there was always a way out, but only for those desperate and overwhelmed. Only they were ready to find it.

They became the folk who stepped from life one day. Vanished, like they had been wiped from existence.

Generally that became the cue for all those who had studiously ignored the warning signs to send up wails of grief. Friends and family. Petitions underlined and tear-stained, demands scored through the paper. The lower levels must be chained off, for the love of God. Cordoned, gassed, something! Plug that hole. Down there. Somewhere between the immense grinding treads that pounded the landscape to rubble.

Like it would do any good. *A New Life* was immense, a grand old lady, and those pilgrims dragging their exhausted hearts could always find a way to slip through and be gone.

For what it was worth, John was determined to do everything in his power to prevent the friend becoming one of them.

He slapped the kettle on the stove, a declaration of war. Coffee. That was step one. Things kept skittering away from him, like cockroaches when you flip on what ought to be an illuminating light.

He fished a couple of mugs from the cupboard. The purple one hers, on its own shelf, as though touch were a contagion a Surgeon could pick up off crockery.

'Hey, Johnny.' She threw a pillow at him. 'You listening?'

'Nope.' He lied. 'It's boring. You're boring.' He waved latex-shrouded hands, conducting an orchestra of one scared woman, bundled up in a guest blanket that had never shucked off its crinkly packaging for anyone else.

She switched tracks. Stopping and thinking were hardly the friend's forte these days; she lived in dread of it. Racing faster through life to beat awareness to the finish line.

'Seems like we never thought about the other cities when we were little.'

'To have identity there have to be others, right? You and me. Us and them. And that's why our city's the best.'

She sighed explosively, a great blowing-out of tension. 'Do you reckon we'll hit the Flagship soon?'

'Reach. Reach the Flagship, not hit.' Very superstitious. 'Weeks at least, they say. We're gaining gradually. You ought to be excited, instead of … whatever you are.'

'I'm reasonably confident *excited*'s not the word. More like starts with *fucking* and ends in *terrified*.' She'd turned green. Her pulse beat visibly in her neck. He was getting sympathy cramps just looking at her. 'After all this time we'll finally know what happened, why they went silent. All those other cities. And when it might happen to us.'

The lights on the comms board stuttering out one by one over the decades. Sometimes heavy breathing came in over the roaring static, and once … once it was a kind of *giggling*, you'd swear. And whispering, the way you do when you're scared of being overhead. Only nobody knew what it was saying.

The final connection to the Flagship had been lost only recently. They were still scheduled to meet, though, and that made her the only chance of finding out what was going on. Nobody was about to stroll out there and look.

'Your morbid nature's showing,' he scolded. 'It's unladylike.' He suffered a chill nonetheless, and ploughed on. 'We don't know *anything*'s happened to anybody. There are at least a thousand perfectly solid explanations why lines or even the navigation squawks might go down. We're all tooling blissfully about on old, old equipment, after all. Ancient stuff. Nobody's manufactured anything wonderful and new since the glory days of Son.'

Her face drooped further. It would be on the floor at this rate. 'We could do with the likes of Son now. You know, when I was a kid I used to pretend I had him as a secret friend. Like he'd been hiding all this time, just waiting for me. Another lonely kid to play with.'

'Of course you did. Children are such egomaniacs. Especially girls.'

'*Son and the Marvellous Machines*, do you remember that? It was my favourite show.'

'You can't seriously wish Son was around. Here, now? I can't think of anything worse.'

She clapped a horrified hand over her mouth. *Blasphemy!*

He hurried to his point. 'No, really, think. We owe him everything, right? Son built the cities and he saved us from Outside, from the Blessed. But all that was such a horribly long time ago.

'Technology just handed to us, so precious and shining, and what have we accomplished? We don't even know how to take care of things properly anymore. It's all falling apart. The masses proved happier with their merry-go-round of shopping, fucking, and raising brats.

'So if you ask me, yeah, it'd be *awful* if Son were somehow alive to see what we've done with all he left us.'

'You're really shit at cheering people up. Anybody ever mentioned?'

'Daily.' He set the mug down in front of her. Enough caffeine and she would slide into sleep, a rag doll on his couch. 'Drink up. If you don't mind, I'm going to get some practice in while there's still night left.'

'Be my guest. It's your house.'

That lasted all of two seconds. Bored, she came to his elbow.

'Uh, would you mind staying over there?'

'Do I look like an idiot? No touchee the Surgeon.'

'Just … step back, then. More.'

'Shut up, I can't even reach you from here. See? *See?*'

Taking off his gloves and exposing the stewed digits to the air always felt horribly lewd, let alone with someone else in the room. Stirred up urges he'd rather do without.

But she wasn't going to bugger off, so he took a deep breath and got on with it.

His patient, a furry little beastie engineered to house a human heart, beamed groggily as he lifted it from the carrier. Warm, soft fur. A faint mousy whiff.

Despite his tension he couldn't help returning the foolish toothy display. The heart animal wasn't about to notice the cracked ruin of his hands. Or flinch, as the friend did, from the high unearthly whine of the laser scalpel heating up.

Couldn't blame her. Even after all these years a thrill of unease shot through him every time the surgical tool woke to life, like *this* was the time he was going to poop his pants. Beneath fissured fingers and visible to his altered eyes only, the scalpel set to bloodlessly parting warm living tissue cell by cell.

Only the ornate silver handle was visible to the friend's sight, there wasn't much point trying to see what he was doing. If it weren't for the drugged little animal gradually skinning open on the bench she would hardly have been aware of the dangerous instrument at all.

The friend had no way of knowing the inflamed needling irritation the blade brought to John's carefully altered sclera. A spike through his head. The Surgeons clasped their secrets close, and that secret was always pain. Pain for experience. Pain for efficacy.

Who wouldn't want every patient to thrive? Who wouldn't cast themselves gladly on a pyre to see suffering scraped out, until in the entire city only theirs was left?

In skilful hands whole structures could be transplanted without a single pierced membrane. Slide to a finer edge and you could shave the axons from a neuron. Finer still and you'd be messing with molecular components, something even a Surgeon needed special licenses for.

LeMars, the laser scalpel's creator, had used the cursed singing prototype on his own arteries, spreading them wide. It was said he'd had a vision of the future. It was true that a live dropped scalpel would plunge through the depths of the city, and everything it encountered. Until it emerged from *A New Life*'s belly to fall, humming and spinning, burying itself in the earth. Earthquakes. Catastrophe.

Nonetheless the inventor was posthumously lauded a hero, patron saint of the circulatory system. Every scalpel carried his name *LeMars*, in ornate curling script on the handle.

Picking coyly at her nails, she found something new. 'Well. I went to High Estate this week.'

Telling heat bloomed in sallow cheeks. He didn't need to glance to confirm her wicked grin, sharp uneven teeth bared at his spine.

High Estate ranked as the greatest of John's obsessions, a guilty moral addiction he mustn't indulge in. Society permitted scant leeway for a Surgeon to be weak. Or human. Cry me a river.

Best crush sweaty daydreams and act his age. No spring chicken. Cram them away in some back pocket and smile, smile as the friend teased his tail feathers. Smile through gritted teeth if necessary.

His long-boned hands never faltered, despite her best efforts. If anyone deserved accolades, it was those Surgeon's hands for dragging the rest of him to success.

'There was a rave, you know.' Coyly.

'There's always a rave!' He couldn't help assuaging discomfort with a jab of his own. 'Why were you flouncing about High Estate parties instead of home with hubby?'

This time her smile came without humour. 'My dear *husband* was working. Be kind to him, Johnny. He always works.'

Instantly ashamed. Bending over his work to hide it. Charles had been his friend, too, back in the day. Nobody made the decision, but she'd inherited him in the end.

Now the happy couple devoted their time to methods of staying apart within the confines of one small flat. Easiest for Charles—he just set about working himself into an early grave. Marital joy being an obligation, the friend's bitter glare reminded him, that a Surgeon stood exempt from. If "exempt" was the word.

The pause gave her a breath to recover. Bringing Charles into it had been cruel, and neither of them were used to him being cruel. It was normally her remit.

'So, do you want to hear about it or not?'

A petulant, unfair question. She knew damn well he lived for these recitals, addicted, stretching out the days. Although she'd taken a bitter edge, when she rambled on about parties the ghost of her adolescent irrepressibility returned. A stupid force of spirit he found frustrating and gladdening in equal measure. Insufferable to his threadbare nerves, he wished a thousand times a day she'd grow up— but it at least proved not everything could be crushed down.

'The rave, it was brilliant. All splashy neon and sound. Loads, and I mean *loads* of people showed up. So many bodies packed in, all breathing and moving together. Sweat thrown up in a spray against coloured lights …'

Breath hissed through teeth a little faster, though he tried to hide it.

'… and I could *smell* all those people, rank funk down the back of the throat, like foul musky animals …'

He wondered where she drew that from. Weren't many animals roaming the city; excluding Frankenbeasties like his little patient here, wriggling impatiently against the straps.

What she described were beasts of nightmare. The very reason for the walls. Great, hulking animals with hot hides and wild smells. Wicked horns. Volcanic eyes.

When he realised his devious subconscious had thrown up the Blessed he hastily squashed the notion. More than enough in the day to be leery of already.

'Exotic animals,' the friend was crooning dreamily, still lost in her neon fantasy. 'So much skin to be seen. Glittering eyelids. Dyed hair in spiked crests. Cocks so heavily pierced they dragged along the ground.'

Bypass practice was almost over, his furry patient doped to the eyeballs and counting its tiny clawed fingers drowsily. Its own heart batted shyly beside the grafted interloper, which bulged monstrously by comparison.

In fact, that human heart filled so much of the chest cavity that lung expansion was visibly cramped, digestion retarded. The miracle of science, hey?

All that remained was to restore blood flow and set the seat of human love pumping again. Easy as pie. Its motion shook the beastie like a motor in a too-frail building.

He set to silently knitting his "patient" back together with mesh.

Returning to her perch the friend snuggled into

the couch cushions. The furnishings of *The Cutters* far outstripped anything to be found down her end of town. 'C'mon, big shot Surgeon. You finished yet?'

John snipped the last wire and thrust his hands in the air like a triumphant gymnast. 'Aaand—I'm done. That's a new time trial.'

Switching the scalpel off, nervously aware of the cooling molecules where the blade had been. Only once had she attempted to touch it. Off her tits on whiskey, she was. Although it hadn't been live he'd still lashed out in a panic as though to slap her away with his bare hand, only pulling up at the last second.

If it hadn't been so serious, the identical shock on their grey faces would have been comic. Never saw her drink whiskey again after that.

'Can I hold him now? Can I? Can I?' She held out her arms, a child eager for its new toy.

On with fresh gloves. 'Sure, but be gentle. Don't put pressure on its belly.'

That earned him a look. 'I'm careful all the damn time. I was born careful.'

The beastie submitted its round body for petting, even blew a few contented spit bubbles. Delighted, she smiled down at it. Curled up on the couch like that, button of a thing in her arms. Was that how she'd look if Charles had given her a baby?

Her next question ever so innocently fired his way. 'Why not tag along next time?'

An air pocket in his glove was more important. He fussed, muttering. 'Uh, sure. Tag along to ..?'

'A rave. Come to High Estate. Stay for the food.'

He scowled thunderously. 'You know better than to suggest that! Especially here!'

'Oh, quit being such a crotchety old grumpy pants. Society peeping through the keyhole, are they? Or are you wetting your shorts that they might suspect the hero of being human?'

'I'm not human. I'm a *Surgeon*.' But his catechism, lately repeated with such despair, rang hollow.

If she noticed his despondence, it earned no further concession than blunt irritation. 'Zippedy-do, bully for you. Look, it's just you've always been so *fascinated* with how the shady half lives. And now, what with the Flagship coming up and all … You may never get another chance.'

'I am **not** fascinated.'

He might as well have stamped his foot. It didn't warrant a response. Only a mental self-kicking; no chance she'd tell him about the rave now. And he'd rather bite his tongue off than ask.

Those wild melee parties always ended the same, anyhow. Some gang, whichever was hot property at the time, took over. And it was all downhill and into the shit from there.

'Johnny, look at it this way. Don't you want to try something exciting before we all die?'

Now he'd reason to trot out the indignant. 'You just watched me hold a *living human heart* in my hands!'

'Uh, hardly attached to a human, though, was it?'

'To date I've performed twenty-nine *highly* dangerous procedures and *hundreds* of tiddlies, with, excuse my ass, a *one hundred frigging percent* success rate! Exactly how exciting do I need to be? Have you got some kind of sliding scale going?'

She wasn't backing off. 'Ever talked to any of them? Given a patient whose life you so *heroically* …' He closed his eyes at the sour spray. '… saved a chance to say thanks?'

'Get to your point already.'

'All you do is repair unconscious meat the way you'd unblock your garbage disposal. What are they to you? Of all things, High Estate at least seems to *matter*.'

When there was no counter-offensive, when he didn't even open his eyes she sighed, visibly trying to let go of her agitation.

'Look, I'm sorry. I know what you do is really important. It just seems unfair, you know?'

Nothing.

'Would you look at me when I'm talking to you? I'm talking happiness, marriage, love. *Fun*. You're always stuck off to one side, or in the distance. Just because there's no other way doesn't make it right.'

Inwardly he quivered at her clumsy attempt at sympathy, but couldn't reply. They were both too old for such emotional flapping about.

She sighed. 'We're getting closer to the Flagship, Johnny. Maybe none of this will even matter once we get there.'

He didn't like arguments, but John's rooms were very quiet after she left.

As quiet as they could be. Not quite the soundproof luxury of the sunlight suburbs at the top of the city—he could still hear *A New Life* groaning all around him.

Most of the city's inhabitants could not consciously register her mechanical pulse. They had known it in the womb, and would die without ever experiencing such a strange thing as silence.

It was a Surgeon's poor luck to move between states, neither fish nor fowl. Unbearably sensitive to such realities.

The gentle vibration caressed the spine, the steady *baoum*

baoum of immense treads. Of those who could hear, some odd ducks were disturbed by it. Tympanic reconstructions were by far the most common surgery done.

On top there was always the dull hissing ventilation, a genius system for drawing the external in safely through a series of spiked traps and filters. The whining lights. And of course innumerable consumer appliances being fired at once.

Only appliances, though. The days of the modern miracles, the living thinking machines, were long past, no matter how covertly longed for. Not even *A New Life* had capacity for thought, although hippies and radicals claimed that she dreamed. Dreamed away her long slow journey. Only Son would have known for sure.

As though she scented the grey trend of his thoughts a message from the friend flashed up on John's screen. Couldn't resist one last dig.

ANOTHER HIGH ESTATE
PARTY TOMO NIGHT
COME PLAY
YOU CAN JUST WATCH
TRY SOMETHING
EXCITING
BEFORE WE ALL DIE.

He tried to clamp down on his anger, and shocked the beastie as much as himself by kicking the couch.

'Fuck!'

Why this infuriating compulsion to stir things up, things that ought to lie decently dead? All ignorant, the friend would end up getting them both killed.

The heart animal burbled in its strange, wordless voice, becoming more active as the ether drained. It groggily rubbed its sutures.

'No!' He lightly smacked the pink paws. 'Naughty!' The damn thing had been unzipped more times than his coat. Ought to know by now not to fiddle with the stitching.

Way back before regulations got so strict about claw length, a heart animal had been found dead at the bottom of its crib. Guts all tangled where it had stupidly tried to flee its mistake. The things were bloody priceless, nobody even knew how old they were. The mysteries of the eternal cell had been lost with the thinking machines.

You never heard so much as a murmur of discontent when you returned them to their plain sterile cribs, where they might wait months. Some kind hearted minder might hang an infant's glittering mobile, for the beastie to coo and chuckle at.

Kind hearted. Certain daft minders were known to cry plenty when their charges got hauled off for surgical practice, and never mind that that was what they were *made* for.

He deposited the rotund creature back in its carrier, all ready for somebody else to practice. It wet the newspaper with a gush of ammonia, and then curled up to sleep with its butt in the air.

When gloved hands lingered on soft fur he resolutely recalled them. Touch. It was so easy for the bloody friend to take for granted. A perfect buddy for a Surgeon, she couldn't stand anyone too close, like she'd been rubbed all over with ground glass. It made John want to scream at her. She never used to be like this.

Of course, she never used to be married.

It wasn't the sort of thing you could say, but in his secret heart he suspected *there* lay the font of all ill. But what else was she supposed to do? Society, the very institution he upheld, dictated marriage. She was hardly in any position to ask "How high?"

Once your date arrived you got a selection, delivered on a list all fancy around the edges. Some of them you would even know. But hell or high water you had to pick one, and marry them. Supposedly all that hardware in the city's cranium only spat out nice clean matches for healthy bouncing bubs, but who knew how it schemed?

So the friend went on her merry way, and John downed taller and taller glasses of chilled vodka in an effort to get to sleep at night. When he dispensed with the glass he knew he was in trouble, but anything topped lying in the dark with visions of High Estate dancing in his head, feeling a right pervert.

The snowballing disaster was en route to see him broken at the bottom of the mountain, if he couldn't find a way to sort himself out somehow.

John's frantic, gnawing thoughts were interrupted by a rap at the front door, which made a welcome change from the friend's more dramatic entrances. But seriously, he glanced at the clock. Didn't anyone *sleep* anymore?

Relief was short lived, as a voice like a decade in the desert crackled through the panels.

'Don't ignore me, Surgeon. I know you're in there.'

He could only hope to live to an age where he could give so few fucks. Sighing, he opened the door to confront the Captain on the front step, before she put a chunk of rock through the window under the mistaken impression she was still spry enough to climb through.

Red rimmed eyes peered at him from a face as grey and lumpy as unstirred tallow. The porch light wasn't doing her any favours. In her prime the Captain would have towered over him, before the years buckled her spine into its present C shape.

Others, especially women, turned to cosmetics or surgery to mitigate time's impact but never the Captain. She shoved her increasing frailty in your face. Each indignity heaped on that snowy head only served to make her sour spirit burn hotter.

A single concession, the silver flask hung around her wattled neck.

'Surgeon,' she acknowledged coolly as though he were the one calling on her for favours at four in the damned morning. Unused to wearing gloves she plucked absently at the void teats at the ends of fingers, with the nerve-wracking squeaking of a freshman.

She always donned gloves when she wandered into *The Cutters* to visit a Surgeon—"blending with the natives," she called it. John felt the gesture sent a darker message: that Surgeons couldn't be trusted to control themselves.

'Captain,' he responded in kind.

Her crumbling body appeared as a series of errors awaiting correction, rather than the result of a natural process, and his fingers itched for the scalpel. She'd rather sip strychnine than take him up on it, of course.

'What can I do for you on this fine chilly morning?' Their steaming breath rose all around them.

'Just making sure you're around.'

He raised his hands. *Where else would I be?*

'Don't be smart, Surgeon. We are expecting some new data in the next day or so, something critical. I'm going to want your expertise when it comes in. So don't go wandering off.'

'New information? On the Flagship?'

The old goat was too canny to feed that rumour one way or the other. By way of response she turned and shuffled her way back down the drive. The cold air couldn't be doing any favours for those joints.

Her purpose had been served—the vigilant neighbours would have witnessed her visit, the interaction noted. He'd just been boosted into a new social circle. Privy to secrets he was sure not to want.

During a crisis the Captain would never sit idle while others flapped about in a tizz; the cunning biddy would be drawing all strings to her. It felt comforting, in a way. No matter what the city faced, she would be ready.

Turning back into his apartment John blanched and for a moment was afraid he might faint. The hallway dipped and swayed.

The friend's innocent-sly, vastly incriminating message was still all over the screen.

He hoped like fuck the Captain's aged eyes hadn't been able to read it over his shoulder.

TRY SOMETHING

With a sweep of his hand he erased it. Would that a thought could be wiped so easily.

BEFORE WE ALL DIE.

Later that day, with an iceberg of clear spirit drifting in the waters beneath his belt, John typed a reply.

He went. God knows why, but he went.

SOMETHING
FOR
EVERYTHING
Automatons Book Two

BP GREGORY

**A Surgeon must not be touched.
The city can never stop.**

Comforting truths to live by. But the other cities have fallen
silent. Fear stalks the streets. And John the Surgeon craves
touch more than anything.

Monsters, machines and roaming cities, insanity, betrayal
and lust: centuries later, the seeds of grim legacy sown in
Automatons have borne strange fruit indeed.

The world is frozen
The animals ascendant
And Jim will do anything
to keep his daughter alive

FLORA
& jim

BP GREGORY

The world is frozen. The animals ascendant. And, locked in desperate pursuit of the "other father" across a grim icy apocalypse, Jim will do anything to keep his daughter alive.